A DEACON NOVEL

AFTER THE END

L. J. STUBBS

World Castle Publishing, LLC
Pensacola, Florida
Copyright © L. J. Stubbs 2023
Hardback ISBN: 9798391773214
Paperback ISBN: 9781960076540
eBook ISBN: 9781960076557
First Edition World Castle Publishing, LLC, May 8, 2023
http://www.worldcastlepublishing.com

Licensing Notes

Cover: Levi Mecham
Editor: Karen Fuller

CHAPTER 1

The thruster was acting up again. Deacon feathered the controller with no response from the defective device. He swore and pushed the knob to the right forcefully. The thruster kicked in and jerked his suit hard to the left. He swore again. He was doing that more and more of late. He blamed his bad language on the aging human technology he was forced to use. Just because he was the only human on the rock shouldn't mean he should have to use the ancient tech. He knew Anzark made him use it because he liked to hound Deacon.

He knew he was different, part of a near-extinct race he had never known. The only other human he had ever seen was his mother, and she had been taken away so long ago that he could barely remember her. All he could recall were diaphanous strands of thought that whispered of a beautiful dark face and black hair like his. Soothing words, an embrace and, of course, her screams for him as they dragged her away that horrible night. Those were his memories. His only connection with his mother and the race he was rumored to be a part of.

It had been two-hundred years since the Tendari destroyed Earth, and the wretched aliens enslaved all those poor souls that escaped the planet. The Tendari were famous for their ruthlessness. They had enslaved many other races and put them to work in the asteroid belt. All other races in the belt were more numerous than humans, and so Deacon had grown up on "the Rock," as its inhabitants had come to call it, alone and persecuted.

The Rock was a large asteroid but small enough that artificial gravity was needed in the station to make living there feasible.

Deacon slowed his approach to the hopper and thanked the Gods that the thruster fired. His mining suit slowed, and he dropped the massive boulder he was carrying into the hopper. Huge metal teeth ground down the boulder, sending chips of ore drifting into the low gravity surrounding Deacon.

Two-hundred years ago, humans had just begun mining the belt when the Tendari came to claim the rich resources there, so Deacon was forced to use the decrepit equipment of his ancestors. The tech was far from efficient when compared to the vastly better equipment used by his alien counter-parts, but here he was. He had to make the most of it.

He pushed off of the hopper's lip and glided over the stone-crushing teeth before beginning his slow descent to the asteroid's surface on the other side. Deacon hopped as soon as he touched the surface and sailed another thirty feet before landing again. He continued like that until he reached his dig area. Anzark, the Tendari's alien foreman on the Rock, had separated all of the slave diggers into their own sections so that they could more easily measure everyone's progress. Anzark was a slave as well, but he had been given privileges and authority over the rest in payment for his management of the slaves. In many ways, Anzark was worse than the Tendari keepers that guarded them. At least the Tendari weren't trying to impress someone with how ruthless they could be.

Deacon reached the pile of ore he had dug out of the cliff earlier and picked up another large boulder. Even with the reduced gravity on the Rock, his suit's hydraulics strained with the effort of lifting the heavy load. He had to push the equipment as hard as it would take to keep up with the quotas. He used the suit's thrusters to help propel him toward the hopper.

Although the work areas were segregated, the hopper was communal, and Deacon tried to time his approach to avoid interfering with other diggers. Getting on someone's bad side was a very real danger that could easily result in his death, especially when he already had two strikes against him. Everyone loved to hate humans.

He patiently waited for his turn at the hopper, and when he finally made it to the giant rock crusher, he pushed his thruster controls all the way down and jumped. He sailed upward toward the top of the hopper. Just then, a deep thrum sounded loudly behind and above him.

Deacon was now over the lip of the hopper and could feel the familiar vibration of the metal teeth chewing away at rock and ore just beneath him. The thrum he heard behind him was louder now, and Deacon recognized it as a heavy ore-hauler that had come to drop its load. Deacon dropped his boulder early in the hope that the loss of the weight would help launch him out of the way of the oncoming ore-hauler.

No luck. The ore-hauler slammed into his suit, pushing him downward toward the hopper's crushing teeth. He heard a series of cat-calls over his headset. He didn't have to wait for his chip to translate them.

"Finally got to kill that little puke-worm." Laughter. They were laughing at him.

He was on the slanted edge of the hopper, sliding slowly down toward the turning blades. The ore-hauler added to his misery by dumping it's load. Ore fell past him into the metallic jaws. Shards of metal ore and stone shot at Deacon with terrifying speed. He was sure the fragments would puncture his suit, and he'd suffocate. What was he thinking? The crusher would do him in long before the lack of air.

The ore-hauler finally crept by overhead, allowing Deacon

a chance to escape. He pushed his thruster in hard, and the thing sputtered, then died.

"Bahg!" Deacon swore.

As he slid down closer to the demolishing stone, the vibration was so intense that it rattled his teeth. Deacon pulled the thruster control back and then forward, trying to get the thing to fire, but it was no use. A large stone flew up from the tumbling chaos just below him and slammed into his knee.

"Bahg, Bahg, Bahg."

Deacon knew, somewhere in his subconscious, that he should have made something far more impactful with his last words, but at that moment, nothing came to mind.

He pulled his hands inside the chest cavity of the suit and punched the chest plate in front of him with all his might. Behind it was all of the wiring for the suit's functions. He hoped that, if it was a short, the rudimentary violence would solve the issue. He prayed to the Gods and put his arms back into the suit's appendages. He pushed the thruster control forward. The thruster sputtered, then caught and fired. He was launched up the side of the hopper and out toward the sparkling stars.

The other slaves that saw the spectacle and laughed at his predicament laughed harder as he was unable to disengage his thruster, and the thing nearly sent him into space before, finally, he was able to angle his flight back toward the surface. He landed in a shower of pebbles and dust.

"Bet he has to clean his suit tonight." Someone laughed.

Deacon seethed. He was young and still small compared to the brutes that drove the other suits and ore-haulers, but he grumbled angry promises regardless.

CHAPTER 2

After Deacon's near-death experience, it was time for shift change, so he limped his way back to the airlock. His knee hurt, and with each painful step, he grumbled some unintelligible oath. He was angry, to be sure, but he wasn't so stupid with rage to not recognize his precarious situation. Deacon was a human, and if he ended up pushed out the airlock or an "accident" befell him in the quarry Anzark and his Tendari task-masters wouldn't even bat an eye.

With his bad leg, Deacon was the last one to enter the lift that would take them below the surface into the barracks. Mugoth, a Carexi with one eye, could be heard complaining that they should "just leave the weakling human on the surface for a night to teach him some humility."

In Deacon's estimation, he was nothing, if not humble. Life had taught him nothing but lessons in humility since the day he was born on this very rock.

Carexi were stout aliens, bipedal like humans, but much larger and ranged in color from green to light blue. They had strange worm-like mustaches that he assumed evolution had given them to sniff out the malodorous food they preferred. As the lift doors closed, the cabin pressurized, and all removed their helmets, including Mugoth. When the helmet came off, Deacon was tempted to reach up and pull off one of his mustache tentacles but resisted the urge. It would only get him killed and be of only momentary amusement. Besides, his true anger was reserved for the driver of that ore-hauler.

Deacon had recognized the voice that had exalted at killing the wretched human though he had not had time to ponder the fact. It was Rullox. Rullox was a Tarpin. Tarpin were wiry and strong, with muscles like cable, but tall and thin, especially when compared to Carexi. Rullox had a flat nose, common to his race, with pointy ears and long human-like hair.

Deacon turned to surreptitiously peek at the stinking pile of reek-weed. The alien stood talking animatedly with a group of his friends, undoubtedly about how he had almost killed Deacon, though the sound of the lift, as it lowered them, was too loud to hear exactly what the Tarpin was saying. Rullox laughed loudly, and Deacon returned his attention to the door in front of him. He gritted his teeth. Rullox would pay, he didn't know how, but the alien would pay for what he'd done.

The doors to the lift slid open, and the dark interior of the barracks waited on the other side. Deacon quickly stepped through, trying to hurry so as not to anger any of the large aliens behind him who would be excited to get to their cots. Deacon didn't have a cot. His was stolen from him years ago. Instead, he slept in the corner behind a sheet of metal that had fallen from the ceiling.

He went with the others to the equipment room, where they all removed their stinking suits. There were different types and sizes for all of the variety of alien slaves that were present. Deacon silently went to the corner and began to remove his suit. He grunted as he lowered the heavy thruster/hydraulic pack to the floor.

As he stripped off the suit, he determined to use some of his water credits to shower. It would feel good to get clean for once. It was rare that he could afford the luxury, and in reality, he was the only one that ever did. All of the other slaves neglected to clean themselves at all, except for the Guzonians, who seemed to do little else but lick themselves clean, though Deacon wondered how clean that really got them.

Deacon thought that maybe the rest of the slaves just didn't have as sensitive a sense of smell as he did. He assumed not since all of the slaves were so pungent to Deacon that he had a hard time being around any of them for long. He sometimes longed to go get into his suit just so that he didn't have to smell the myriad aromas that emanated from them. At least his own smell, he could change.

Another problem with the smell in the place was the reek-weed. It grew in the corners and low-traffic areas of the facility. No one seemed to care enough to try and clean it up because the stuff had been there for at least as long as Deacon. Maybe no one touched it because of the increased odor the plants ejected upon contact. Either way, Deacon supposed the problem was pretty low in priority for them. Slaves had enough to deal with to worry about noxious weeds too.

Speaking of reek-weed, the showers were full of it, and Deacon had to carefully clear a spot. Luckily, the showers were far from the sleeping area, and no one should complain about the added smell. They were all nose-deaf anyway.

He turned the handle on the shower and flashed his wrist across the scanner to give him access to the water. The water spurted and then sprayed out in a hot cloud. Deacon stepped under it and fought the urge to step back out. It started out too hot, but as he stood under the stream, the heat began to feel good, and he luxuriated in the feeling. Steam quickly filled the cool interior of the showers.

There was nothing to use to help wash his dirty body, so he used his hands to scrub clean his dark skin. He didn't waste time because time was water, and even though the Rock was covered in ice, water credits accumulated slowly. He turned off the water and sat on a bench nearby to examine his knee. It was swollen and already showing the discoloration of a bad bruise. He was surprised that the seal on his suit had held. Maybe humans weren't so useless after all. They had, apparently, created a suit two-hundred years ago that could not only withstand the ravages of time but could also hold up under the assault of hopper debris.

His whole life, he had felt ashamed for being a human. It was hard to feel anything different the way everyone ragged on his race, but now he felt an odd twinge of appreciation for his ancestors for the very same suit that, an hour ago, he had cursed for its ancient technology.

Deacon stood and went to his locker, where he got dressed in his cover-alls, the same cover-alls that all of the slaves wore with alterations for anatomical differences. Once he was dressed, he went back to the equipment room and pulled his mining suit from the closet. He hefted it onto the low table in the center of the room and examined it.

The suit would have been white if it were two-hundred years younger, as it was the suit had taken on the same color as the surface of the Rock. Deacon rubbed a finger over the white, red, and blue rectangular patch on its shoulder and wondered, not for the first time, what it meant. He liked the patch and had endeavored to keep at least it clean over the years.

He picked up a screwdriver from his stash of tools and worked on removing the screws from the wiring panel cover. Once inside, he gingerly lifted the panel and carefully pulled out the jumbled wiring harness that fed the suit his commands. He had worked on his suit before but never on something so complicated, and he prayed that he wasn't making the problem worse.

He slowly separated the wires and examined each one, looking for any explanation for the thruster issue that nearly killed him. The work was tedious, and Deacon contemplated putting the plate back in place and hoping for the best, but then he felt it. There was a small segment of red and white wire that had a break in its plastic insulation. There would have had to be a second wire with bad insulation to complete the circuit unless the red and white was a supply that was grounding out on the metal inside the panel.

Deacon taped the spot and then searched for more wires with breaks in them with no luck. All in all, he was impressed with the condition of the two-hundred-year-old wires. He gently stuffed them back into the panel and secured it with the screws. Now there was only to wait until tomorrow's shift to test it out. He lifted the heavy suit off the table and stowed it in the closet, then turned toward the barracks. It was past time to get some shut-eye.

As he walked through the row of bunks and cots, he had a strange feeling that something was different. He looked at the beds and saw eyes focused on him as he walked. The other slaves seemed to be giving him far too much attention. He began to worry. What if Rullox, or some other degenerate, waited for him by his sleeping spot? He supposed that there was nothing he could do about it if they were. He walked slowly to the back of the barracks and looked around.

No one waited for him. He checked under the sheet metal where his bedroll still lay rumpled on the floor. Nothing seemed amiss.

He was about to lie down when the sight of a figure in the opposite corner stopped him. It was hard to see in the darkened room, but something about it made him curious. There had been no other slave there before his last shift, and something about the figure seemed familiar. He walked slowly over to the figure. As he drew closer, Deacon could see that it had pale skin beneath the gray hair that covered his face. Something brought Deacon even nearer despite the obvious awkwardness in him being so close to the strange figure. But it wasn't strange. It was...right.

"Are you human?" Deacon heard himself say.

CHAPTER 3

The man sat on the floor and stared back at Deacon with piercing blue eyes. His hair, although abundant, was well groomed, which was at odds with his dirty skin and clothes.

He frowned and looked away from Deacon, ignoring his question.

"Are you human?" Deacon asked again. The man didn't move.

He tried Tendari thinking that maybe the translator chip hadn't been installed in the man's head yet, but the man still didn't move.

Deacon moved closer and crouched down to be on the same level as the man.

"Leave me alone, boy." The man's voice was deep and raspy.

The sound of his own language being spoken and not just translated in his head was surreal. The words made him excited. He wanted to ask the man a million questions, but from his demeanor, Deacon knew that it would be no use. Maybe he could try again another time. He raised himself slowly to his feet and turned back to his own corner.

Deacon had a hard time falling asleep. The thought of having another human so close excited him. He thought of all the questions he had and imagined the answers long into the night until, finally, he drifted off to sleep.

The next morning Deacon awoke groggy and exhausted. He shuffled to the bathroom and relieved himself, then went to the alcove, where they doled out the daily food. A fat Carexi named Strobi handed out tubes of nutritional paste. The stuff was gray and completely unappetizing, but it would be the only food he'd get for the day. He opened the tube and slurped up a mouthful, then folded the top over and pocketed the rest. He'd take another mouthful later on in the day to try and stave off the hunger pains.

Meals on the Rock were not planned with humans in mind, and most of the aliens didn't normally eat more than once a day. Some didn't eat but once a week. Deacon felt like he was dying of hunger most of the time, but the protein supplement was designed to give the highest nutritional value with the least cost, hence the single nutrition-dense serving per day.

Deacon went to the equipment room and waited for the crowd of slaves to move out of the way of his closet. He suited up and was actually looking forward to a day under the stars mining ore when Anzark came into the room trailed by the other human.

Despite looking ancient with his gray beard and wrinkly face, the man seemed in good shape and walked straight-backed without a limp. Anzark brought him to a locked closet and swiped his wrist over the pad. The door slid open. Anzark shuffled to the back of the closet past racks of old suits.

"Now, I know I had a spare human suit. I could have sworn it was right here. Deacon heard a series of curses followed by the sound of Anzark as he rummaged through spare suit pieces and tools that were discarded at the back of the closet.

"There it is!" Anzark pushed his way back out of the closet, dragging a battered suit. The thing looked like it was in even worse condition than his was. Deacon didn't think that was possible. Seal tape hung off the suit in rotting strips.

"Anzark, surely you have something better for him. He won't last a day in that thing." Deacon said. He wasn't sure why he said it. He hoped that he hadn't just put a target on himself.

"He's human, so he gets a human suit," Anzark smirked.

Anzark was a Kupelti, and Deacon had yet to meet one that wasn't fat. They had green skin and scales that were always coated in a kind of slime that stunk. Anzark's neck was so fat that he had rolls that completely hid it, and that made his head look like it was just the top of a mound above his shoulders. Deacon didn't know how the Kupelti grew so fat on a single meal a day. Maybe they just truly didn't need as many calories as humans did.

"At least give him a day to seal it up tight before he has to go out there." Deacon pressed.

"I don't answer to you, weakling. He goes out. If you're so worried about your new friend, then you can give him your suit." Anzark chuffed and waddled out of the equipment room.

"Bahg," Deacon said.

"Please, don't curse," the man said softly.

Deacon looked at the man. He was confused. Why was the man concerned about his language when his life could very well end today. The man saw his look.

"Listen, I appreciate you trying to help me, but I will be alright.... Or I won't. In any case, it's none of your concern."

Deacon knew that he was right. He should have just left well enough alone, but this was another human. It seemed foolish, but Deacon felt like the man might be able to shed some light on who and what he was.

"Right, well, good luck," Deacon said. He grabbed his helmet and strode toward the lift.

The man was the last one to board the elevator, and he barely made it before the doors closed and the lift started its slow ascent. It was a strange feeling, worrying about someone. Granted, Deacon recognized that at least a portion of his worry for the man was selfish. He needed answers, as foolish as it seemed.

He shrugged it off. Such things lost all importance when you were struggling day-to-day to survive. He still hoped the man survived but would not let it crowd his thoughts. Even though he had been doing this every day for years, mining was dangerous work, and it took a steady head to stay alive. He wondered if the man had ever done it before. Of course, he had. He had probably been a slave on another asteroid that had been mined out or one of a dozen reasons slaves were transferred between asteroids.

Deacon didn't know much about his own kind, but he did know that most, if not all, of the remaining humans were slaves here in this very asteroid belt. The lift halted, the conversation paused, and all of the slaves fixed their helmets in place. Deacon couldn't help but look toward the man as the air was sucked out of the room.

He'd seen an alien's suit fail once. It was not a pretty image. The alien was dead before they could override the airlock and return air to the room. The experience haunted Deacon ever since. Every day, he half anticipated his own suit to fail, his own eyes to bulge, and his own life to leak out of him. Now, he watched the man for the first signs that his suit failed him, but nothing happened, and Deacon let out a breath he didn't know he was holding.

They left the lift and set out to their individual digging areas. Deacon was excited to see if fixing the wire in his suit made any difference to his thruster, and as soon as he could, he pressed the control. The thruster punched him off of the surface of the asteroid instantly. There was no sputtering delay like there had been. He smiled to himself.

He dug for hours, using the digging arms he left in his area each day for the next shift to use while he was gone. Once he had a substantial pile of ore, he began to carry it to the hopper. His thruster performed wonderfully, and he was excited to not have to risk death with every trip over the hopper.

At about mid-shift, Deacon pulled his arms out of the suit's arms and pulled his food tube out of his pocket. There were some benefits to being smaller than what the suit was intended for, he thought and fished the tube up into his helmet where he could suck out a mouthful of the goop.

Deacon thought about Rullox and wondered what he could do to get back at the alien. He felt he couldn't let him get away with almost murdering him. He had to make a stand, or he wouldn't last much longer on the Rock.

He thought of the wiring in his own suit and thought that would be the easiest way to do it. If he could find the right wire, then it would be an easy thing to fix it so that Rullox's rebreather shorted out or his thrusters didn't work.

A part of Deacon didn't want to kill Rullox. He felt that killing the alien would be wrong somehow. Nothing in his life had told him that such an act of revenge was wrong, but he felt something tell him that he shouldn't, though logic and experience told him to seek retribution against Rullox. If he did nothing against the alien, then the law of the slaves would be broken, and he would be seen as nothing but a target. The weakling that they all accused him of being.

He had to do something. Tonight.

With the resolution made, he proceeded with his work half-heartedly. He pondered his life, the new man, Rullox and his own decision to get revenge on the alien. The shift change sounded sooner than he would have ever expected, and he set off toward the lift. His knee felt better than it had the night before though he still walked with a limp. It was good that it seemed nothing serious was wrong with it.

He wasn't the last back to the lift, at least, and was happy to see the man standing toward the back of the airlock. His suit had surpassed his expectations, just like Deacon's had. For that, alone, he was grateful to his ancestors. Deacon nodded at the man, a simple acknowledgement that he had survived, yet the man didn't return the nod and continued staring straight ahead.

He didn't know why he had expected that the man would be nicer to him than the rest of the slaves. Shouldn't a human be nicer to a human than to someone of another race? It seemed to Deacon that all of the Tarpins hung out together, as did the Carexi and all other alien species. Sure, some aliens were friends of differing species, but in general, they usually stayed in their groups.

At least the man hadn't threatened to kill him yet or call him a weakling. Maybe that was all he could hope for.

Deacon waited for all of the other slaves to remove their suits before he entered the equipment room. He hoped that no one would suspect him of anything since he usually kept to himself as much as possible anyway. Once the room had cleared, he entered and slowly extricated himself from the cumbersome suit. The whole time he disrobed, he steeled himself for what he'd decided to do.

No one should see him as no one came back into the equipment room after their shift was done. Deacon was the only one that ever had to worry about his equipment failing, and so it wasn't out of the ordinary for him to stay behind in the room.

After he was out of his suit and stood wearing only his coveralls, he nervously looked toward Rullox's closet. The lock by the door was green. He hadn't locked it as Deacon knew he wouldn't. No one ever did. He moved over to the closet and pressed the button to open the door. The interior was dark, and the Tarpin's suit was hanging high above his head.

Deacon stepped into the closet and reached as high as he could but couldn't reach the hook that the suit hung on. He stepped on a narrow ledge at the bottom of the closet and was just able to reach the hook. He heaved and was able to pull the suit from its hook.

"What do we have here?" A voice said behind him. The initial language before it was translated was Tarpin.

CHAPTER 4

It was Rullox's voice, Deacon was sure. He turned. Sure enough, the ropey Tarpin was flanked on either side by two other slaves. Another Tarpin to his right and Mugoth the Carexi to his left. Rullox stepped forward and grinned broadly.

"Imagine my surprise. I went through all the effort of gathering up those that hate you most to come to witness your end, and when we find you, you have already given us a reason to kill you," Rullox said.

Deacon stepped to the opening of the closet, still holding the alien's suit in his hands. He felt ashamed and resigned to his fate. He didn't truly believe that he would survive much longer in this hellish place, at any rate. In all honesty, he should have died years ago.

"Let's get this over with," he said in Tarpin. The sound of the guttural Tarpin language coming out of Deacon's mouth must have surprised Rullox because he hesitated in his slow walk forward.

"I'm surprised you know any of my language," Rullox said as he continued toward Deacon.

"Gods know I've heard you talk enough to have learned," he said. Rullox's smile broadened.

"Your Tarpin is good. Better than I would have imagined

from one of your race. It will almost be a shame to kill you. But not quite."

Rullox's fist slammed forward without warning. The alien's long arms gave Deacon just enough time to raise the suit in front of his face. The force of the blow rocketed through the suit and slapped into Deacon's head. He couldn't imagine how bad it would have been had he not blocked it. His hands tingled from the shock of the strike.

Deacon fell back into the closet. He heard something high-pitched and wondered what it could be. He thought maybe he'd knocked his head, and now he was hearing things, but then he realized it was his own wail. He stifled the sound. There was no point in adding to Rullox's enjoyment. There was no stopping the tears that welled up in his eyes and began to streak down his face, however.

Deacon waited for Rullox to finish him. He could do it with one punch, he realized. He hoped it would be that fast but didn't think he was that lucky.

He felt Rullox grip his ankles, and before he could think, Deacon reached out to either side of him and gripped the grated metal sides of the closet to try to keep the alien from dragging him out. When the alien tugged on his legs, Deacon felt like his shoulders would come free of their sockets, and he quickly tried to release his grip, but his fingers caught and bent, then broke as Rullox's overwhelming strength came to bear.

Deacon cried out again in pain.

He lay there and cried. Over his own noise, He realized that the three aliens were laughing. He lay there in pain and fear as they laughed. Rullox made the same noise that Deacon had heard over the comms as he slowly slid down the inside mouth of the hopper.

He heard other voices farther away, laughing as well. He turned his head and saw a group of watching slaves, drawn by his misery, pointing and laughing at him. They were blurred from his tears, but they were there.

Deacon's breathing changed, and soon he was growling instead of crying. He felt something under his back. He reached behind him and gripped a screw-driver with his broken fingers. He kicked out with all his strength and caught Rullox in the shin with his boot.

The alien roared in pain and anger. He bent over and reached down to finish Deacon.

Deacon sat up, meeting Rullox halfway and jammed the screwdriver into the alien's upper bicep. Rullox swung his other arm in rage and caught Deacon in the chest with bone crushing force, sending him spinning across the floor.

The rest of what happened was kind of a blur. Deacon struggled to maintain consciousness through the pain, and what happened next seemed more like a fever dream than reality.

The man. The human man pushed his way forward through the crowd of onlookers and entered the equipment room behind the three large aliens.

"Leave the boy alone," the man said.

Rullox turned angrily toward the man, furious that someone dared speak.

"Ah. The other one." The comment dripped with scorn. "Glad we could get rid of both of you at once."

Rullox reached up with his left hand and pulled the screwdriver from his muscle, and flung it across the room.

The man spread his legs in a wide stance and brought one arm forward, hand raised in a strange way while his other was brought back beside his head. In it, he held a long dagger fashioned from a piece of discarded scrap metal and sharpened to a razor point.

Deacon watched as Mugoth launched himself forward, determined to overpower the much smaller human before he could use his knife. A fist, twice the size of the man's head, swung out. Deacon thought, for sure, that the man had been obliterated by the blow, but he couldn't see now, as the big Carexi's body was blocking his view of the fight.

Mugoth swung again, slowly, then went still, and Deacon wondered if the man was dead, but then the Carexi slumped to his knees and fell forward on his face. The man stood there, still poised and waiting for another attack in the same stance he had been in before, covered in the blue blood of the Carexi.

Rullox and the other Tarpin looked at each other, picked up a tool from the table in front of them, then circled it and approached the human, one on either side of him. They came at the man at the same time, and Deacon thought there was no way that the man would survive, but he was a blur of motion all of a sudden, and he leaped and danced his way out of reach of the tools' deadly arcs.

The Tarpin grunted in anger as they struck out in vain. The other Tarpin, the one that Deacon didn't have a name for, let the frustration get the better of him and lifted his torsion wrench high. The man used the opening and slid between the alien's legs and severed the Tarpin's tendons that stretched behind the knee.

The alien cried out in pain and fell to the floor, seeping gray blood out over the smooth metal tiles. The man stood behind the kneeling Tarpin, knife held against his throat. Despite the Tarpin being on his knees, the man was still shorter than the alien and had to force the alien to slouch with its head cocked to one side.

"This is the one chance I give you. Take your man and leave us alone, or pick up his dead body." The man said. His words were quiet and seemed all the more menacing because of it. Rullox looked at the watching slaves.

"Take him!"

A couple of slaves made as if to comply, but the sound of heavy boots behind them brought them up short.

Anzark pushed his way to the front of the crowd, followed closely by a squad of Tendari guards. The guards wore their customary black riot gear and carried batons that they used to push the crowd of slaves out of the way. Tendari were large, though not as heavy as Carexi and not as wiry as Tarpin, but they were a match for both. Patches of red skin showed under their black clothing, and their frightening razor teeth snarled under their helmet visors.

Tendari were testy aliens, even more so than the other races that Deacon had known. They were just as likely to raise their visors and rip out the throat of a slave that seemed too slow as they were to tell them to speed up. Every alien on the Rock showed the Tendari guards deference, not just because they were the ones with the guns.

Deacon hurriedly pulled his legs out of the way of a Tendari that ran past him, moving to secure the opposite side of the equipment room. He may have been on the verge of passing out, but he knew better than to get in the way.

The man looked around him and then tossed the blade onto the ground and raised his hands.

"It looks like the new human doesn't put up with your bahg Rullox." The deep rasp of commander Grato echoed through the silent equipment room.

"I should kill you all and have done with it," Grato said so casually that Deacon had no doubt that he would do just that without a second thought.

"But...I suppose we need all the hands we can get to mine the Rock. We're short-handed as it is. So.... What should I do?" Commander Grato began to walk slowly forward.

"Rullox, this isn't your first indiscretion. It seems you don't play well with others."

"Sir...I." Deacon was surprised. He never would have imagined Rullox as being afraid of anything, but now he stammered a weak defense that highlighted his fear of the Tendari commander.

"Sir, they're just humans, sir," he tried again.

Grato seemed to ponder this as if it was the most rational

explanation he could have received.

"True, Rullox. They are just humans," he pulled his side-arm and pointed it at the man still standing behind the Tarpin. Unlike Rullox, the man stood confidently, ready for whatever judgment was given. Stoic. Rullox sneered his approval of the commander's new trajectory.

Grato pivoted without warning and pointed at Rullox's head, then pulled the trigger.

A hole the size of Deacon's fist punched through the Tarpin's head. Gray blood and worse sprayed out of the body, then it tumbled, lifeless, to the floor.

"And you are just a Tarpin," the commander said. He looked around the room at Deacon and the injured Tarpin.

"The wounded receive only half rations until they are well enough to work."

Grato made a jerky motion with his right hand, and his men pulled out of the equipment room without a word and formed up on him. They left as quickly as they had come, leaving the slaves to pick up the pieces.

The man came over to Deacon and knelt beside him. He placed his hands on Deacon's chest and probed with his fingers.

"Does this hurt?" He asked.

"Yeah." Deacon didn't want to let it show just how bad it hurt. "It also feels like I can't get a full breath."

The man nodded.

"I think you have a broken sternum and possibly some ribs. You should be ok if we can keep an infection from setting in."

"How do you know that?" Deacon asked.

"I know a lot of things." The man smiled. It wasn't an answer, but Deacon accepted it.

"Looks like your nose is broken as well."

The man reached up to Deacon's face. He put his thumbs on either side of the crooked nose.

"This is going to hurt." And before Deacon could respond or ready himself, the man forced the nose straight. Deacon let out a groan.

"That wasn't so bad, was it? Now let's get you up." The man got his feet under him, then bent and lifted Deacon in strong hands. The movement sent shockwaves of pain through Deacon's chest, but he kept from whimpering...just.

They walked slowly through the barracks toward the back, where their pitiful beds were located. Surprisingly, slaves got out of their way as they moved, and no one made jibes or angry threats as Deacon would have anticipated.

The man lowered Deacon to the floor by his own bed.

"I think we should probably sleep next to each other, you know, so you can watch my back." The man winked at Deacon.

"What's your name?" The question was a whisper since it hurt to speak.

The man hesitated as if deciding whether or not to tell Deacon. Finally, he answered.

"My name is Elijah," he held out his hand.

Deacon looked at it. He didn't hide the confusion that he felt at the gesture.

"Give me your hand." Deacon gingerly placed his broken hand in Elijah's.

Elijah shook his hand. Deacon winced at the pain.

"Ooh." Elijah looked at the mangled hand in his. "We're going to have to set these as well.

CHAPTER 5

"I don't have anything to splint those, so you'll just have to be careful not to re-break them until they heal."

Deacon didn't really know what he was talking about, but he nodded anyway. He was sweating and breathing hard from the pain he'd just experienced. He knew Elijah was trying to help, but bahg, he wasn't sure he wanted this kind of help.

Elijah sat back against the wall and reached for his ration of water. He handed the bag to Deacon.

"Drink."

Deacon took the water gratefully. He reflected that this was the first time someone had given him anything in a very long time. He drank the water with difficulty until he raised himself up on his elbows with groans of pain and was able to gulp the liquid down.

"I honestly don't know how you stayed alive down here for so long by yourself. How old are you anyway?" Elijah asked.

Deacon handed the empty bag back to him and laid back once more before answering.

"I am not sure exactly. I think I'm about five and a quarter Tendari cycles." Deacon said.

"That would make you about thirteen, maybe fourteen Earth years old. Far too young to be on your own."

"How do you know what an Earth year is? For that matter, how do you know how to fight? I've never seen anything like it."

Elijah hesitated again before answering. "I am a keeper of memory. I have been tasked with storing knowledge of our past, culture, and identity in my mind. I have devoted my life to mastering certain aspects of humanity and then sharing those pieces of human identity with other humans. After being caught by the Tendari and put here, I forgot my purpose for a while. I apologize for how I treated you before." Deacon shrugged the apology away.

"Believe it or not, it was still the best someone had treated me in a long time."

"I believe it. The way those slaves went after you, you'd think you'd murdered their brothers."

"Nope. Just my presence." Deacon smiled. The gesture felt strange.

Elijah's explanation had only opened up more questions for Deacon, and he attempted to curb some of his enthusiasm so as not to annoy his new friend.

"So you weren't a slave? How is that possible? I thought all humans were slaves."

"That's what the Tendari want you to believe." Elijah looked around the interior of the darkened barracks.

"I don't dare get into it here, but you should know that there are others out there, not just those in the clutches of the Tendari."

"What made you help me?" Deacon still couldn't believe that someone would put themselves in harm's way for him.

"You did. You reminded me what it is to be human."

"What, to get your butt kicked by a bunch of big aliens?" Deacon said with scorn.

"No. To fight back no matter the odds."

Deacon thought of that for a while. He was proud, he realized, of how he had acted. He had always wondered how he would act in that scenario. The scenario where certain death loomed moments away. He was proud that he had not tried to run or cry. Sure, he'd cried, but that was only after the pain set in. He had stood up to Rullox, and now the alien was dead. Rullox was dead. Deacon felt as if a heavy weight was lifted off of him.

"Get some rest," Elijah said. "We will have plenty of time to answer questions another day." He patted Deacon's shoulder gently.

Despite the pain he was in, Deacon slept better than he ever had.

The next morning Deacon awoke to Elijah bringing him his half ration of food.

"Do you mind if I use your suit today? I didn't really have time last night to reseal mine."

"It's the least I could do."

Deacon felt even more sore today than he had yesterday. Everything hurt, and when he repositioned himself to a more reclined posture, he thought he might start to cry at the stab of agony in his chest. He was able to hold back the tears but not the whimpers.

"You gonna be okay here by yourself?" Elijah asked.

"Of course," Deacon said.

"Even so, take this." Elijah handed him the sharpened metal piece that he had killed Mugoth with. "I still don't know why they didn't take it from me. Maybe they knew I would just make another one. Maybe they just want me to stay alive for other reasons. Either way, you have it now, so don't gut yourself with it, please." Deacon felt there was more to Elijah's comment, but he didn't pursue it.

Deacon held the long knife carefully. He gently scraped his thumb over the blade to judge its sharpness. Though he didn't have much experience with knives, this one seemed very sharp, and he wondered how he had gotten such a fine edge on it so soon after arriving.

"How did you do this?" he asked.

"I took it with me yesterday out to my area. I used the rock grinders to put an initial edge on it."

Deacon was surprised. He didn't know how Elijah had gotten the weapon past everyone, but he was impressed.

Deacon burned with questions for Elijah but now wasn't the time. Maybe they could talk more after Elijah returned from his shift. It was strange having someone to talk to. Even the few short conversations he had had with the man were the most that Deacon had had in a long time.

"Be careful out there. Rullox had a lot of friends," Deacon said.

Elijah nodded. "You too."

"The opposite shift is coming in now. I don't think his circle included the other shift."

"Don't underestimate your enemy, even if he's dead," Elijah said. He patted Deacon on the shoulder and left for the equipment room.

Deacon lounged against the wall for as long as he could until the need to visit the bathroom was too great. He slowly climbed to his feet, holding his ribs and chest as he did. He knew that the act of physically holding his abdomen wasn't necessarily helpful, but it just hurt so bad that he felt the need to try and support it. He walked carefully to the bathroom and relieved himself.

On his way out of the bathroom, Anzark saw him.

"Good, you're up and about. Follow me." The fat alien turned and waddled away.

Deacon groaned inside, but he knew better than to complain out loud. He followed Anzark. They approached a door Deacon had never been through, and Anzark opened it. They went down tunnels that were filled with pipes running above their heads. Every now and then, a spout of steam would erupt from a valve in one of the pipes, and it would fill the tunnel with a cloud of fog. The tunnel was poorly lit, and Deacon had difficulty seeing down the smaller, branching side-tunnels. He wondered how far the tunnels went when it, all at once, opened up into a large room filled with conveyor belts and myriad other equipment that Deacon didn't recognize. The noise was intense.

Deacon heard a series of pounding and cursing. Someone was taking their rage out on the equipment, it seemed. The ringing blows of metal on metal reverberated through the maze of equipment, giving Anzark a constant bearing. Finally, they came around a large box with a metal grate over the top, and he saw her.

She was atop a stopped conveyor belt, splayed out to keep her balance. She swung a large wrench angrily at the wheel along which the conveyor belt was meant to move. The wheel was obviously out of place and needed to be returned to its cradle before the belt could be turned on again. He knew that he shouldn't stare, but she was beautiful. The most beautiful thing he had ever seen.

She was a Kalix. He recognized the species though he had never seen one. Kalix were almost as rare as humans. That wasn't the only thing their two species had in common. Kalix were very similar physiologically to humans. This Kalix had pale blue skin, gills behind her ears and larger than normal eyes. Other than that, she seemed like she could be human. She was obviously female. She had long golden hair that she had pulled back in a tail behind her head to keep it out of the way as she worked. Her coveralls were the same as his, except they fit her so well that Deacon felt the blood rise to his face.

He felt strange.

This was the first time he'd ever felt this...attraction.

Deacon realized that Anzark was talking. The Kalix girl had stopped her battery of the equipment and was listening to him.

"I know he's human, but that's all I have. You'll have to

make due. By the way, he's technically in recovery, so he may complain, but he should be able to turn a wrench. Oh, and don't kill him. I need all the miners I can get."

Anzark turned without another word and walked away.

Deacon guessed he was supposed to stay and help this Kalix girl. Despite his sore chest, he tried to stand up straight.

"What's your name?" The girl asked.

"Deacon. What's yours?"

She made a sound through her teeth and ignored his question. He got the distinct impression that she did not like him. He, all of a sudden, had the undeniable desire to win her over.

"What can I do to help?"

"Help? I don't need the help of someone like you. I was hoping for a Carexi or a Tarpin...a Guzonian, anything but you."

Deacon didn't really understand the hatred that most alien races had for his race, but he had experienced it far too often to be surprised by it.

She hefted the heavy wrench once more and began swinging it hard into the side of the wheel. With each ringing blow, another expletive burst from her lips. Deacon hadn't heard such language, and that was saying something. None of the slave miners had particularly good manners, but their language was down right clean by comparison to this.

The Kalix girl paused in her efforts and glanced at him.

"What the bahg is wrong with your face? It looks like you got between a group of Kupelti and their food."

Deacon touched his tender nose.

"It seems that my existence was too much for a bad natured Tarpin to bear."

"Bad natured, huh? It wasn't Rullox, was it?" She asked.

Deacon was surprised that she knew him.

"Uh, yeah."

"I'm surprised you're still alive if someone like Rullox doesn't like you."

"How did you know Rullox?" He asked. He hoped that he hadn't been her friend.

"Listen, there are some slaves it pays to steer clear of. Rullox is one of them. Not that I can't handle myself," she quickly added. She began swinging the wrench into the wheel again. Finally, after Deacon had learned a few new words, the wheel slipped back into place.

"She nodded down at the conveyor belt with a slight smile on her beautiful face. Her overly large eyes were a bright green, and they contrasted wonderfully with her skin.

"Maybe you'd be happy to know that Rullox is dead," Deacon said.

She looked up. It was her turn to be surprised.

"Not you. You couldn't have done it," she said, looking down at him with scorn.

"I stabbed him, but Grato himself finished him off," Deacon bragged.

She looked at him differently now, as if re-evaluating him. He swelled with pride under her gaze.

"You're one dumb mud-thumper, aren't you?"

Deacon deflated.

CHAPTER 6

The rest of the day passed in silence. Deacon was sullen. She hadn't been impressed. On the contrary, she seemed to be genuinely disgusted with him. To make his time with her more difficult, she wouldn't let him help her with any of her maintenance and repairs. He supposed he should have been grateful. He hurt. His chest, ribs, face and fingers all felt like they had his heart pounding away inside. He throbbed with pain. He couldn't be sure, but he felt that the agony he was in now was worse than when it had actually happened.

Despite the pain, he attempted to be there for her if she needed him, and so he would follow her from place to place, and each time, she would sigh and shake her head and mumble under her breath.

Finally, after a long day of sitting around, she looked at him. Deacon perked up.

"Don't come back tomorrow," she said and pointed toward the entrance to the room.

Deacon took it for what it was and stood to leave. Took a step toward the door, then stopped.

"You know, I didn't choose to be human," he said over his shoulder.

He left then, angry at her. Angry at Anzark. Angry at the

Tendari, but mostly, angry at himself. Deacon arrived back at the barracks an hour before shift change, and so he laid down and was asleep almost instantly.

He awoke to Elijah sitting down next to him.

"Hey, kid. How you feeling?" he asked.

"I've been better. Doesn't help that Anzark couldn't let me rest today."

Elijah's eyebrow lifted. Deacon told him about his day.

"I knew a Kalix once. She was a fire-brand as well. Must be part of their allure." Elijah smiled at the memory. "Did you know that Kalix are mostly female? One male for every hundred or so females. That's why they're so rare now, what with the Tendari putting their males to work and not allowing them to spread their seed..."

Deacon yearned to ask the question that had been bothering him most of the day and most of his life, but he didn't want to sound like he was whining. Finally, he just said it.

"Why do they hate us?"

"Who, the Kalix? I suspect they hate everyone or at least pretend to."

"No, I mean...everyone. Why is it that everyone hates us?"

Elijah paused and gathered his thoughts. The question seemed to trouble him. Finally, he cleared his throat and began to speak.

"Earth was right on the edge of major inter-planetary development when the Tendari attacked. They had just begun to mine these very rocks, and they had started small colonies on mars and were looking toward Titan, the moon off Saturn. Humans would have rivaled the Tendari in size and strength in a few generations. The Tendari attacked Earth without warning and obliterated it within hours. What humans were left were either here, in the mines, or on mars. Rumors persist that an expedition to Titan was underway when the attack hit and that there are other humans out there somewhere, but those are probably just hopeful fancy."

Deacon was spell-bound. He had never learned any of this before, and the story was enthralling, but it had little to do with his question. He decided he didn't care and watched the old man as he recounted their history.

"The Tendari weren't done with us. After destroying ninety-nine percent of all humans, they took the mines and expanded the operations that were already here. With the resources they gather here, they have grown quickly. Their scientists, if that's what you could call them, studied us. They found something very interesting about us. At some point in our very distant past, humans fought off a very robust disease. This disease became a part of humanity without our knowledge. It hitched a ride, so to speak, on our very genetic makeup, our penance for surviving it."

The old man seemed to look into the near distance for a time as if he didn't really believe what he was saying, Deacon thought.

"The Tendari brought it out of hiding and weaponized it. The disease was very effective at reducing a civilization's population quickly, allowing the Tendari to swoop in and enslave the survivors and take over the planet with minimal damage to the infrastructure. The pattern worked so well that they jumped from place to place, enslaving a hundred civilizations of varying technological advancement and inheriting all of their knowledge. Now, the Tendari are the strongest, most ruthless culture in the universe as we know it, and we were the ones that made it possible for them.

"The Tendari were ruthless before we were involved, as evidenced by what they did to Earth, but we were the crucible with which they forged their greatest weapon. Of course, it wasn't our fault, and anyone who thinks about it rationally will tell you that the Tendari would have found some other way to perform their atrocities, but you have to admit these truths are hard to get over. Especially when they named the disease 'telum terrae.'"

Deacon's translator translated the name 'Earth weapon,' but he didn't recognize the language.

"What language is that?" he asked.

"It is Latin, an ancient Earth language. The red bellies even used our own language as a sort of jab at us."

"That's why they call us 'Groloxi'- carriers," Deacon realized aloud.

Elijah looked surprised. "That's right. You have a good head for language. If you would like, I can teach you other Earth languages that have all but been erased from our history."

"I would like that," he said. Deacon had always enjoyed listening to the words before the chip in his head had a chance to work and then compare it to the translation. Then, later while he worked alone and with his comms off, he would often recite and compose conversations in various languages trying to perfect his pronunciation of the alien words. He was proud that Elijah recognized his efforts. His high spirits, however, were mitigated by the news that he had just learned. Of course, everyone hated them. Because of them, their planets were captured and enslaved. Because of humans, the Tendari were ravaging the universe.

Deacon felt bile rise in his throat, and he swallowed it down.

Elijah noticed the effect the news had on Deacon and placed a comforting hand on his shoulder.

"Listen, the only thing left is for us to go on. We cannot help who we are. We cannot help who the Tendari are. The most we can do is fight back where and when we can."

"Fight back?" Deacon had never even heard the slightest mention of a rebellious comment like what Elijah had just said so casually. Even the most hardened slaves, slaves like Rullox and Mugoth, were cowed entirely by the Tendari.

"I won't talk more about that now, but know that we are stronger than anyone gives us credit for." Elijah looked around the interior of the darkened barracks, again, trying to pinpoint the location of hidden cameras and microphones that would reveal his rebellious talk to their Tendari watchers.

"Now, get some rest. Your body needs to heal."

Deacon had more questions but figured he had enough of them answered for tonight. Besides, he was exhausted despite not having worked all day.

The next day Anzark came for him again and ushered him to the Kalix girl, he tried to tell the fat Kupelti that she didn't want his help, but he wasn't having any of it. He just huffed and kept walking. Deacon got the distinct impression that the alien taskmaster didn't care if the Kalix had reliable help or not and that he was just filling a quota.

When they found her, she was stretched out under a pipe. The sound of a ratchet clicked away as she tightened some unseen bolt. She grumbled when Anzark announced their presence. She was not happy to hear that Deacon was there again, and he couldn't say he was too keen on the idea either. After learning what he now knew about his history, his perception of her animosity had changed, and he felt almost embarrassed to be there.

Anzark left without speaking to him, and Deacon stood uncomfortably until she finished with the bolt and wiggled out from under the pipe.

"I thought I told you not to come back today?"

"I didn't have a choice." She didn't seem to believe him. "I tried telling Anzark I wasn't needed, but he didn't seem to care."

"Yeah, he wouldn't, would he?" She sighed and turned around, then motioned over her shoulder for him to follow. "Come on, then. We'll see how useless you are."

She took him to an equipment closet filled with mechanic's tools. She reached for a grease gun and handed it to him. He took it gingerly with both of his broken hands.

"Bahg! What's wrong with your hands?" she said.

Deacon looked at her sheepishly.

"Rullox broke them," he said. After yesterday he didn't dare embellish at all.

"Gods, you're useless," she grumbled and took the gun back. She reached for a manual lever type and handed that to him. "Maybe you can use both of your useless nubs to work this one."

She led him to a long conveyor belt and pointed out the same wheels underneath that she had been working on the day before.

"These need to be greased so that what happened yesterday doesn't happen again. Each wheel has a port for you to inject the grease. Do both sides. We'll see if your dumb hands will work well enough to be of some use to me. There's more grease in the closet if you run out. Now, don't bother me. I have to go work on the skid." With that, she walked away, leaving Deacon looking at the ridiculously long conveyor belt in dismay.

He found it near impossible to place the fitting over the port with enough force that the grease didn't come spilling out everywhere when he depressed the lever with his two palms. After ten minutes of working and swearing at the first wheel, he finally gritted his teeth and pushed. The pain was intense, but the fitting slipped onto the port with a satisfying click. When he depressed the lever, the grease injected into the wheel's interior bearings for a time and only began to spill out when the insides were full.

Deacon yanked the hose off the port and went to the next port down the line. He gritted his teeth again and swore at the pain as he forced the fitting over the port. It went like that for twenty or so ports until he ran out of grease.

He went to the closet and changed out the tube of grease, and grabbed two spare tubes. He looked up at the wall of tools. He had always enjoyed fixing things and had always been interested in tools, but he didn't have a name for many of these. He began to turn to leave, and his gaze fell on a roll of seal tape. The tape gave him an idea.

A half hour later, he was back to work on the conveyor belt with newly taped fingers. The work progressed much quicker after that. The tape hardened into a durable second skin that supported his broken digits. He had left his joints free of the tape so that he could still bend his fingers, but the broken segments of bone had been casted in the stuff. The pain was still there, but it did not hurt nearly as bad when he put pressure on them.

He worked on greasing the wheels all day. By the end, his chest and ribs hurt abominably, and despite the tape, his fingers had almost gone numb with pain. The Kalix girl came back just as he was finishing up with the last two wheels. She watched him for a minute, and Deacon had to force himself to continue working and try to ignore her presence. After a while, she saw his fingers.

"You idiot! That stuff is going stay on your fingers for years!" She looked incredulous.

"Well, at least I won't be useless."

Her mouth opened and closed, then opened again. She obviously struggled with what to say. Finally, she tilted her head and peered at him through those two beautiful green eyes.

"I am Nah-leesi," she made a weird gesture with her hand and gave him a very slight bow.

"Deacon," he said and held out his hand as Elijah had done to him. He was pretty sure he was doing it right. She hesitantly gripped it, and he shook it as Elijah had his. She smiled briefly before a scowl returned to her large eyes.

"Tell Anzark that he doesn't need to accompany you, all he does is slow you down, and that's no good because you're already so slow. See you tomorrow."

Deacon floated back to the Barracks.

CHAPTER 7

Deacon was so sore he wondered if he would ever feel better. He lay in the corner by Elijah's bed roll, waiting for the old man. He stretched his fingers out straight with a groan. Using them today had probably been a mistake, but he knew that the Tendari didn't support the weak or injured for long. He had to make sure that he was doing something productive, or Anzark would probably request that he be thrown out of an airlock.

Deacon thought about what he'd learned from Elijah and wondered how the man knew so much. He said he was a Keeper, whatever that was. Soon, Deacon was imagining other humans. What they looked like, how they spoke, and even what colors they were. It had been a surprise for him that Elijah was a different color than himself. His mother had been dark-brown like him, but Elijah was light-skinned. He supposed that he should have anticipated the differences since most alien species had occasional differences in their color or physical appearance.

Deacon was suddenly brought back to himself when he noticed a large figure standing close by. It was the tall Tarpin that Elijah had injured in the fight. Deacon tensed. He should have been paying closer attention. He shuffled under the blankets for the knife that Elijah had left him, cursing when it eluded him.

"That's right, little boy. Are you afraid? You should be,"

the Tarpin said.

Deacon's fear subsided slightly as he realized that if the alien had wanted to kill him, he wouldn't be talking. He looked at the Tarpin and saw that the alien's leg was tightly bandaged, but he put as little weight on it as possible and stood there leaning to one side.

"That's interesting...I was going to ask you the same question," Elijah's voice came from behind the Tarpin.

The Tarpin spun, almost losing his balance in his haste. Even so, he hopped awkwardly on his good leg. The alien snarled at Elijah's words, but when Elijah took a step forward, the Tarpin shuffled quickly back. It was evident that the Tarpin was, indeed, afraid of this much smaller human.

"Let me make this very clear. This part of the barracks is off-limits to you or any of your friends. Any of you step foot past that corner," he pointed toward the nearest corner of their alcove, "then I will kill you in the most painful way I can come up with... and I am very creative."

The Tarpin stood there shaking with either fear or rage. Deacon wasn't sure which.

"What is your name, Tarpin?" Elijah asked.

The alien didn't answer right away. Deacon understood his reluctance. The politics of this place were far more complicated than anyone would guess. If the Tarpin answered, it might seem like he was subservient to this human. On the other hand, if he didn't, then he might be humbled once again by Elijah. The Tarpin weighed his options. Finally, he responded.

"Silax. You will remember it," he said.

Not bad, thought Deacon. He answered but included a subtle threat that would disguise his obedience to the human.

"Silax. If you wish to live, you will leave now and never bother Deacon or me again."

Silax didn't rush to obey. His pride wouldn't let him, that is, until Elijah took another step toward the alien.

Silax hobbled as quickly as he could past Elijah, grumbling Tarpin swear words as he went. Deacon let out a breath he didn't know he was holding.

He had no doubt that if Elijah hadn't arrived, the scenario would have ended up quite different. He smiled at the man as he came over and squatted beside him.

"Thank you, Elijah. Even wounded, I would have been easy prey for him."

"Don't mention it. We have to look out for each other. It's the only reason humans haven't gone completely extinct already. How are you feeling today?"

Deacon told him how he may have overdone it working with Nah-leesi. He held up his hands to show him as if Elijah could see his pain.

"I see that you wrapped them. You did a decent enough job, too, except you did it with seal tape. The stuff makes excellent casting material, but you're going to have to wait a long time before they come off."

"I know, but I needed them to work," Deacon said, somewhat defensively.

Elijah waved off Deacon's terseness. "We need to begin your education, and since you are injured, we'll have to just focus on the mental aspects and not the physical, although we will need to give you some training soon before you're Silax meat."

Deacon sat up a little, excited that Elijah would be teaching him anything. He had received no proper education, of course, and what training he'd received was in the rudiments of space walking so that he was more useful as a miner.

"Let's begin with history."

Elijah talked while Deacon listened intently, for the most part, only occasionally interrupting the older man with questions. Hours seemed to pass in a blink of an eye, and they were both yawning before they knew it.

"That will have to be enough for tonight. We have work in

the morning." Elijah said, putting an end to the lesson.

As Deacon settled down to sleep, he realized just how tired he was just moments before he succumbed to the comforting embrace of unconsciousness.

The next few days passed quickly. He spent his days doing what he could to help Nah-leesi maintain the mining equipment and his nights learning what he could from Elijah. As they talked, Deacon began to feel the magnitude of what he was learning. He felt, somehow, responsible for the survival of his species' culture and that, through him, humans could withstand the torment of slavery and subjugation. He concentrated and did his best to learn quickly.

For the most part, Elijah seemed impressed with his passion and willingness to learn, but Deacon felt antsy, like he needed to do more. Since Elijah materialized in his life, Deacon had become more and more convinced that his life could be more. He knew that he would most-likely live the rest of his pathetic existence on the Rock, but he had something more now. When he attempted to diagnose the feeling, he realized he finally had a definition for the word 'hope.'

He *hoped* that someday, maybe, he and all of humanity would find their freedom, and who knew, maybe he would be a part of that. He found himself day-dreaming more and more about the possibilities that awaited him. He began to feel a sense of happiness, slight as it was, that he had never felt before, and he knew that there was an existence beyond the Rock, beyond Anzark and beyond even the Tendari.

One day Anzark trundled down the corridor and found Nah-leesi and Deacon working on an electric motor that had seized.

"Deacon, I think it's time for you to get back to the mine. You've milked your down time long enough. Tomorrow you will start your shift like normal."

Nah-leesi looked to Deacon, then to Anzark. She scoffed

and chuffed angrily.

"Don't you even start with me," Anzark said, raising a hand to forestall her protests. "I give you a lot of leeway, Nah-leesi, but you're walking a fine line. You push it, and you'll be space hopping with the rest of them."

"Do you really think I can do all this by myself?" She said, motioning at the surroundings vaguely with both hands. "There is far too much down here to manage for just one person."

"I thought you did not like the human," Anzark said. He folded his short arms and smiled at Nah-leesi as if he had scored a point.

"Well, for a human, he's not bad. He's better than nothing."

Deacon, oddly, wasn't offended by her response. In fact, knowing Nah-leesi, this was high praise.

"Well, *nothing* is what you're going to have to deal with for a while, Nah-leesi. We just don't have enough people to spend them on maintenance. The quotas are just too high."

Anzark exploded, without warning, in a coughing fit that doubled him over. Slimy spittle glistened in a long line toward the floor. For a moment, Deacon wondered if this would be the end of the task master and silently wished it would be, though he doubted Anzark's replacement would be any better. Finally, Anzark was able to take slow, shuddering breaths and straighten. He wiped the drool from his gaping mouth.

During the episode, Nah-leesi and Deacon had done absolutely nothing, they had just watched the alien struggle to breathe, and Anzark glowered at them after he gained a degree of composure.

"Bahg, but this dust is horrible. You should do something about it," Anzark said to Nah-leesi, and with that, he turned and ambled off.

Nah-leesi let out a string of curses in Anzark's wake. She turned to the motor and kicked at it angrily.

"If it helps, I don't want to leave."

"Of course, you don't want to leave, you dumb mud-thumper. I imagine work down here is slightly less dangerous than it is out there in the vacuum, chipping rocks in ancient tech."

Deacon smiled. He couldn't help it. His time with Nahleesi had somehow made her insults endearing.

"What are you smiling at?" She poked him hard in the shoulder.

"I'm going to miss you, I think," he said, then felt embarrassed by the admission. He was sure she would hate him for it.

She stayed quiet for a while, staring at him as if gauging if he told the truth, then she burst out laughing.

"You've got to live one sad life if you are going to miss this," she punched him in the shoulder, still chuckling to herself and turned back to the motor.

Deacon was still sore, and it pained him to do certain things, but he definitely felt better than he had. He wouldn't say that he was ready to go back to work mining, but he supposed that they had let him 'idle' longer than he expected them to.

As Deacon walked back to the barracks that night, he realized that he was nervous to go back to work with the other slaves. He had been successful at staying away from most of the aliens since his fight with Rullox, but tomorrow he would face them all, at least for a short time, and he worried about what they might do or say. At least Elijah would be there. It was a strange feeling to have someone that would help him. He had been so long without anyone to look up to that the feeling felt foreign but entirely welcome.

CHAPTER 8

This time when he made his way to the window where they doled out the rations, Deacon received a full tube of the grayish nutritional paste. He swallowed half of the tube and kept the rest for later like he used to before he was injured. Despite his anxiety about the other slaves, there was something comforting about resuming his duties. This is what he was used to. What he knew.

Deacon followed Elijah into the equipment room. He didn't want to seem like he was hiding from the other slaves, but Elijah's presence was a comfort. When they entered, there was a cacophony of conversation among various different alien species, and the noise was intense, but as their presence was realized, the alien's talk subsided into a chorus of whispers.

A hundred eyes of differing sizes, shapes, and colors stared at him. He paused for a while near the entrance and waited for his heartbeat to settle. Ahead of him, Elijah continued on to the locker next to Deacon's, where his suit was stored. Deacon breathed out once, forcefully, then followed.

Soon the conversations resumed their previous volume, and the stares were fleeting rather than prolonged. Deacon needed help from Elijah to lift the heavy section of the suit that covered his abdomen as the movement sent stabs of protest through his chest and ribs. Deacon couldn't help but overhear comments criticizing his weakness as Elijah lowered the piece into place.

Eventually, he and Elijah were ready, and they made their way to the lift, where most of the other alien slaves waited to begin their shift. After a few minutes of wait, the massive door rumbled closed, and the lift began to ascend slowly toward the cold surface of the Rock.

When the air was sucked from the room and the door rose once more to reveal the barren surface and the black expanse above, Deacon ritually exhaled his pent up breath. It seemed he would not face a complete suit failure today, at least not yet.

"Take care of yourself," Elijah said before exiting the lift and, using his thrusters, skipping across the surface toward his mining area.

Deacon headed off toward his own area, being careful to stay out of the way of the other slaves as they all scattered to their designated work zones. He was happy that his fix on the thrusters still held, and he was able to count on them when he needed them.

The digger was where he had last left it, and it didn't appear that anyone had been working in his area since he had been injured. He clipped-in to the machine and began separating the stubborn ore from among the useless rock and frozen water, cursing when the articulating teeth of the device caught in the craggy surface.

He worked nonstop for half the day, breaking up the ore into manageable pieces and piling it until he had enough ore for his daily quota. He paused and pulled his arms back into his suit and pulled the rest of his rations from the front pocket of his coveralls, and fed the tube up into the helmet of his overly large suit. It felt good to have full rations again.

With his miniscule meal finished, he detached the digger and picked up a large boulder of ore, then set off toward the hopper. As he drew near the huge ore crushing machine, he queued up behind Denzink, one of the fat Kupeltis. The alien plodded along slowly in front of Deacon, and he was tempted to pass the alien but thought that that would undoubtedly anger the Kupelti, so he slowed his pace and waited for the alien to drop his load. Denzink would never have been able to keep up with his quota if it hadn't been for the Kupelti strength. The alien held a massive boulder, one so big that the alien suit had extensions on the arms to grip the huge rock.

When Denzink was directly below the lip of the hopper, he set his feet wide and took an agonizingly long time to engage his thrusters. Finally, the alien lifted off the surface with a jolt. When the thrusters engaged, however, an air hammer fell from a clip on his waist and trailed behind Denzink by its hose that connected to a tank on his back. The tool drifted twenty or so feet behind and below the alien.

Deacon saw the danger immediately and fumbled on the comms switch.

"Denzink! Denzink! You have a hammer hanging from your back!"

Deacon heard static and then a mumbled response he couldn't understand, then panic.

"No! No!" Denzink yelled.

Deacon didn't hesitate. He dropped his boulder and hit his thruster controls. He rose like a rocket and was soon over the lip of the hopper, but Denzink wasn't there. He spent precious seconds searching for the alien until he looked below him.

Denzink was being pulled relentlessly toward the crushing teeth by the tangled hose of the air hammer. A flash of fear shone up from under the tinted visor of the alien's helmet, and Deacon was reminded of his own terror when he had been nearly killed by this same death-trap.

Deacon cut his thrusters and dropped inside the edge of the hopper. Denzink yelled incoherently up at him, his fear making the words too garbled for the translator to work, and yet his meaning was all too clear. Deacon reached down and gripped one of the long extensions that Denzink had used to grip the ore, pointed his feet down and punched the thrusters.

They rose a few feet as the added tension stretched the hose but stopped as all of the slack was used up. Deacon cranked up his thrusters to the max and held on with both hands. He doubted he would have the strength to hold on for long but made a silent promise to hold on as long as he could. His fingers screamed in agony, and he was sure that if it had not been for the seal tape, they would have rebroken under the sudden strain, but he held on.

For a second or two, Denzink seemed to calm slightly, hope having been restored with Deacon's help, but as the teeth began to draw them inexorably downward, the alien screamed with renewed terror.

Deacon knew all too well the fear that gripped Denzink's heart and gripped the extension with all the strength he could muster, but it didn't seem to be enough. The metal extension arm slid slowly through his grip, and it would just be a matter of seconds before Deacon lost his grip entirely.

Something gave, and they were launched with surprising speed out of the hopper, both of their suit's thrusters propelling them up and out into the darkness of space. Deacon cut his thrusters almost immediately, but Denzink didn't, and his thrust sent them into a frightening spin.

Deacon almost let go of the alien, but he was afraid that, in his current state, Denzink wouldn't be able to orient fast enough to get back to the Rock.

"Cut your thrusters!" Deacon yelled at Denzink.

The Kupelti just continued his wailing, unintelligible scream. Deacon pulled on the extension and brought himself closer to Denzink. He reached up and gripped the alien's helmet in both hands and yelled at him face to face.

"Denzink! Cut your thrusters!"

Denzink's far-away look of despondent terror resolved into understanding, and a second later, his thrusters shut off. Their spinning had not subsided, of course, but now, perhaps, Deacon could correct their deadly course. He turned his head around, trying to orient himself with the asteroid, and when he finally found a quick glimpse of it, his heart sank. They had traveled so far, so fast.

Deacon concentrated on their spinning and adjusted himself so that his thrusters pointed in the opposite direction of their spinning and gave it a few short bursts. The forces that seemed to want to pull his insides out of him seemed to lesson, and he accepted that as a good sign. He reoriented himself and saw the Rock over his left shoulder, spinning around to his right. He gave his thrusters another tap, and their spin stopped. He could only assume they were still moving away from the Rock at nearly the same speed they had been, and he repositioned his legs so that they pointed away from the asteroid.

"Hold on," Deacon told the trembling Denzink.

The alien's grip tightened around Deacon's already wounded ribs, and he coughed out in protest.

"Not that tight."

Deacon held his breath and hit the thrusters.

The Rock began to drift out of view, and Deacon had to adjust himself quickly to bring the asteroid back on target. For a while, he wasn't sure if they were making any progress toward the distant target, but soon the Rock was coming toward them quickly, too quickly.

Deacon began to panic, only a little at first, but more as the asteroid came on, larger and larger until it was the only thing in their view. He tucked his knees up and cut his thrusters, then twisted and engaged them again. Luckily he had gauged it correctly, and they had spun just enough to bring them flying feet first toward the surface of the Rock. He cut the Thrusters and let them descend, slowly now, to the surface.

He remembered back to a time when he had been out at his mining area working away at the ore when a small asteroid shot down into the surface of the Rock. The impact sent pulverized rock out into space to forever travel farther from the crater of its origin. Now, he felt a little like that asteroid and hit the thrusters again at the last second.

They landed hard, but Deacon flexed his knees and didn't seem to break anything on impact. Denzink sagged to the ground breathing heavily. Other slaves skipped across the surface of the Rock toward them. Out of nowhere, Deacon realized that voices echoed in his helmet. Their comms were still open, and the slaves chattered in excitement.

To Deacon's knowledge, many slaves had made the terrifying flight out into open space, but none had ever made it back. There had been many different methods by which they had been sent on their flights. Some had thruster malfunctions. Some had been launched off the surface by a malfunctioning piece of mining equipment, but all had died screaming in the cold darkness.

It was secretly the biggest fear of every slave on the Rock, and each alien that approached couldn't refrain from lifting Denzink from the ground and hoisting the heavy Kupelti onto their shoulders in celebration. Some of the slaves even slapped Deacon on the back in congratulations. He wasn't delusional enough to accept their excitement as a new-found friendship. He knew that it was the act of defeating the fear of certain death in all of their minds that had freed them to approach him so openly, and yet he couldn't help but smile.

CHAPTER 9

It was surprising to Deacon how much his act of saving Denzink had changed his own life. It started with simple nods from those who had completely ignored his existence before. It grew to one-word comments from slaves who had never before considered him worthy of speaking to. This change seemed like such a big difference in his life that he felt like a different person altogether.

The other slaves were still not what Deacon would call friendly, but they seemed to accept him, while other slaves, like Silax, hated him more than ever. It was like his act of saving the alien had pushed his standing with Silax over the edge into near hysteria.

One day, not long after the incident, a Guzonian spoke to Deacon in the lift. He had been within hearing of Silax, and the two word sentence that he'd said to Deacon was enough to send Silax into a rage. He threw his helmet against the lift door repeatedly until the visor was shattered.

Deacon was sure that that infraction probably cost the Tarpin a week's worth of water rations, something that he was sure Silax would blame on him. He was convinced that if Elijah hadn't been there, looking on, Silax would have torn Deacon to pieces.

Deacon wouldn't have ever guessed the phrase: "Move,

please." would elicit such a reaction. Maybe it was because the Guzonian said the word, please. He was worried for the alien's safety, and judging from the look on his face, the Guzonian was equally worried. He obviously hadn't anticipated such a reaction from the hysteric Tarpin either, and the outburst undoubtedly gave him something to stress over.

Elijah had been more concerned with Deacon's safety than that of the Guzonian and began training him in self-defense and martial arts that very night. Deacon hadn't known what those things were until Elijah explained, at length, that they were ancient forms of human hand-to-hand combat.

Now, a week later, Deacon was breathing hard in the dim light of the barracks, sweat running down his face. Elijah was barely breathing hard. It wasn't fair. The old man should be gasping. Everyone knew that when things got old, they started to fall apart. Why was Elijah still so strong?

Deacon had been punching the air for hours, and his muscles were burning. His shoulders ached with the need to put his arms down, but his pride kept them up far longer than he would have thought possible.

Elijah did the exercises right along with Deacon and critiqued his technique at every opportunity because... "It's easier to teach you the basics correctly than to go back later and try and fix them." Deacon didn't really understand, but he went along with it.

What was even more aggravating was the fact that Elijah could still speak while doing the routine. More than that. He could and did give lectures. The lessons were mostly stories of the past. History that instilled in Deacon a sense of belonging. Knowing the stories that made up his dormant culture helped him cope with his feelings of loneliness and worthlessness, and it gave him purpose.

As he learned, he grew more and more determined that he would leave the Rock. He would leave and join what free humans he could find and try to make a future with his people. His people. He had never thought of them like that before. Never before had he viewed other humans as anything other than some phantasm made of half opaque mist. Before Elijah, he didn't even have a clear mental picture of what humans looked like.

Sure, he had seen his own reflection, but as he learned upon Elijah's arrival, he looked quite a bit different than the old man. Were there other humans that had blue or green skin like the Kalix? Or perhaps red like the Tendari?

When Deacon asked Elijah this question, between gasps for air, the old man chuckled good naturedly.

"The skin tones don't vary to the wide degree you have described, unfortunately. Our two extremes are about as varied as it gets in humans. When humans lived on Earth, they had many races and cultures. Many of the races differed physiologically, though none were so varied as, say, the Carexi. Unfortunately, many of the races died out with the destruction of Earth."

Deacon couldn't believe how bad his muscles burned with these exercises. It's not like he was lifting anything heavy, he was just lifting his arms and legs, but the movement drove fire into his appendages. His muscles had never been so sore as they had been these past few days.

His goal had been to go until Elijah called an end to the sessions, but so far, he had collapsed in a sweaty heap every night before the old man gave the word.

Deacon began to think that the old man would never call an end. Maybe it was supposed to keep going for as long as Deacon could go. If that was the case, why was he pushing himself? He should just stop now and save himself from the added torture, but something pushed him onward.

Deciding it was better when his mind was occupied, he queried Elijah once again.

"How do you know so much?" He gasped.

Elijah didn't answer right away.

"After Earth was destroyed, and it was evident that the Tendari were hunting the remaining humans in the solar system, our ancestors hid their educational resources to keep them away from the enemy. Word eventually got out where the caches of information were hidden, and free humans were able to rescue much of the data."

"Years later, it was decided that the information was too vulnerable, and so a secret education program was started. Free humans would elect Keepers to learn all they could from the store of Earth's data. It was thought this would disperse the knowledge, making it more difficult to eradicate."

Deacon paused in his shadow sparring and turned to Elijah.

"Should you really be saying all of this out loud?" He scanned the room's dark corners, sure they were being watched.

"The Tendari already know of the Keepers. They already know of the program and the information, but apparently, it doesn't really concern them no more, at any rate, than the prospect of free humans. They still hunt those of us that are free, but there is little distinction for them between a Keeper and anyone else. For that, I am grateful."

Deacon was surprised. In his mind, the Tendari should be targeting the Keepers and hunting for the data. Without it, humans were a lost and lonely bunch, dispirited and broken. Deacon was learning first hand the importance people like Elijah were to the rest of them. For the first time in his life, he felt anchored, and he, too, felt gratitude for the Tendari's ignorance.

Elijah clicked his tongue against his teeth and motioned for Deacon to continue the exercise. He sighed and punched the air. It was soon time to change stances, and Deacon felt momentary relief as different muscles were targeted. This motion, Deacon assumed, was a block of some kind, but Elijah hadn't gotten into what each piece that he learned was for. The old man had just said something about how he had to teach his body to do these basic motions so that later they would surface naturally.

It didn't take long for Deacon to reach his limit once again, and he stopped the movement and bent over, gasping. They had been at it for hours. Surely Elijah would want to finish soon.

"Well, it seems that you are done for the night," Elijah said, lending credence to Deacon's theory that he would always go as long as Deacon was able to.

Deacon heard a scuffling sound and glanced up to see Anzark shuffle into their corner.

"Exercise, huh?" Anzark said. "That is good. We always want to encourage such initiative in the miners."

Deacon stood up straight, and they looked at the taskmaster without saying a word. Anzark obviously expected some sort of small talk in return, but the silence grew awkward. Finally, Anzark continued uncomfortably.

"I am to accompany you to commander Grato."

Elijah made to follow the big alien, but Anzark raised a hand.

"Not you," he pointed at Deacon. "Him."

Deacon exchanged a worried look with Elijah and then strode toward Anzark.

The Kupelti led Deacon through corridors he had never been down before, but unlike those leading to Nah-leesi, these were devoid of the unsightly pipework and valves. The corridors were altogether nicer than anywhere he had been before. They were clean and well-lit, and there was a distinct lack of odor.

"Denzink is my friend, you know," Anzark said. Deacon was shocked. He didn't expect Anzark to talk so openly with him about anything personal, and yet he got the sense that the alien wasn't done.

"I...I didn't," Deacon finally responded.

"I must say your stunt out there seemed to have caught a lot of people's attention. If you play your cards right, you may come out of this atop the heap."

Deacon wasn't sure what he meant but nodded anyway. He hoped that the attention that he got wasn't from someone like Silax. As they walked, Deacon noticed that the air seemed to get heavier and warmer, far warmer than he was used to, and despite the heat, he shivered.

Anzark must have sensed Deacon's discomfort.

"Don't worry. Grato can be harsh, but he is reasonable. I was on Canto 72 before I came to the Rock, and the commander there was far more...strict."

Deacon nodded again. He had heard the stories and seen some of the aftermaths of Grato's "harshness." It was enough to intimidate anyone, but the last time Deacon had seen the Tendari, he had been spared, so maybe Grato wouldn't kill him this time, either. Despite the logical side of his brain testifying to him that his nervousness was unwarranted, the unease would not leave and the sweat that the exercise had begun continued unabated.

CHAPTER 10

Deacon was led to a large door guarded by two vicious-looking
Tendari Marines. They growled at Deacon when they saw him
but put in the access code to allow Anzark and him to proceed
regardless of their obvious contempt for him. They proceeded
through warm halls that, for the life of him, felt wet. As they
walked, more and more Tendari appeared. It was here that
Deacon saw his first Tendari, not dressed in the armor of a
soldier. The alien was just as tall and muscular looking as the
rest, but he wore a plain-looking suit that Deacon assumed must
be a uniform from the bars across his chest that he thought must
indicate some kind of rank.

　　The alien sneered at him as he passed, and Deacon couldn't
help cringing from the sight. Anzark took him to a small room
and motioned for him to sit in a chair. Deacon hoisted himself
into the giant chair and let his feet dangle. His back didn't reach
the chair's back, and so he sat slightly hunched and completely
aware of his diminutive size. He felt exposed in the small room
that, despite its size, was busy with Tendari coming and going.
It seemed that every Tendari that passed through eyed Deacon
angrily. He soon decided it was best to just keep his head down
and try to ignore the growls and rude comments. He yawned. It
was late. Did the Tendari ever sleep?

Finally, after what seemed like an eternity, a wiry Tendari with more of a pink complexion than the red that was common among their race stepped out of a door to Deacon's left. He came to Anzark and growled to get his attention.

"Commander Grato will see you now," the Tendari said.

Anzark nodded, the fat rolls encompassing his neck jiggling with the motion. Anzark stood and signaled Deacon to do the same.

Deacon jumped off of the chair and followed Anzark to the door. Anzark exhaled loudly, then pressed the button next to the door. It slid open without a sound, and they stepped in.

The room's interior was darker than the corridor and the room outside, but it was just as hot and wet. The room was larger than the one they just came from, and at the far end sat Grato. He was behind a massive metal table upon which sat scores of the digital tablets that the Tendari carried. Deacon wasn't sure what they did with the things, but they seemed important. Grato was looking at one, and the pale blue light that shined from the device made his red skin look purple.

Anzark and Deacon stood with their hands in front of them, waiting for the commander to acknowledge them. Deacon tried but couldn't hold back a yawn. Anzark glared at him.

Finally, Grato set the tablet aside and looked up at them.

"He's small," he said. There was silence for a spell until Anzark decided that Grato expected a response.

"Humans are very small, sir," Anzark said uncomfortably.

"I know they're small!" Commander Grato exploded. "Do you think I'm stupid?"

"No....No sir," Anzark stammered.

"Boy, are you small for your age?" Grato asked Deacon.

Deacon swallowed nervously.

"I don't know, sir." Deacon waited for the Commander to respond, but as with Anzark, it was clear that he wanted more. "I am the only human I have to go by. I suppose that by that standard, I am exactly the right size."

Grato stared at Deacon for a few seconds. Seconds that felt like an eternity. Then he roared. The sound frightened Deacon, but he soon realized the alien must be laughing. The sound was a disturbing snarling cough that was about as far from jovial as Deacon could imagine.

"I like this human," Grato laughed.

Anzark smiled and half-heartedly joined in the laughter. A chirp sounded from the door, and Grato pressed a button on his desk. The door slid open, and a soldier entered carrying a tray of something that smelled amazing. Deacon craned his head to try and see what was on the tray, but he was too short.

"The galley said that you hadn't eaten yet, sir, so I took the liberty to bring this to you," the Tendari said.

"Put it on the desk," Grato said.

'Desk' was a new word for Deacon. When the soldier placed the tray on the table, he realized it must be another word for table, though he didn't know why two words were needed for such a simple object.

On the tray was a pile of gray-brown...something. Despite the heat in the room, steam rose from what Deacon assumed was food. He scrutinized the tray intently until Grato did his snarling cough-laugh again.

"It looks good, doesn't it?" he said.

Deacon only nodded, embarrassed by how he was acting.

"Would you like to try some? Anything has got to be better than that nutrient paste that they stuff in you slaves."

Deacon was awe-struck. This must be a trick. Why was he being so kind? It seemed incredible that the Tendari Commander of the Rock would offer him food from his own tray. Deacon hesitated and glanced side-long at Anzark, who didn't return his gaze. Finally, Deacon nodded slowly.

Grato smiled. His massive razor teeth made the spectacle intimidating rather than comforting. He picked up a piece of the food and tossed it to Deacon. He barely caught it. It was greasy and hot. He passed it from hand to hand till it cooled. He examined the food and saw a hard white-grey shaft coming out of the brown that looked like it could be...bone. He almost dropped it. This was flesh of some kind. His mind was flooded with a million possibilities for the origins of this...meat. He had to search his brain for the correct word.

He had only heard about meat through an occasional translation from some home-sick alien who pined for the food. He knew it was an animal, but to a Tendari, was he an animal?

Could this meat be some poor human? His thoughts drifted as he looked at it. Maybe it was Carexi or Guzonian or one of the myriad other aliens on the Rock. Maybe this was some of the remains of Rullox. He was disgusted by the thought, and yet, the smell was intoxicating.

He knew that he could not refuse Grato's generosity. Even if it was human flesh, he would be forced, by unspoken law, to eat it. And so, he took a bite. The taste was unlike anything he had ever experienced.

He had bitten his tongue once so badly that it bled profusely, and he had imagined that meat would taste like that metallic blood and tough as the muscles in his arms or legs, but this was not. This meat was tender and juicy, but the juice was not blood. It tasted salty but not like sweat which was Deacon's only experience with the flavor.

The texture was a whole other level of experience for him. He soon realized he was unused to using his teeth, but this felt natural. He tore a second bite from the hunk of meat and groaned with pleasure.

Commander Grato laughed again, entertained by Deacon's ignorant exuberance. He finished the scrap of meat and sucked on the bone. He grew embarrassed as he came back to himself. He put the denuded bone to his side and stood stiffly in front of Grato once again.

"I'm glad you enjoyed it. Some are not so reticent to accept my hospitality," he said.

Grato picked up a small piece of the meat from his tray and sat back in his chair while he nibbled at the food. It looked almost comical. He was giant sized, with razor sharp teeth that extruded past his lips, and yet he ate delicately.

"I'm sure you're wondering why I called you here," Grato said. "Your recent heroics have caused quite a stir among the other slaves. While there is nothing wrong with that right now, I must warn you about further incitement regardless of the reasons. You have been in the spotlight too much of late, and that is never a good thing in your profession."

Grato paused and leaned forward in his chair once more.

"Now, that's not to say that I was not impressed by your level-headedness during a time of crisis. It's not often that a slave of any race can handle himself in the same way as you did when faced with the open blackness of space. That is something that is highly prized by any good commander, and so I have deemed that your time in the mines is over."

Deacon's heart raced.

"We have an opening in one of our exterior maintenance crews on board the Gorski."

Deacon frowned, unfamiliar with the name, and Grato picked up on his confusion and pressed on.

"The Gorski is the corsair ship that is tethered to the Rock as this facility's naval support."

Deacon nodded his understanding, and Grato continued.

"You will be required to space walk along the hull of the Gorski and perform all manner of functions. You start tomorrow. You will continue to sleep in the barracks with the other slaves, but you will leave every morning and come to this section of the compound where you will be shuttled to the Gorski. Any questions?"

He had a million questions, but none he felt comfortable

bothering the commander with. He shook his head.

"Anzark, you will still be in charge of feeding him, but all other responsibilities fall to me and those that will be over him in the maintenance crew." Anzark looked slightly perturbed but quickly schooled his face and nodded his acceptance of the commander's wishes.

Deacon wasn't sure what the commander meant by 'responsibilities,' but it sounded like he had just been promoted if a slave could be promoted. He smiled.

CHAPTER 11

The next morning, Deacon awoke still tired but excited and nervous to start his new position. Elijah had been more than a little skeptical about the whole thing and warned Deacon repeatedly to be careful. Everyone knew that the Tendari were touchy, to say the least, but Elijah's warnings seemed more to do with his reluctance to believe that Grato and the Tendari would do anything positive in the life of an alien slave. He seemed suspicious of their motives.

Deacon hurried to the window where they passed out the rations and grabbed his with a smile and a word of thanks to the female Carexi that hunched behind the opening. She seemed surprised by his mood and glared at his retreating back.

After wishing Elijah a good day and receiving yet another admonition for safety, he made his way down the corridors he'd walked through the night before. The closer he came to the Tendari annex, the more nervous he became. He turned a corner and swallowed when he saw the Guards and the intimidating door waiting to receive him.

The Guards growled at him, and unlike every other time, a Tendari had growled at him, this time, he felt chilled to the bone. Before, their aggression had been mitigated by the fact that at least some other alien had been present to disperse the Tendari ire, but now he was alone. There was no question to whom the growls were intended, and the sight of such a small and seemingly weak specimen might just initiate their only slightly repressed predator/prey instinct.

Deacon paused in the hallway and contemplated running in the other direction but shook it off. He squared his shoulders and proceeded toward the door.

"My name's Deacon. Commander Grato told me to come here," he was ashamed at the way it had come out more like a question than a statement.

The two growled again, more fiercely, but Deacon held his ground. He was sure his resolve would win him some kind of respect from the two, but their threatening posture didn't subside. Finally, after a lifetime of being viewed as a tray of meat by the two, Deacon...growled back.

He was doing it before conscious thought could tell him it was a bad idea, and upon later analysis, he would feel embarrassed by the action. He must have looked ridiculous, standing on his tip-toes with a puffed-out chest, growling at the two massive sentries, but he didn't care. He didn't even think, in that moment, how he looked or how they could have ripped him apart in a matter of seconds. In that moment, he did what he felt was needed. There was no other way to explain it.

The guards' reactions were instantaneous. Their growls cut off, and they stood back in shock. Deacon finally ran out of breath and let his growl fade away with his wind. The two sentries looked at each other and then began a far more intense version of the laugh that commander Grato had done the night before. The snarling, coughing laugh would have scared Deacon had he not gotten a glimpse of it beforehand. Even so, it was still troubling. Drool escaped one of the guard's mouths in his fit, and it traced a glittering trail from one long tooth down to a hanging globule of saliva that swung back and forth with his head until the pendulum-like motion broke it free from its glistening tether and it fell to the floor below.

Finally, the guards gathered themselves enough to open the door, though residual coughs of laughter echoed through the doorway after him. After the door closed and silence filled the corridor once more, Deacon was half certain that the two would still be laughing about it that night when he returned from his shift. He was surprised at how much these scary aliens laughed and how little the laughter softened their image in his mind. After all, their laugh was more intimidating than most aliens' rage-filled rants.

He had been told which corridor to take to go to the shuttle the night before, and he turned left as the instructions indicated. Several groups of Tendari passed him. All seemed to glare at him, and most growled. He began to wonder if they had all been trained to confront humans and any other 'inferior' aliens in this way. After all, they had become predictable with how consistently they treated him.

He came to a room where a Tendari wearing one of the suits, rather than the armor that was far more common, sat behind a...desk. Deacon nervously approached the desk. The giant sitting on the other side glared, unsurprised, down at him. Deacon shifted under the gaze but refused to avert his own gaze.

"I am Deacon. Commander Grato said to come here for transport to the Gorski."

The alien growled, then spoke through the rumble, somehow conveying words while simultaneously fulfilling his obligatory crossness.

"I know who you are. How many humans do you think come through here? Here is your security badge. If you lose it, I will kill you." The Tendari reached over the tall desk and handed down a plastic card that hung from a tether that Deacon hung around his neck as he had seen Anzark do with his.

"I am lieutenant Grusel. You will report here every morning at this time, where I will enter you in the log, and then you will leave for your shift on the shuttle. Sergeant Trask will be waiting for you on board the Gorski. He will be your shift supervisor. Any questions?"

Deacon was relieved that the growl had subsided, but he knew better than to ask any questions. He was told to wait for the next shuttle, and so he sat down on another oversized chair and swung his legs. Other passengers arrived in the waiting room, all Tendari, and did their customary growls of disapproval before sitting down as well.

After about ten minutes, the doors at the far end of the room opened, and an electronic voice sounded, urging the passengers to board in Tendari. They all entered a small compartment that Deacon realized was a small spaceship. He supposed he didn't know what he had anticipated when they had talked about a 'shuttle,' but this wasn't it.

He hesitated on the threshold, scared to enter. He was bodily thrust forward by an agitated Tendari who used words that his translator didn't bother translating but that Deacon recognized as curse words that described methods of violence that the alien wished to unleash on him. Deacon ducked his head in a suitably chastised manner and crowded into the shuttle craft. He wished for his space suit as the doors slid shut with a squeal, and he felt the craft detach from the airlock. His feet began to lift off of the metal floor, and panic set in. His arms and legs began to windmill as the artificial gravity that was present in the facility was left behind.

He felt his boot strike something, and an angry growl was preceded by giant hands that grabbed him from behind and pressed him against the wall of the shuttle. He could feel the hot breath in his ear as he imagined the Tendari's giant teeth sinking into his horribly exposed neck.

"Do you wish to die, human?" The voice was so close that the ominous whisper sounded loud in his ear.

Deacon shook his head vigorously.

"Then Don't ever touch me again." The Tendari said, then forcefully shoved Deacon back to the floor. Deacon scrabbled for something to hold on to so that he wouldn't accidentally strike another Tendari, and found a ridge in the metal wall of the ship.

After he was able to calm himself and assert some control over his appendages, he looked around, curious as to how the others stayed upright. It was their boots. It seemed that all of the Tendari had boots that stuck to the floor and they held handholds high above Deacon's head that kept them in place. He held on as best he could, trying desperately to stay out of the way of the testy Tendari.

It only took a few minutes for the ship to make the journey to the hull of the Gorski and another four to attach itself to the docking collar, but it felt a lot longer to Deacon. Finally, the door opened, and the Tendari pushed themselves past him with the customary growls rumbling in their throats as they passed. Once he made it out of the shuttle, the corridor before him emptied swiftly, the passengers quickly making their way to their various duties, except for one Tendari, who was easily the largest he had ever seen.

He decided that the giant must be Sergeant Trask, the Tendari he was supposed to meet. He approached the lone alien with all the confidence he could muster. Sergeant Trask did more than growl at the sight of the approaching human. He thundered. His shoulders hunched, and it looked like he would jump on Deacon at any second. He was visibly upset beyond anything he had ever experienced among the Tendari before. Despite his resolve to display confidence, he couldn't help but hesitate at the sight of the angry Sergeant.

"They said I was getting an alien slave, but not a human! And a boy at that!" His voice was like the grinding, crushing bass the hopper made as it demolished ore boulders.

Deacon understood the disappointment that the Sergeant must be feeling. He knew how weak and insignificant he must look to the giant. No wonder they didn't tell him more about Deacon. Trask probably would have smashed the skull of whoever gave him such news.

Deacon thought of Elijah's warning and wondered if this was some joke, some comical way to dispose of Deacon. He knew that commander Grato enjoyed a good joke, and maybe he had something in for Trask. A hilarious prank among the Tendari, but at the expense of Deacon's life. It did make sense, considering they neglected to tell the Sergeant about Deacon.

Trask moved toward Deacon, flexing his massive arms. Deacon began to back pedal, holding up his hands.

"I am small. I can fit in places that your other workers can't." It was the only plus that he could think of for being him. He didn't think the argument would work on Trask, though and closed his eyes in anticipation of a bone-crushing and, perhaps, life-ending blow.

It never came.

He slowly opened his eyes.

Trask towered above him, still glaring hate down at Deacon, but the anger in his eyes wasn't necessarily for him, but for whoever insulted Trask by assigning Deacon to his crew.

Deacon slowly lowered his hands and stood straight.

"Perhaps, keeping me on would prove that you are the better man?" Deacon was reaching and talking to the Tendari like this was a risk, but he hoped it would pay off.

Trask looked down at Deacon, and for an instant, Deacon thought that he had overstepped. Then the alien squinted and seemed to think about what he had said. A moment later, the Sergeant was headed in the opposite direction, toward a corridor busy with passing Tendari.

"Come." Trask rumbled.

CHAPTER 12

Trask led Deacon through a section of the ship, giving him a glimpse of the interior of the Gorski. It was incredible. The corridors were clean and shiny, reflective metal everywhere. The proportions of the Gorski were huge, but not necessarily designed with the large Tendari in mind, but Deacon felt miniscule walking its interior. They passed dozens of Tendari, who all growled their greeting at him with undisguised disgust.

They entered a large room that felt familiar to Deacon. It reminded him of the equipment room back at the mining facility. It was crammed full of space-suits, tools, and repair materials like wire and sheets of metal plating. Deacon looked around the room in awe. The equipment here was pristine. He had never seen suits that were in such good condition.

He lifted his hand to touch one of the suits, and Trask smacked it away from the suit with surprising speed. His hand throbbed from the impact. Deacon held it against his chest protectively.

"Don't touch anything." Trask's rumbling voice whispered. A more ominous command was never given to Deacon, and he nodded quickly to assure the Sergeant of his subjugation.

"Stay here. I need to find you a suit." Trask said. He left Deacon alone in the room.

Deacon wanted to stroll around the room, looking at the equipment, especially those things he didn't recognize from where he was. Instead, he put his hands behind his back and stood still. He was afraid that if Trask came back while he was walking around the room, he would never believe that Deacon hadn't touched anything.

Soon, ten minutes had passed, then twenty. Deacon was feeling tortured by the boredom of having to stay in one place while in such a new and interesting place, so he began shifting his weight from foot to foot, then after another ten minutes, he threw in a little hop. After forty-five minutes, Deacon was seeing how long he could stay balanced on one foot. He wondered if Trask had forgotten about him. What would he do if someone other than Trask came in? Surely they would wonder why a small human had invaded their work area, and, for most Tendari, that would be enough to rip out his throat.

Deacon wondered how far around he could turn in a circle while jumping. He paused his balancing game and crouched, then extended his legs, launching himself into the air. As he rose, he twisted his body as far as it would go and spun. Half way through his rotation Deacon glimpsed Trask's giant form behind him. He had already committed to the spin, and his momentum carried him through the rotation until he was again facing the way he was when he began.

He paused, terror creeping down his spin. He turned to face the alien Sergeant, ready to apologize, but the look on Trask's face brought him up short.

He stared at Deacon, bewildered. Deacon gathered himself once again to apologize, but Trask spoke first.

"They said humans were strange, but I guess I underestimated you."

Deacon looked away, embarrassed.

"Here, I found this in one of our escape pods. It is for a Tendari infant," he held a suit in one hand. Deacon had, of course, never seen a Tendari infant, but surely they were not that big. The suit looked like it would, indeed, fit him. At least, it would probably fit much better than the suit he had been using for years.

He held out his hands, and the Tendari dropped it unceremoniously in his hands, the weight of which nearly bowled him over. His still healing sternum and ribs protested the sudden jarring weight, but he resisted showing any sign of his discomfort.

"Put it on. I have a job for you." As to-the-point as ever, Deacon thought.

Deacon struggled with the new suit. It was different from anything he had ever used or seen. None of the alien slaves had Tendari suits, and he had to figure out the fasteners by himself. Trask climbed into his own suit, and Deacon watched surreptitiously for hints on how the thing worked. Finally, he was done and stood, holding the helmet under his arm. The suit fit perfectly, and Deacon had to hide the smile that came to his lips. He looked at his feet and was pleased to see the same boots the Tendari passengers had in the shuttle.

Trask shouldered a pack and motioned for him to follow, walking out of the room. They went down the corridor to the right and came to an exterior wall of the ship where an airlock waited. Deacon swallowed as they entered. Trask definitely wasn't one for preamble. In a way, Deacon was glad. Getting the actual work out of the way would ease a lot of his anxieties and, hopefully, prove his usefulness to the Sergeant.

Deacon followed Trask's lead, securing his helmet in place. Deacon was surprised to see lights flash across the visor in front of his eyes. Deacon couldn't read in any language, let alone Tendari, and the letters that appeared in front of him were totally foreign. He supposed that some may even be numbers, of which he was equally ignorant. He hoped the suit wasn't trying to tell him something important, like, 'your helmet isn't on all the way, you idiot.' There wasn't much time for him to worry because Trask pressed the decompression button as soon as the inner doors were closed.

Deacon held his breath. No alarm sounded in his helmet, but the lack of it didn't ease his anxiety entirely. After about a minute, the lock was devoid of air, and Trask opened the outer doors. Darkness faced him. Cold, uncompromising space. Stars glittered faintly. The view began to drift slowly, down and to his right. He looked around him and was shocked to see that he had risen off the airlock floor and steadily floated away from the Gorski. Panic started to set in. He began windmilling his arms and legs, trying in vain to find something to grab.

Trask's giant hand closed around his calf and pulled him back into the airlock and down onto the floor.

"Stupid human. You have to engage your mag boots." Trask grumbled and kicked one foot against the other, and with a click, the lights on the sides of his boots turned off, and he began to float off the floor. He kicked again, and the lights turned back on, and he was sucked back down to the floor.

Deacon kicked his foot against the other as Trask had shown him, and the lights on his boots turned on. He pushed his foot down toward the metal floor, and once they were close enough, they were drawn down to it, first one, then the other. They connected to the floor with a loud click, and he instantly tried to lift one of his feet again experimentally, but it was stuck fast.

Deacon looked up into the shadow where Trask's face would be behind the visor as if to ask for some continued guidance. Trask cursed a string of profanity that Deacon committed to memory, then pointed at his own feet and lifted one foot off the floor. It didn't look any different than how Deacon had done it, so he waited for the alien to oblige him further. The massive Sergeant began walking in place, grumbling the whole time. As Deacon watched, he realized that Trask seemed to push down with his heel before lifting his foot. Deacon tried it, and his leg lifted from the floor. He laughed excitedly.

As if unable to resist, Trask swatted the back of Deacon's helmet at the sound of the laughter. The blow would not be much for a Tendari, especially one so large as Trask, but it nearly sent Deacon spinning into space. He prayed that his one boot held firm to the floor. He was finally able to bring his other foot back down and was pleased when the boot sucked down to the floor with a reassuring click.

Trask stepped through the doors and swung his foot over the edge, and then stood so that he was now perpendicular to how they had been standing. Despite the alien's bad temper, Deacon smiled at the strange sight.

"Come," Trask said.

No more encouragement was needed, which was good because Deacon didn't think Trask had any in him. Deacon tried to mimic Trask's technique, but the odd sensation of changing planes was disorienting, to say the least. After some effort, he was able to swing his leg over and attach it to the metal panel that acted as a piece of exterior shielding for the ship.

He sucked in a breath and pushed his left foot's heel down, disengaging the boot and swinging it up to be alongside his other. He knew that he had not done it as cleanly as Trask had, and his wobble as he stood proved that, but he was proud, nonetheless. He looked out ahead of him and saw the long side of the Gorski, and past the end of the ship, he could see a portion of the Rock brightly reflecting light from the distant sun. Light from the Rock highlighted the side of the ship well enough that Deacon could make out the seams and rivets in the metal panels. He marveled at the view and was surprised when he saw Trask walking casually down the ship's side far ahead of him.

Deacon hurried to catch up, but Trask stayed far ahead until he finally stopped and waited impatiently for the small human legs to make up the distance. He was leaning against a piece of the ship that angled out for a span, and once Deacon was alongside the Sergeant, Trask made a show of standing up straight again.

"Now that you have decided to join me, maybe we can finish this job before I'm dead."

"No hurry then?" Deacon said, then panicked. He couldn't believe that it had escaped his lips. Maybe Trask wouldn't hear him.

Trask's blow to the back of his helmet made stars shine in his eyes and his head tingle. Despite his feet being secured by the special boots, Deacon swung forward. If there had been gravity, he would have fallen for sure, but with the boots as his anchor, he went as far forward as his stretched hamstrings would allow and then he teetered back in the other direction. He was sure he looked comical, swinging back and forth like this, but it took several vacillations to get control of his body.

When the ringing in his ears stopped, he could hear the now familiar, snarling cough of a Tendari laugh. He looked at Trask, who didn't seem upset in the least. In fact, he seemed to have enjoyed Deacon's jibe. Deacon was confused until he realized that the Tendari must have slapped him out of startled joviality and not anger. It seemed to Deacon that he would have to watch his jokes as they could cause him more pain than inflicting annoyance on the giant.

Once Trask had finished, he straightened.

"We have a job to do. Actually, you have a job to do," he unshouldered the pack he wore and was careful not to let it go as he pulled an unfamiliar object from it.

"This is a new transponder coil. The old one is bad. You need to remove the old one and replace it with this."

It seemed pretty straightforward, and Deacon nodded his understanding.

"It's down there," Trask said. Pointing to a narrow gap in the exterior of the ship. Deacon approached the crevice and looked down. It looked like a tight fit, even for him, and he gulped. He was far more used to the wide open space than he was to any type of confinement, but he knew that he had to do this. He shimmied down until only his abdomen extended past the lip of the gap, and Trask handed him a small wrench and the replacement coil.

"Oh, and be careful not to touch the ends of the hoses that go in and out of the coil."

"Why?" Deacon couldn't help asking.

"Because, if you do, I will have to explain to my Lieutenant why an infant-sized suit was melted into the life-support relay."

CHAPTER 13

Deacon prayed to the Gods that he didn't snag his suit on something sharp down here and puncture it. What little light had reflected off of the Rock had not made it down to the bottom of the gap that he now climbed down, and he had to rely on the lights on his helmet to see anything. He heard nothing but the sound of his own breath coming too quickly.

He looked up and was surprised by how far he'd come. Why was this crevice in the ship so deep? It seemed like a bad design to Deacon. Though he knew nothing of the complexity around him, it didn't change the fact that the Tendari would, obviously, struggle to reach anything down here. He supposed that he should be grateful. Trask could have killed him and probably would have had it not been for this troublesome coil weighing on the Tendari Sergeant's mind.

If Deacon could replace the coil without 'melting' himself to the ship, then maybe he would be accepted by the Tendari Sergeant and his maintenance crew. Maybe, if he was accepted, he could leave the Rock and have some degree of freedom in his life. Deacon reached the bottom and looked around him. He searched through the myriad foreign parts that were crammed into the space for a similar part to what he held in his hand.

Hoses of all different diameters laced back and forth

through the crevice, and Deacon cautiously moved some to the side to see what lay behind them. Something round but entirely different from the coil he was to replace was affixed to another round thing. He had no clue what the objects were, but he moved his hand to allow the hoses to cover again. He moved on around the cramped space, trying to find the broken part.

"What is taking so long?" Trask's harsh voice echoed through his helmet. Deacon winced at the tone in his voice.

"Uh. I am trying to find the old coil." Deacon replied lamely.

"Well, hurry before I leave you out here."

Deacon sighed and continued his search.

He had made his way down one length of the wall as far as he thought was a reasonable distance from where he initiated his search, then went back and started on the other side. Finally, after peeking around a large metal box that extended from the wall, he saw a coil. It looked the same as the one in his hand, but this one had sporadic flashes of light pulsing through it. He smiled and examined it more closely. It was difficult for him, and he had to allow his legs to float up so that he could get the right angle.

He could see that it was fastened to the wall with a single bolt, and, comparing it to the new one, he could indeed see that there was just one way it could be inserted. He pulled the wrench out of his pouch on the outside leg of his suit and ratcheted out the bolt. It was frustrating work as there was only room for a quarter rotation of the tool, and the bolt came out slowly.

Finally, he could turn it with his fingers, and he spun it the rest of the way out. Before he realized his mistake, the bolt floated away toward the opening high above him.

"Bahg!"

He reached up and just missed the bolt as it floated out of his range.

"Bahg Bahg Bahg."

He pushed off the wall and launched himself toward the bolt. He managed to catch it before stopping himself with a hand on the opposite wall. He worked his way back down the crevice until he reached the old coil again. He put the bolt in his pouch and prepared himself for, what he assumed, was the most dangerous part of the job. He had to remove the hoses off each side of the coil, being careful not to touch himself or anything else with the ends.

He flexed his fingers and reached out to the old coil. Slowly, very slowly, he twisted the bushing on one of the hoses where it connected to the coil. Every muscle in his body tensed as the hose came free, and a flash of light nearly made him drop the thing. He slowly let go of the hose, hoping that, with the lack of gravity, it would stay put. Deacon exhaled sharply in relief when it floated obediently out of the way. He went to work on the other bushing and did the same as before. He smiled as he gently left the old coil floating next to him.

He put the new coil against the wall and took the bolt from his pouch. He figured that it would be easier to screw in the bushings if the coil was fixed in place first, and so he twisted in the bolt with the wrench, careful to stay well clear of the ends of the hoses as he worked.

Once it was secured, Deacon carefully grabbed the hose on the left and pressed the end into the coil and began twisting the bushing. When he was done, he exhaled and took a second to breathe, aware that he hadn't been for some time. Deacon collected himself and then did the same with the hose on the right. He luckily didn't kill himself, but when the thing abruptly lit up and began to hum loudly, he almost had a heart attack.

He watched it for a minute or so to make sure that the thing was working and then began pushing himself back up to the opening above him. Trask stood, boots rooted to the ship's exterior, arms and hands floating limply. Deacon wondered if the alien had died. Trask's body swayed slightly from side to side.

Deacon approached the Sergeant slowly, fearing the worst. If Trask had died, then Deacon was marked for death as well. He wasn't even sure he could operate the airlock to let him back into the Gorski. He stepped around Trask to peer into his visor. The Tendari's eyes were closed, mouth slightly opened, and black tongue lolling out. He looked dead to Deacon.

He poked the alien with his hand. Nothing. He prodded harder, and Trask exhaled with a snort and opened his eyes.

"Ah. You're not melted. Did you finish the job?" Trask had said it as if he'd been awake the whole time.

Deacon nodded slowly, still unsure about what the Sergeant had been doing.

"Are...Are you okay, Sergeant?" Deacon asked.

"I am now that you're finally done. Had to take a nap to pass the time." The giant sighed good naturedly. "A nap in zero-G is always sought after but rarely obtained."

Deacon was shocked by how nice Trask seemed after his nap and wondered if the entire Tendari reputation was based on those who hadn't napped.

"I must say that your size may, indeed, be advantageous. We would have had to dismantle half of the life support to get to that coil. I suppose...I won't push you off the Gorski and allow your body to float for eternity through space like I had planned if you failed."

Deacon swallowed. He had to try to remember to stay on Trask's good side, even when he was in a good mood.

By the time Trask and Deacon made it back to the equipment room on board the Gorski, other members of the maintenance crew had arrived, all Tendari, as Deacon had assumed. He had wished for another foreigner to be there, if for no other reason than to divide the Tendari temper between them, but it was not to be. Deacon's arrival caused quite the stir among the Tendari.

There were six besides Trask and himself, and they seemed in genuine distress at the sight of this human boy trailing behind their leader. It was almost as if they viewed Deacon as an invader, and they seemed hurt that Trask was accepting his presence.

He had gleaned a surprising amount from their snarls and growls. Maybe this was part of their language, and he was finally learning it, and as he thought of it in that light, he began to see the truth in it. Feeling was attached to every nuance in the Tendari's actions, feelings that were impossible for the translator to convey, feelings that sent a chill down Deacon's spine as he realized their complexity.

He prided himself on his ability to learn the myriad languages on the Rock, but this was altogether different. He didn't think he would ever be able to mimic what he was beginning to recognize as communication. At least, his new understanding might help him stay alive around the Tendari.

"What is this pit stain doing on the Gorski?" said one Tendari, who's scaly skin seemed less red than most.

"He replaced the bad coil in G section," Trask said. The other Tendari's attitudes shifted slightly for a second or two, long enough for Deacon to recognize their feelings toward him had changed. Not a lot, but enough that he could breathe again.

Trask could see that more explaining was desired, and he growled. Trask's rumbling eclipsed the others, and, one-by-one, they fell silent.

"I do not explain myself to you. He is part of this crew now. Gorkalak knows that there are more than enough tight spaces we can send this thing into."

A few of the Tendari chuckled in their odd way and eased noticeably, while others didn't seem convinced, but Deacon didn't think mere words would convince them anyway. They would need more results.

Trask went to his locker and removed his suit without another word, and Deacon followed his lead. Once it was off and stowed in his new locker, he waited for permission to go but was too afraid to ask, so he stood there, waiting. He awkwardly lingered close to Trask as he discussed some needed repairs with other crew members until, finally, the Sergeant noticed him.

"What are you still doing here? The last shuttle is in five minutes. You'd better hurry." Trask looked down at Deacon's ratty boots that he had replaced the new Tendari boots with and tsked.

"You'd better put your mag boots back on, or we'll be scrapping your brains off the inside of the transport."

Deacon smiled, ran to the locker, pulled out the boots, and then ran for the door.

CHAPTER 14

"Nice boots, space boy." The comment was originally in Bulrathi, a short species compared to most aliens, but they were extremely strong and had spikes that ran up their backs and around their heads like a crown. This Bulrathi was named Janisar, but Deacon didn't need to see who had said it to know that it was not said as a legitimate compliment. Scorn dripped from the words like the saliva that hung from Janisar's mouth.

"Hey, Janisar," Deacon said, not slowing as he passed.

"Where did you get them?" Janisar called after him.

"Oh, you know. Around," Deacon evaded.

He heard a string of Bulrathi curses trail after him and cringed. He should have realized that the other slaves wouldn't take kindly to his new footwear, especially if they knew their source. He had a spark of fear as he thought of what Silax might do if he saw Deacon in the new Tendari mag boots. He searched the barracks ahead of him for signs of the Tarpin and increased his pace. Silax was nowhere to be seen, and he sighed in relief.

Two more aliens noticed his boots and mentioned them, a Carexi and a Guzonian. The Carexi was as angry as Janisar, but the Guzonian was characteristically unimpressed and went back to licking himself...herself? Deacon was never really sure of a Guzonian's gender.

He found Elijah, and he listened to Deacon's day while seated in their alcove, opting to give Deacon his undivided attention over trying to discuss the events while practicing martial arts as had become the custom. He showed less emotion than Deacon had anticipated, and for some reason, that disappointed Deacon. From Deacon's point of view, his day had been a constant barrage of excitement and suspense, but Elijah acted less interested in his near death experiences and more interested in odd details that Deacon barely remembered noticing.

He asked about how the guards opened the door and what he had seen on the shuttle. He asked about how many Tendari he had seen on the Gorski and how many on the Rock. Deacon began to grow annoyed with the questions and rushed through the remainder of his day without the excitement he had begun the story with.

Elijah seemed to notice the change in mood.

"I am proud of you. It sounds like you handled yourself better than anyone could have hoped." The words brightened Deacon's soured mood, and he smiled up at the old man.

"A lesser person wouldn't have made it past those guards. There is strength in you, boy. Now, should we give that strength some teeth?" Elijah said.

Deacon's smile broadened, and he lifted himself to his feet. They started with the usual round of forms that Elijah promised would eventually allow him to react without thinking. Soon, Deacon was covered in a sheen of sweat, and Elijah spoke of Earth's history. Usually, Deacon picked up little of what Elijah said during his lectures because he was forced to give most of his attention to performing the exercises correctly, but tonight, he moved more smoothly and was able to pay closer attention to the lesson.

This lecture was about a man named Leonidas in an ancient place called Greece. The story seemed too fantastical to be true. Leonidas and three-hundred of his soldiers held off an entire empire in a desperate attempt to buy time for his countrymen to raise an army to confront the vast enemy forces.

Deacon was enthralled as Elijah recounted the methods of fighting that the Greeks employed and how they used the terrain to force the enemy to attack their front and not surround them. He had a hard time imagining Earth's topography, so it was difficult for him to visualize a canyon or how the Greeks could use it to their advantage, but he got the gist of the story and was awed by it.

"Okay, looks like we're done for the night," Elijah said, ending what he called the kata.

Deacon was shocked. He had made it through an entire evening of exercise, and he hadn't even wished for it to end once. He was breathing hard, for sure, but the entire experience had been far more enjoyable than ever before.

"Tomorrow, we can advance past the beginner's kata." Deacon frowned.

"That was for beginners?"

"Well, yes. You are a beginner, after all." Elijah smiled. "Don't worry, you are learning very quickly, and your stamina will come."

Deacon shook his head, incredulous that it would only get harder. He leaned against the wall and breathed heavily. He was tired, but he also felt good. His muscles felt like they had worked hard, but they also felt...satisfied? He was about to slump to the floor when Nah-leesi passed by, crossing the barracks floor.

He was stunned. He watched her as she walked and marveled at her graceful lines.

"I'll be back," he mumbled to Elijah and set off in her wake. Elijah clicked his tongue in disapproval behind him, but Deacon didn't care and jogged to catch up.

She passed through a door on the far side of the barracks, and Deacon reached it just before it would have locked him out and slid through. He had barely made it through the door when he was slammed, bodily, against the corridor wall and something sharp pressed against his throat.

Nah-leesi glared at him through suspicious eyes.

"Why are you following me?" She was clearly annoyed.

"I, I just wanted to...see you." As the words echoed back, they sounded lame in his own ears, and he almost groaned at the response he anticipated from her.

She laughed. It wasn't a simple chuckle or a polite ha-ha, but a roar that doubled her over. She released him and wiped her crying eyes.

"You sound so pathetic. 'I just wanted...'" She mocked him.

Deacon growled in frustration. He felt his face heat up with embarrassment, and he hung his head rather than try to convey his anger through words. Words that would only betray him.

She straightened and began to walk away. Deacon watched her go for a second, then slowly turned back to the door, defeated.

"Are you coming?" Nah-leesi called back to him.

He spun. She had turned back and stood in the dark twenty feet away, backlit by the corridor's widely-spaced lights.

Deacon hesitated for only a second. His pride warred with his desire to see more of her. He jogged to her side, and she resumed her path.

"I haven't seen you in the barracks before. What brought you?" He asked her, hoping to start a conversation.

She sighed, as if talking to him was a chore.

"I have a broken inductor in section D." Was her only response.

"It's late. Couldn't it wait?"

"You 'wanted to see me,' and now you are saying I shouldn't have come?" She said his words in a comical male voice that made him sound hopelessly stupid.

"I don't sound like that," he said. Smiling at her tone.

"You're right. It's more like...I wanted to see you." This time the deep male voice was broken sporadically with higher pitches. He laughed despite his embarrassment.

"Apparently, you know nothing about inductors, which, I guess, I shouldn't be surprised by," she said. "If the magnetic field loses cohesion, then the energy stored inside will have nowhere to go but out," she made an expanding motion with her hands and made an explosion sound with her mouth.

Deacon was concerned.

"How big of a...problem is this?"

"Well, if I can fix it in time, then not much, but if I can't, then the entire facility will decompress and kill everyone."

Deacon nearly tripped. Nah-leesi recognized his fear.

"Oh, don't worry, we'll be vaporized, so none of that...." She put both hands to her throat and mimicked someone choking to death. "...painful stuff," she looked over at him. "You're welcome to head back, though, if you'd rather decompress."

No, that is something that he definitely didn't want to do. Decompressing was one of his biggest fears, and he'd much rather get vaporized and not have to suffer through the agonizing fear that accompanied asphyxiation, but he wasn't sure knowing about the impending doom was better. Maybe he should have stayed in the barracks, ignorant and most likely asleep, while Nah-leesi saved everyone. Now that he knew, however, he might as well keep going.

They came to a small room that was little more than a widening of the corridor. A large mechanical...thing was crammed in the center. It hummed intermittently, and Deacon felt the fine hair on his arms raise each time it thrummed. Nah-leesi approached the thing and pressed her palm against a screen. The display lit up, and she navigated through different options confidently while he looked on, completely oblivious to the meanings of the runes and characters that flashed on the screen.

She made sounds with her mouth as she worked, which he was sure she was unaware of. She came to a screen that was flashing red, and she swore loudly.

"What's wrong?" Deacon asked.

"What's right? Bahg! We have less time than I thought. The field is dropping, and the shutdown sequence is muddied," she grabbed an empty barrel from the corner and dragged it over to what Deacon assumed was the inductor. She climbed up on it while Deacon steadied it. She reached over the top of a giant cylinder and struggled with something. She swore and tried again.

"It's stuck. Bahg!" Her body jerked, and her feet lifted off the barrel as she fought with whatever it was. Deacon carefully climbed up beside her and reached above his head. The curve of the cylinder hid the object from his view, but he felt where her hands were, and it seemed to be some kind of lever. He gripped it tightly and pulled. It began to move but then stopped. He grunted and took a breath.

"On the count of three. One. Two. Three." They pulled together, and the lever shifted and then moved. They strained, and all at once the lever flipped, and Deacon and Nah-leesi tumbled from the barrel and hit the floor hard.

When the lever was thrown, the thrumming slowly faded away, and Deacon dared to hope that the crisis had been averted. Nah-leesi was breathing heavily. She turned to him and smiled. He smiled back. Surely it was a good sign.

"Is that it?" Deacon asked.

"Well, we won't die right now, at least," she got up and pushed the barrel back to the corner, then went back to the inductor.

"I have to shunt power off this line, or there will be a build-up. Hand me those cutters."

They worked for an hour on the problem before Nah-leesi was sure they were safe from impending doom.

"I'm glad you came with me. It turned out I needed the help."

Deacon was surprised by the admission. Nah-leesi was not the type to admit any kind of weakness. The comment, however, only made her seem stronger to Deacon for some reason.

"I'm glad I did too. Although I had better get back. Sergeant Trask will kill me if I fall asleep tomorrow."

"Who's Sergeant Trask?" She asked.

Deacon explained his new role, and her eyes widened.

"I'm impressed," she said. "Working with the Tendari though... I don't know that I could do it."

"It is scary. They are an intimidating bunch, to say the least, but I'm beginning to suspect that most of it is a show."

"What do you mean?"

Deacon explained the constant growling and his theories about possible non-verbal communication between the Tendari.

"Well, I don't think I could do it because I hate them so much."

Deacon had to remind himself that Kalix, Nah-leesi's home planet, was defeated by the Tendari only five years ago, well within her memory. For Deacon, the visceral hatred for the Tendari wasn't there. He knew nothing else. He would have loved to spite them for having imprisoned him on this asteroid, making him a slave, but it was his life. He had no memories of torture and death that so many aliens had on the Rock. To Deacon, the Tendari were only slightly more troubling than any other species that constantly tried to tear him down or kill him. He understood Nah-leesi's hatred, though. He couldn't imagine having lived free, with a whole planet as beautiful as Kalix was rumored to be, and having all of that taken from you.

"What's an ocean like?" Deacon asked. He knew that Kalix was supposed to have massive oceans, and he couldn't imagine the scope of something like that.

Nah-leesi didn't respond. He turned toward her. She was

looking away from him, and her hand went to her face like she was wiping tears away.

"I'm sorry. I didn't mean to...."

"Go," she said, pointing toward the dark corridor. "We don't want you to be too tired to help those mud thumpers," he saw that she was indeed crying.

He turned to leave but then turned back and embraced her. Surprised by the hug, she jerked, but then she softened, and he felt her shudder against him as she sobbed. Finally, after several minutes in the comfortable closeness, she pulled away, wiping her face. She looked beautiful. She smiled at him.

"You stink," she said.

CHAPTER 15

Deacon woke up in a daze. He had only gotten a couple hours of sleep after spending most of the night helping Nah-leesi with the inductor, and now he felt like he would fall asleep walking to the shuttle.

The Guards had been less aggressive than the day before, but they still growled. Deacon ignored them and stood patiently waiting for them to open the door. After it was clear that Deacon was not going to react to their bravado, they punched in the code. He tried to see the keypad as the symbols were punched, but it was covered by the guard's torso.

He sighed and walked through the doorway, and proceeded to the shuttle waiting room. His experience with the transport to the Gorski was markedly better than it had been, thanks to his new boots. The same Tendari that he had accidentally kicked was present in the shuttle, and Deacon clicked his feet together proudly, engaging the magnetism, then he nodded to the Tendari. The alien merely sneered and turned away. As far as Tendari went, that was downright cordial. Deacon smiled to himself.

He made it to the Gorski without incident and found the equipment room nearly empty. Trask sat on one of the Tendari-sized benches fiddling with a lamp that could be fitted to the inside of a space helmet. He looked up when Deacon entered and growled a greeting. Deacon took it in stride and nodded his own greeting to the giant alien.

Trask was nearly twice Deacon's height, and he was sitting. Deacon looked up at the Sergeant and yawned. He couldn't help it. Trask looked at him, confused for a second, as if unsure what this new human custom meant.

"What do we have on the schedule for today?" Deacon asked, trying to divert attention away from his own tiredness.

Despite his fatigue, he was excited to get out in his new suit and practice his space walking.

"I don't need you today," was Trask's brusque response.

Deacon stood next to Trask, waiting for something else, some direction or orders. Trask just kept fiddling with the lamp.

"Should I go back to the Rock?" he finally queried.

Trask grunted as if surprised that he was still there.

"No, of course not. You need to clean up this place," he motioned to the room around him. Tools and equipment were scattered around the table and floor. The state of the room was daunting. He didn't know where to put any of the stuff that lay unorganized around the space. He sighed, then quickly glanced at Trask to make sure that the Sergeant didn't read his hesitancy the wrong way. Trask glared at him, his interest in the lamp temporarily forgotten.

"Do you think you can come here and do only the best work?"

Deacon didn't think that was fair. In his mind, risking being melted to the outside of the Gorski wasn't 'the best work.'

"No, sir, I just don't know where to put any of these things. I don't even know what a lot of it does," he said.

"Well then, I suppose this is the perfect time for you to get familiar with it. I will be back before the last shuttle. This place had better be immaculate by then."

Deacon didn't know what 'immaculate' was, but from the

context, assumed that it was something like 'clean.' He nodded his understanding, and Trask left the room.

He sighed again and leaned against the too-tall bench. This was going to be bad. He could see this going only one way. All of the Tendari ripping him to pieces when they got back to the room that night and found their favorite wrench out of place.

"Well, I guess I'd better get to it," he said to no one.

He began with the things he recognized and tried finding the best places for the objects. When he was done with that, there was a depressingly large amount of debris still left on the floor, table and benches.

"Bahg," he swore.

At first, he just shuffled around the room, kicking objects in frustration. What was he supposed to do with this stuff? He picked up a long handled...something, then dropped it back to the floor.

He sat for a time in the corner and contemplated the best course of action, but he began to fall asleep, so he forced himself up, and he continued his useless tour of the room, examining items as he went.

Finally, he decided to work on his own locker first. That way, maybe he could work out any bugs along the way. He pressed his palm against the button on the wall, and his locker opened. His suit hung there, but there was nothing else. No tools. No equipment besides his single suit. This wasn't going to help him figure out any of the other lockers, which were completely full of stuff.

He sighed and turned to leave.

Something caught his eye, and he paused. A black line was scribed on the wall, probably by the previous occupant. He followed the mark with his finger and couldn't figure out what the line represented. After a few minutes of examination, he realized that it must be the outline of a tool. Sure enough, as he examined the interior of his locker more closely, he could see marks showing how some previous crew member had organized his space.

He went to the locker next to his. All of the Tendari had left their lockers open, probably because they knew he would be given this impossible task, and he stepped over a pile of tools to look at the interior walls of the locker. Nothing. There were no lines that traced the invisible tools, but that didn't mean that he couldn't use his as a template.

He smiled. He had a plan.

Deacon worked quickly, trying to make up for the time he'd wasted earlier. The first locker or two sent him running back and forth between his locker to copy the format, but he soon had it down and could place the tools precisely without help. He was sweating and breathless when he finished hanging the last object in the last locker, but he wasn't done yet.

He was pretty sure that 'immaculate' meant cleaner than the room's current condition, and he went to the closet that he noticed earlier had cleaning supplies. He dragged out a mop and jugs of stuff that he assumed were used to clean the grease off the floors. He poured the liquids into the bucket and used rags that were piled in the corner to begin scrubbing the greasy metal floor.

The stuff worked pretty well, but it was hard work, and the chemicals made his head swim. He worked for hours and was proud of his progress. Deacon estimated that he would finish the floor before Trask returned. He scrubbed, and as he went, he thought of Elijah and the training he was receiving, and when he had tired of that train of thought, he thought of Nah-leesi. Her beautiful skin, her big wonderful eyes.... His mother screamed as they dragged her away from him. He felt the tears run down his cheeks as he realized he was all alone.

Deacon crashed back to reality. Where was he? What was that yelling? The translator kicked in, and he heard the recognizable words form sentences.

"You fall asleep on my crew?"

It was Trask. He was standing in the doorway to the equipment room, hands on hips. He clacked his teeth angrily, and saliva dripped from his mouth as he worked it in a rage. Deacon was lying on the floor. He struggled to remember what he had been doing or why he was being yelled at. The pieces began falling into place as the giant Sergeant thundered into the room.

As he came, he grabbed a canvas strap from a peg on the wall. The strap was used to secure loads on carts, and it was thick and heavy. Deacon raised his hands, trying to defend against the obvious threat. He pleaded with a shaking voice.

"Please, I didn't mean to. I." He couldn't say more because the force of the first blow knocked all rational thought from his head. He saw stars, and a line of agony slashed down his face where the strap cut into him. He ducked his head to protect his face, and the next blow landed on the side of his head. Somewhere in his subconscious, Deacon came to the conclusion that Trask was taking it easy on him, after all, his logical brain reasoned, if he hadn't been, he would have already been dead. Then his nerves sent another batch of damage reports to his brain, and all logic was once again replaced by fear and pain. He blacked out then, his brain opting to go dark rather than be submitted to more punishment.

When he woke, his head felt like nothing he had ever experienced. It felt heavy and...thick somehow. He tried to flop it to the side to get a look at where he was, but he couldn't see. Panic started to set in. He began feeling around himself and felt nothing but cold metal.

He felt his face and eyes trying to identify the source of the obstruction. His eyes were swollen shut and crusted with blood. He swore.

"Look, Gorat, the baby human woke up finally."

The sound startled Deacon. He knew that voice. It was one

of the Tendari guards outside the blast doors on the Rock. How had he gotten back here? Someone, or a string of people, must have carried him this far but didn't seem to think he was worth taking all the way into the depths of misery that was the slave barracks.

"Better be running along then," the guard said, and Deacon felt the guard's boot poke at him, trying to coax him up.

A groan escaped his lips as he slowly lifted himself onto unsteady feet. He tried hard to open his eyes and could barely see through the narrow gap in his left eyelid. He stumbled away from the Tendari guards, holding his hand against the wall to both steady himself and guide him toward the barracks.

He knew he was close when he could smell the pungent air wafting down the hallway. The smell never smelled stronger than when coming back to it. He shuffled through the open doorway and carefully entered the crowded barracks.

"Whoa, what happened to you, space boy?" Janisar's familiar voice sounded from his cot by the door. "Your Tendari friends turn on you, eh?" The alien chuckled to himself.

Deacon could hear more alien's comment as he walked. He stumbled forward, having caught his toe on something. He couldn't be sure, but he suspected someone had tripped him. More laughter washed like a wave around the watching slaves. Deacon wanted to just curl up in a ball and disappear. He lingered on the floor, unwilling to subject himself to more humiliation than those watching, doubtless, intended.

Hands gripped under his armpits, and Deacon struggled against their hold until Denzink's voice whispered in his ear.

"Don't worry, Deacon, I have you," the Kupelti said.

The laughter subsided, and Denzink was allowed to usher Deacon away toward his and Elijah's alcove. A few aliens voiced their disappointment in Denzink's intervention, but most seemed to have been embarrassed by his actions. More than ever before, Deacon was glad he had rescued the alien.

"Thank you, Denzink," Deacon managed through thick, bloodied lips. His view through his one partially dimmed eye took in Denzink's response. The Kupelti seemed to be self-conscious all of a sudden.

"What I did was nothing in comparison to what you did for me," he said. "It was the least I could do."

Elijah stood when he saw Denzink and Deacon approach, and as the Kupelti lowered him to the floor, the old man nodded his thanks to the alien. Denzink left before Elijah said anything.

"What happened?" the old man queried.

"I shouldn't have helped Nah-leesi last night. I should have just let everyone die. This is what I get for my efforts."

Elijah didn't say anything. Deacon suspected that the man knew he had to vent and didn't necessarily believe it would have been better to let everyone die. To be honest, Deacon wasn't sure if he was just venting, though. He felt torn down. Sure, there had been good things that had happened to him lately. Still, there had been definite tragedy in his life as well, and he felt that the constant disparaging comments and physical abuse had worn him thin. He sighed.

"I think I understand why everyone hates the Tendari."

CHAPTER 16

Elijah dabbed at Deacon's face with a cloth he found and washed out with his own precious water rations. Deacon winced as the old man came painfully close to the gash that ran down the side of his face.

"This will scar," Elijah said.

"Maybe it will make me look meaner," Deacon said. Elijah smiled.

"I've found that women quite like the occasional scar," Elijah said.

Deacon made as if to say something, then hesitated, thinking.

"What are women like? Human women, I mean," he said. Elijah paused in his work and looked at Deacon.

"They are both the greatest thing in the universe and the most difficult to understand. They are equal parts bewildering and enchanting. A beautiful woman puts the beauty of a nebula to shame, while a woman scorned is one of the most dangerous things in the universe."

Deacon recognized the attributes that Elijah spoke of in Nah-leesi, and he smiled at the comments.

"Do you speak of a specific woman?" Deacon asked.

Elijah returned to cleaning Deacon's face. "There is always

one that stands out...she was killed by the Tendari a decade ago."

Deacon grabbed the old man's hand. It trembled in his grasp. He looked into the old man's eyes and saw the pain there.

"I'm sorry," Deacon said.

"Don't be stupid. You have nothing to apologize for. It is the Tendari that will have a reckoning." Deacon nodded his agreement. Elijah continued his work on Deacon's wounds until it was time to sleep.

"I think we will forgo any exercises tonight." He smiled at Deacon and patted him gently on the head. "Get your sleep. Your body needs all it can get if it is going to heal."

Deacon was asleep almost as soon as he laid down, and it had seemed like he had just closed his eyes when he was gently prodded awake by Elijah the next morning. He sat up and regretted it. His head felt like it had been crushed and then reassembled, its fragments held together by seal tape. His hands went to his temples, and he tried, unsuccessfully, to ease the pressure there with his fingertips. His vision swam, and he leaned over and wretched.

He had nothing in his stomach, and the vomit consisted mostly of bile. He ran the back of his hand over his lips and groaned.

"You shouldn't go to the Gorski today. I'm sure they won't expect you after having your face smashed so thoroughly." Elijah said the words, but even with Deacon's clouded thoughts, he could tell that the old man didn't really believe them. The Tendari were past compassion or understanding when it came to the 'lesser' species.

Deacon shifted and slowly lifted himself to his feet.

"You don't believe it any more than I do. I'll do my best to take it easy," he said, more to comfort the old man than anything. Elijah nodded sadly.

"I'll go get your rations and help you to the corridor." Deacon grimaced at the thought of eating, but Elijah scowled at him. "You need food. You don't need to eat it right now, just take it with you and eat it later." Deacon nodded, and Elijah walked off toward the ration line.

After Elijah dropped him off at the corridor, Deacon made his way easily enough. The swelling around his eyes had subsided enough for him to see clearly, and if it hadn't been for the occasional bout of dizziness and pain, he would have made good time, but as it was, he feared that he would miss the shuttle.

When he came in sight of the blast doors that separated the Tendari occupied section of the facility from that of the miners, he paused. He didn't hesitate out of fear but curiosity. Every other time he had gotten to this point in the corridor, the two guards had challenged him with their customary growl. This time there was no such greeting. He moved closer, and still nothing. Finally, at a distance of only ten feet, the guards clicked their tongues on the roof of their mouths oddly and tilted their heads. Deacon paused.

"You are nothing if not persistent... stupid...but persistent." The guard on the left said. He went to the control panel and punched in the code. Deacon caught sight of the keystrokes and tried to memorize the sequence. The Guard stood back and let Deacon shuffle past. "You had better hurry if you want to make the shuttle," he called after Deacon.

The experience was odd. The guards had been almost kind in how they had treated him. Respectful, maybe. Deacon hurried his pace and saw surprised Tendari faces as he passed the occasional foot traffic. Apparently, he looked as bad as he felt. Some Tendari growled, but most did some approximation of the greeting the guards had performed.

When Deacon entered the equipment room aboard the Gorski, his nerves were on edge. He imagined possible reactions to his appearance the whole way to the room, and most were grisly. Trask had definitely taught Deacon the meaning of fear, and as he stepped through the doorway, he nearly trembled with nervous energy.

Trask looked up at his entrance, and a look of shock, quickly schooled, crossed his face. The Tendari sergeant had been talking to a short crew member, and the conversation halted as Deacon walked slowly across the newly cleaned floor. As he approached, Deacon saw a splash of blood, his blood, dried to the metal floor beneath Trask's giant feet.

The crew member was not short, he realized. Trask was just that much taller than the average Tendari. The crew member had turned to see what had caught his superior's attention, and upon seeing Deacon, he tipped his head and clicked his tongue as had so many other Tendari that morning.

Trask looked at the back of the crew member's head with anger for a second, and he made to speak but then thought better of it. Another crew member caught sight of his mangled face, and he joined his clicking to the first, then another. Soon all of the Tendari were clicking their tongues and tilting their heads in unison. All except Trask.

Finally, after seeming embarrassed, Trask joined in for a few seconds, and then all the clicking ended together. Deacon didn't understand what had just happened, but whatever it was, it was better than the macabre imaginings he'd had on his journey to the room.

Trask looked down at Deacon, and he had to force himself to return the huge alien's gaze without flinching.

"I did not expect you back. To be honest, I had thought I had killed you. Your species is so weak that, although it was not my intent, I assumed that the punishment had been too much for you."

Deacon didn't know what to say, for it was evident that Trask expected him to respond. Was this Trask's poor attempt at an apology? Surely not. Why would a Tendari ever apologize to him?

"Different aliens have different nicknames for us, humans.

The Kupelti call us slug-worms, the Bulrathi call us trash-dogs, and the Kalix call us mud-thumpers. They are all names taken from their own planets. They are things that disgust or annoy. Things that, despite the inhabitant's best efforts, cannot be eradicated. We are stubborn."

Silence followed Deacon's short speech. It was obviously far more than had been expected, and once again, Trask was stunned. Deacon wasn't sure if he should feel pride at what he had just said, but he did. Given everything humans had been through in the past two-hundred years, they should have been extinct already. It was hard to imagine any other species doing better under the same circumstances.

Trask smiled broadly and reached out a hand to slap Deacon's shoulder, but before he could register the Sergeant's intent, his arm shot up to block the giant hand, and his body shifted to the side to evade Trask's reach. Deacon paused, afraid that he had offended Trask. He stood back up straight and tried to resume the same stance as before, hoping that Trask hadn't noticed the training behind his reflexes.

Trask stood back up straight and looked at Deacon with a sidelong glance.

"You, my boy, are full of surprises."

Deacon glanced around the room and was surprised to see all of the other crew members watching him. He shifted, uncomfortable with the increased scrutiny. He looked back to Trask.

"If it is okay with you, sir, I would like to finish cleaning the floor," he said, more to divert attention from himself. He pointed at the square of dirty floor he hadn't gotten to and the specks of his blood that sullied the otherwise shiny surface.

"I have something more important for you to do," Trask said. "Are you up for it?"

"Of course, sir," Deacon responded. Just a day before, such a phrase would have sent a thrill through him. He desired knowledge and enjoyed learning what the Tendari had to teach him, but the excitement he had felt just the day before was gone. He had craved advancement in the eyes of his Tendari masters, but not now. Now he seemed to have a different goal, which he wasn't sure of. It was more of a feeling than a course of action. A nebulous wish. The only word that he had for it was freedom.

He didn't truly know what that word meant. As Elijah had taught him of his human history, Deacon had put together that most of the stories of conflict could be boiled down to that one word. Even Leonidas and his three-hundred had fought for it in a way. They resisted the vast empire that desired control over them.

Yes... freedom. He knew now that no matter how ingratiated he may become to the Tendari, his life with them would never allow him to reach a fraction of his potential.

"You will go with Golith today. He will show you what you are to do. Just make sure you don't sleep on the job again." Trask pointed at him with a giant finger for emphasis.

Deacon thought that Trask was quite the hypocrite, and as he looked into the huge alien's eyes, he could see that Trask knew it as well. Shame, buried deep behind layers of pride, was still visible there. Deacon couldn't bring himself to verbally respond to the reprimand, so instead, he just bowed his head slightly.

Deacon geared up and pulled his suit out of his locker. He still felt woozy, but he forced himself to slurp down his rations before confining himself in the suit. This suit was the perfect size, so there was no room to pull his arms in to eat.

"I don't know how you can eat that slime," Golith said with a disgusted face.

Deacon knew that anything he was to say on the subject would probably only get him in trouble, so he just looked at the alien, unamused.

Golith actually looked chagrined at the look.

"I suppose they probably don't give you much of a choice?"

he said. The conversation shocked Deacon, but he kept his face stoic and only shook his head, confirming Golith's suspicions.

"Have you ever had anything other than that?" He pointed at the empty tube in Deacon's hand.

He wasn't sure why this Tendari was being so genial, but it was a welcome change. Still, he decided he should be wary.

"I had some type of meat once," Deacon said.

"Once? You don't even know what it was?" Golith said.

"No." Deacon had a flash of the same sickening thought that he had had before, that he had been eating some poor slave that had died.

Golith sat in silence for a span. He was already suited up but for his helmet, and he waited patiently for Deacon to get ready. When he was done, they both stood and wordlessly made their way to the airlock. They remained uncommunicative until they got out of the airlock and, with the help of their mag boots, made their way...somewhere. Deacon just followed the Tendari to wherever his small size would be of use.

"I still can't believe how relieved Trask was that you had lived," Golith said.

Deacon was confused. "He was relieved?" Deacon asked. To him, it seemed that Trask had been somewhat ambivalent. Sure, he had been more...interested than perhaps Deacon would have expected from a Tendari, but he wouldn't have called it relief, and definitely not the level of relief that would instill incredulity in Golith.

"He was beyond happy to see you." Golith didn't expound on his comment, so, finally, Deacon prodded him.

"He was? Why?" Deacon asked.

"I forget that other species don't have the same methods of communication that the Tendari do. It is often hard for others to see our words, and so we have to say them." Deacon was intrigued but decided that he wanted to hear about Trask more and so he didn't interrupt. "Trask had lost honor when he attacked you

with a weapon. It is beyond reproachful to attack one so weak as
yourself with anything but your hands. More than that, you were
lying down, unarmed, and pleading for mercy." Golith paused
and stopped walking. He turned to face Deacon.

"That is not to say that you were not in the wrong.
Sleeping on the job, for anyone, let alone a slave is egregious, but
his actions were too much. Some say that slaves don't deserve to
be honored in the code, but more say that because they are slaves,
they deserve it more. This is why we leave most of the dealings
with slaves to other slaves. Tendari are above it," he said proudly.

They were hardly above it, Deacon thought, but it
fascinated him that the Tendari had any 'code' that guided them.
It had always seemed the opposite to him, and he wondered if
Golith was supposed to be telling him all of this, but he kept his
mouth shut, hoping that the Tendari would continue.

"Trask could have faced demotion for his actions. If you
had died, then there would be no recourse other than a court-
martial." Deacon didn't know what 'court-martial' was, but it
didn't sound good. "The fact that you lived indicates that you
are not as weak as we all assumed. Whatsmore you came back
the very next day, walking on your own and ready to work. This
pleased Trask because your heartiness saved him from certain
dishonor."

Golith turned around and started walking again, and
Deacon had to hurry to catch up.

"What does the clicking noise mean you all did when I
came in?" Deacon asked, encouraged by Golith's openness.

"Respect."

Deacon was stunned.

"Respect for an underestimated enemy, to be more
specific," Golith said.

Silence returned between the two, and Deacon smiled to
himself as he thought of the Tendari all showing him respect.
Respect that he had never before experienced. Finally, after ten

minutes of walking, Deacon asked Golith what their project was for today.

Golith looked at Deacon over his shoulder and smiled.

"No project."

Deacon looked at him quizzically.

"We have nothing to do today, but Trask wanted you out working to reaffirm his stance that you are a strong enemy. He wanted me to 'train you,' whatever that means." Golith said.

CHAPTER 17

Golith had run Deacon through a bunch of different techniques of space walking around the exterior of the ship, and by the time it was time for him to go, his already weary body was ready to collapse. For his part, Golith seemed impressed.

"I think I will call you Grak," Golith said, as they returned to the airlock.

"Why is that?" Deacon said.

"Because a Grak is a small, hideous creature that is surprisingly hard to kill. I guess they would be the Tendari version of those creatures you mentioned to Trask." Golith smiled down at Deacon, relieving some of the sting from his words. To be honest, Deacon was proud of the nickname. He had taken pride in the way his return to work had been received, and despite his miserable fatigue, he smiled back.

Once they were back in the equipment room, Deacon shrugged out of his suit and hurried to the door. He was anxious to return to the barracks and rest, but a giant Tendari hand reached out and forestalled him.

"Did you do this to my locker?" A voice grumbled in Tendari. Deacon looked up at the face of the alien that accosted him and didn't recognize him. He must have been part of a later crew that he had yet to see in the room, unsurprising, as the separate teams seemed to come and go at odd hours.

"Uh...yeah...Sorry," Deacon managed. He didn't know what to say. When he had organized the lockers, he had done so with no direction other than a mysterious template he had found in his own locker. At the time, he didn't have much choice, but he had been nervous to see how the Tendari received his work.

The Tendari started to snarl and cough in the way that his species laughed, and Deacon relaxed.

"It is masterful!" He yelled and slapped Deacon a little too hard on the back. Deacon stumbled forward and just managed to catch himself before falling on his already bruised and swollen face.

"Careful Srak," Golith called behind him. "The boy has been through enough today."

"I forget how weak other things are sometimes," Srak said, and manhandled Deacon back upright. "I am just pleased. I have been asking Trask to make a change with this place. It was becoming difficult to work in such a mess. This...." He motioned to the organized lockers. "Is exactly what we needed. A little organization." The big alien inhaled deeply as if catching a whiff of something good.

Deacon had never seen a Tendari so pleased, and he was happy that he was the cause of it.

"I'm glad you like it," he said.

"Like it! I like it so much I could eat you!" And for a second, Deacon was worried he might do it.

"Probably not something you should say to a human, Srak," Golith said.

Deacon must have had a worried look on his face because Srak looked at him, then laughed again and apologized.

"I will not eat you, don't worry. I hear humans are too bony," he said with all seriousness, and then he lifted Deacon's arm, and his other hand tested the theory by prodding at his muscle.

Golith reached over and freed Deacon's arm from Srak's grasp.

"Go ahead, Grak. I will see you here tomorrow," Golith said.

Deacon was grateful to Golith and nodded up to him before going for the door.

"Grak? That's perfect." Deacon heard Srak laugh behind him.

As he walked to the barracks that night, he couldn't help but marvel at the crazy ups and downs his life had been pulled along of late. He was surprised to feel like he had had a good day. He never would have anticipated it. In fact, he had been dreading going just this morning, and yet he was happy. He had to remind himself of the pain still aching in his head and face. He had to make himself remember the horrible anger he had felt the night before.

Confused about everything but his desire for rest, he entered the mining facility and was drawn to the bathrooms. He thought he'd at least wash himself as best he could in the basin with what water rations he had before hitting the sack.

He stepped up to the sink and pressed his palm against the wall above it. The water kicked on, and steam from the heated water began to drift up as it hit the cool metal of the sink, but he didn't notice. He stared at the screen where he had pressed his palm. There was a readout that always showed how many rations were available as the water was used, and Deacon had had a rough estimate of how much he had, and the screen was wrong. It had to be.

He wasn't good with his numbers. The characters were in human form, adapting themselves to match his profile, but he had never had much call to learn, and so the number that he saw on the screen seemed...impossible.

1.0.0.0.

The screen normally read 0.0.0.2 or maybe 0.0.0.3. Deacon

knew enough about counting to know that his new number was more than hundreds. He was shocked. He stood for a long time, just looking at the wall until water began pouring over the basin's edge.

The water splashed on his legs and feet, breaking him out of his trance. He rushed to turn it off. The water in the basin hadn't even used one of his rations. He was rich. He laughed, turned slowly around, and stripped off his clothes as he walked toward the showers.

The water was miraculous. It seemed to revive him in a way. For the first time in his life, he let the water cascade, uncaring of the amount he used. He reveled in the feel of it over his skin.

After a while, he noticed that the pads on each finger had begun to wrinkle, and for a minute, he was worried. Maybe he had overdone it. He turned off the water and stood, relaxed, waiting for the water to dry from his skin and hair.

He exited the showers and pulled on his coveralls again, thinking that next time he would wash them in the basin or wear them into the shower to try and clean them as well. He made his way back to the rear of the barracks, where Elijah was waiting for him.

The old man had obviously been worried, and Deacon felt a stab of guilt at having prolonged his absence to take a shower. Deep creases etched Elijah's face, and he seemed to have aged since that morning. At the sight of Deacon approaching, however, the old man smiled broadly and stood.

"Well, I'm glad they didn't finish the job," Elijah said, and pulled Deacon into a hug.

Deacon hadn't been hugged like this since his mother, and the sensation was strange. At first, he didn't know what to do with his arms, and they hung limply by his sides. Then, as if of their own volition, they returned the embrace. Deacon felt Elijah's hands pat his back, and he felt safe, comfortable.

They released, and Elijah held him at arm's length,

examining his face.

"You have had a hard day, I'll wager. I think we'll forgo the exercise portion of our training."

Deacon was too tired to have even thought of it as a possibility and just nodded his head in agreement.

Deacon laid down on his blanket, and Elijah sat next to him.

"Elijah?" He asked.

"Yes?"

"What is ten one-hundreds called?"

"Ten hundreds is called one-thousand...why?" Elijah asked.

"That's how many water rations I have," Deacon said. The old man's face blanched.

Deacon told Elijah about his day and about his theory that Trask had given him the rations as a sort of peace offering.

"That's why you smell better," Elijah said. Deacon felt embarrassed. "Don't worry. You don't ever smell any worse than anyone else around here. You must have made quite the impression on them." The old man paused. "Or maybe they really don't like the way you smell," he smiled.

Deacon did as well.

Without another word, Deacon settled in to listen to Elijah's soothing voice as the old man started in on a lecture about physics. He was talking about gravitational pull when Deacon drifted off to sleep.

The next week went by at an incredible pace. Each day, Deacon would wend his way through the Tendari corridors to the maintenance crew's equipment room aboard the Gorski, and each night he would find his way back. The Tendari had begun to accept his presence without reaction and even talked to him on occasion.

Back at the barracks, Deacon would cram what information he could into his tired brain while simultaneously practicing martial arts. After Trask, Deacon had felt even more motivated to learn Elijah's deadly skills, and despite his still-sore face and body, he pushed himself to his limit.

On the Gorski, Golith would teach Deacon the fundamentals of space-walking while working on the occasional small project that just seemed like busy work to Deacon. It surprised him how much Golith talked as they worked. The alien seemed genuinely interested in Deacon's life, though it was impossible for him to understand why. It hadn't been a full week before Deacon was sure he had covered everything in his life with Golith, and yet, the alien continued his long conversations with him until Deacon began to feel comfortable asking his own questions in return.

Deacon was surprised to learn that Golith was over seventy years old. Apparently, their species lived for one hundred and fifty to two hundred years, far longer than Deacon had ever heard of any species, at least among the slaves. He had a hard time imagining a life that long.

"I don't think I would want to live that long," he said.

Golith looked at him, their faces separated by their helmet's visors, and patted his shoulder.

"If I were a slave, I'm not sure I would either," he said simply.

CHAPTER 18

He collapsed to the floor, breathing hard. Sweat covered his exposed chest.

Elijah had begun sparring with him, and what Deacon had thought was hard before paled in comparison to the rigors he now had to look forward to each night. His stomach ached where the old master's punch had landed.

The sad part was that Deacon was sure that the old man was holding back a lot to not to hurt him. He sat back on his heels and rubbed his sternum. Elijah had assured him that he would not hit him hard enough to reinjure his freshly healed bones, but it didn't feel like the old man remembered his promise.

"Are you sure I'm ready for this?" he asked between gasps.

"We don't really have much choice. I'm amazed that you've lasted this long without any training. You said it yourself. Most of them still want your blood." Elijah waved his arm in the direction of the slave filled barracks.

It was true enough. After Trask had beaten him, the slaves had, for the most part, been excited to see him in such a state, and if it hadn't been for Denzink, he was sure they would have finished him off.

Deacon nodded his acceptance and picked himself up. If nothing else, he was learning how to take a punch, he told himself, though the thought of taking a punch from ninety percent of the aliens was a devastating notion. Elijah had told him time and time again that he had to learn the ancient human fighting techniques so that he could evade the blows of his enemy, not so that he could 'take' them.

He readied himself once again, standing with legs spread wide apart and hands raised in front of him in a stance that Elijah had said was from the discipline of Krav Maga. To Deacon, the style of fighting that Krav Maga employed seemed to be the most intuitive and useful, though he also tried to mix in other favored moves from Tai Chi, Judo, and Aikido.

Elijah struck fast, without warning. A quick double strike almost landed on Deacon's face, but he had just been able to turn aside with an outstretched hand. The old man didn't pause in his onslaught but followed up with a knee aimed at his sore stomach.

Deacon saw the move just in time and blocked it with both hands while simultaneously stepping back to get out of Elijah's effective range.

"Good," Elijah said. Though the old man spoke, it didn't mean that he wasn't still moving, and he launched a quick jab that Deacon was sure was only meant to distract him, but he wasn't sure from what. Instead of thinking about it, he just reacted and ducked.

He felt the wind from a fierce spinning backhand part the air where his head had been a second before.

"Very good," Elijah said as he stepped back. Deacon realized that the old man had stepped back, not to give Deacon a break, but because his duck had put him in an excellent position to counter-strike with a Muay Thai upper-cut. He kicked himself mentally for not seeing it sooner.

It was rare that Deacon was able to even attempt a strike against the seasoned fighter, and every opportunity he missed was a stinging blow to his pride. Despite not following through, he had bought himself some time to re-center.

Elijah continued with the Muay Thai and opened his fresh assault with a step-up kick that Deacon dodged, followed by a brutally quick punch that he wasn't quick enough to stop. The old man's closed fist came within a half inch of Deacon's face and stopped. For a moment, Deacon could do nothing but marvel at the old man's amazing control.

The fist slowly lowered, and Deacon, recognizing his failure, slumped to the floor.

"You are improving exceptionally," Elijah said. He was smiling and seemed genuine in his praise of Deacon's progress, though Deacon felt less than proud of his abilities. They had been sparring like this for weeks, and he had yet to even lay a finger on the old man.

"I think that's enough sparring for one night," Elijah said. "Should we work on your numbers or letters?"

Deacon groaned. The old man had been teaching him how to read and something called arithmetic. He hated the latter, but after such a grueling sparring session, the thought of reading was almost as bad.

"Letters," he said, knowing the old man would favor the numbers if given the option.

Elijah smiled.

"Very well." The old man began scratching words into the packed dirt that coated the floor. Deacon assumed that if someone were to chip up the hard soil, they would find the metal sheeting that made up the floor in the rest of the mining facility. Years of mineral dust being tracked in without apparent care given to cleanliness had hidden the flooring completely, giving them an acceptable make-shift writing surface.

Elijah finished a sentence and sat back, giving Deacon a clear view of the words. Deacon worked slowly at them, sounding them out. He knew it was better if he took a long time but got the words right than if he hurried and got them wrong.

"Water is wet." Deacon read slowly. He felt foolish at how

difficult it seemed for him to read something so simple.

"Good," Elijah said. He went back to the dirt and began scratching away again.

"I saw the code they put into the door," Deacon said. Elijah paused in his writing and turned back to face him. "I actually saw it a while ago, but it took a few more times to memorize it."

Elijah smiled. "What is it?" he asked.

"The characters are Tendari. I don't know their names," he scooted over to Elijah and took the bit of wire that the old man was using to write with and began tracing the Tendari runes in the order that the guards punched in every morning.

When he was finished, Deacon looked at Elijah and watched as the old man screwed up his face in concentration, obviously memorizing the code. In a matter of seconds, he seemed content and rubbed out the runes, destroying the evidence of Deacon's defiance.

"Excellent," Elijah said, and clapped Deacon on the shoulder. "Now, we just need to know about that shuttle."

Deacon wasn't sure what pleased him more, that Elijah was happy about the code or that he had derailed his lesson. He pulled on his undershirt and stuck his arms in his coveralls. Now that he had been sitting for a while, the sweat on his skin now chilled him, and he zipped up his coveralls.

Elijah sat back against the wall, overcome with visions of freedom, it would seem, and Deacon was content to let him ponder. Deacon had nothing upon which to base such visions, try as he might, and so he contemplated Nah-leesi. During his more logical moments, he would criticize himself for how much he thought of her, but thoughts of her were too rich to abandon. She was unlike anything he had ever experienced.

Nah-leesi had awoken in him feelings he didn't know existed. He thought of their hug and smiled. Self-conscious all of a sudden, he sniffed under his arms. She would definitely say he stunk. He resolved to take a shower tomorrow.

Despite his wealth of water rations, he had been reluctant to indulge fully in his riches. The sudden obvious increase in his ablutions would be both noticed and loathed by his slave colleagues. Deacon didn't need any more violence directed at him, so he refrained from taking as many showers as he craved. Still, once a week wouldn't hurt, he rationalized.

"Well, I guess we'd better get back at it." Elijah interrupted Deacon's thoughts as he leaned forward and began writing once again in the packed soil.

Deacon sighed. At least he had gotten a few minutes reprieve.

"What does that say?" Elijah queried.

He worked at the phrase with all the patience he could muster.

"Eat or be eaten?" Deacon said.

CHAPTER 19

Gorat and Slik, the two Tendari guards that waited each day outside the heavy blast door, stood up straight at his appearance around the corner.

"Good morning," Deacon said in his best Tendari. The rough language hurt his throat to imitate for too long, but he had wanted to practice.

"You're sounding better, baby human," Gorat said. Slik just smiled a toothy grin at his attempt and turned to input the code.

Deacon didn't like being called a 'baby,' but both guards had found it humorous, and he knew that it would be so much worse for him if he asked them to stop, so he walked past them without another word.

While boarding the shuttle, Deacon tried to see everything he could of the interior. The exterior of the shuttle was always hidden by the facility's walls, so it was impossible for him to gather any information about it. Instead, he focused on the inside. He craned his neck to see past the hulking masses of aliens that crowded the passenger compartment and was able to make out the dark outline of a closed hatch toward the front of the craft.

He assumed that if there were any pilots, that would be where they were. He didn't see an access display that was common outside of all the doors Deacon had seen in the Tendari facility. Maybe they had made it impossible to open from this side, and maybe no code was needed to open the door.

Deacon didn't know that it mattered in any case. The giant, fierce-looking aliens that surrounded him seemed like more than an adequate deterrent to any attempt he could conceive of in taking the shuttle. Elijah was a force to be reckoned with, to be sure, but even if Deacon could match the old man's abilities, he failed to see how they could overcome the Tendari in the spacecraft.

Despite his doubts, Deacon continued his 'reconnaissance,' a new word Elijah had taught him. He counted the Tendari in the shuttle, careful not to make his spying obvious. Thirteen. Thirteen of the meanest-looking aliens in the universe stood in the cramped compartment, swaying in unison with the ship's movements as it docked with the Gorski.

Deacon was the first to exit, and he quickly got out of the way of the testy Tendari as they rushed out of the shuttle. There were two more Tendari aboard today than there were yesterday. He, so far, hadn't been able to see a pattern to explain the difference in numbers he saw from day to day, but he dutifully reported them to Elijah each day anyway.

Deacon was on his way to the maintenance room when alarm klaxons began a cacophonous serenade, and lights flashed above his head. A voice speaking Tendari came over the hidden speakers in the corridor.

"Prepare for emergency burn. All crew, prepare for emergency burn."

He was terrified and unsure of what he was supposed to do. No one had ever told him anything about a 'burn' emergency or otherwise. He had no clue how he was supposed to 'prepare.' He began to panic as he saw the Tendari in the corridor begin to run. He'd never seen one of the giants run before, and the sight was beyond intimidating. He had an intuitive reaction as one came closer. He wasn't proud of it, but he crouched down and covered his head with his hands until the Tendari had passed.

Finally, after he gathered his nerves and his wits, he stood and decided that he would continue on to the maintenance room. He tried to match the Tendari's alacrity and ran to the room, but he was much slower than the aliens around him. By the time he arrived, the room was already empty, and the corridor was cleared.

"Bahg!" He yelled, as the fear that had gripped him so firmly in the corridor began to reassert itself. His chest felt tight, and he almost screamed as the deck plating beneath his feet began to tremble as it never had before.

The scariest part for him was the unknown, he realized. He had no idea what was happening or what was expected of him. He was totally at a loss. The only thing he knew was that whatever could make a Tendari run to obey must be serious. He turned circles in the doorway to the maintenance room, searching again and again for what was obviously not there, help. He needed help, and searching for it among the Tendari was a hopeless pursuit.

Finally, depressed by his probable fate and dejected by the disappearance of his Tendari taskmasters, Deacon slowly sank to the floor and put his head in the crook of his arms. He listened to the reverberations of the ship around him amp up, and he trembled along with the Gorski as it prepared for its 'burn.'

All of a sudden, hands, big and strong, clamped around his arms and lifted him from the floor. Deacon couldn't see much until he was set down, none-to-gently on a too-large seat in what he recognized as the closet where he had found the cleaning supplies, but now seats were lining the walls, each with harnesses, hoses and wires connected to them.

The seats were filled with Tendari, who all stared back at him as he looked around him worriedly. Golith stood above him and had apparently been the one that had rescued him from the floor where he had succumbed to his fate. Golith worked on strapping Deacon to the seat, but it had been designed for a much, much larger being, so Golith swore and tied straps here and there, trying to fasten Deacon in place.

A countdown began over the hidden speakers, and Deacon was sure they would need to be secured before the count reached zero. He heard several of the Tendari yell at Golith to secure himself and to "leave the little grak," he looked at the other occupants of the small room. They had all placed masks over their snouts, so Deacon pulled the mask from beside his chair and tried to fit it over his mouth. He was able to adjust the straps so that it was tight enough, but the mask itself covered his entire face and had gaps besides. He was sure this was inadequate, but he figured it would have to be good enough.

Golith continued to fuss over his straps, but as the count reached five, Deacon gripped the alien's hands and pushed them away. Golith looked him in the eyes and nodded. The alien ran to his seat and only had one arm through the harness when the count reached zero, and the ship around them thundered violently.

Deacon was nearly thrown from his seat in the first few seconds, regardless of the effort Golith had put into securing him. He held on as tight as he could to the straps, which burned his palms as the material pushed and pulled through his grip. He swore as a sudden, intense concussion passed over him. He felt like his head would explode as the pressure wave surged through the room.

He began to feel woozy, and his vision swam. The violent jostling that had nearly torn him from his seat seemed to be subsiding, though the occasional jolt would toss him around with frightening ease. Through his blurred vision, he tried to assess Golith's status. He worried that, by saving him, the alien had doomed himself, and the sight of him being tossed to and fro around the interior of the room only confirmed his fear.

Deacon watched helplessly as his unlikely ally went limp,

the occasional bounce of the ship no longer triggering a defensive response from the obviously unconscious Tendari. He watched as the torpid body slammed headfirst into the room's ceiling with a sickening crunch. Slowly, Deacon's vision deteriorated to the point that he couldn't make out the insensate movements of his savior, and he realized that only part of his difficulty was the mask and lack of oxygen.

As his tears filled his eyes, he prayed that Golith was still alive. Darkness crept into the corners of his eyes, and the last thought he had before it took him was.... What would Elijah say if he knew I was praying for a Tendari?

CHAPTER 20

A fuzzy, pain-filled cognition slowly awoke Deacon's senses, and he put his trembling hands to his head, attempting to still the thunderous thudding at his temples. His vision gradually improved as he became aware of his surroundings, and memory flooded his thoughts. He remembered Golith and searched the room for the alien.

Turning his head made him wince in pain, but he spotted his friend lying on the floor. The rest of the Tendari had seemingly, abandoned their comrade. All of the seats that ringed the room were empty. Deacon struggled out of his restraints. The process was surprisingly difficult for how close he had been to flying out of his chair during that hellish burn. He still wasn't sure what a 'burn' was, but he knew he didn't want to experience another.

He crouched next to his friend and tentatively held out a hand to feel the scaly skin for some sign of life. Golith felt cold, which shouldn't be surprising since his species was cold-blooded. Instead, he laid his hand on the alien's chest and waited for movement. Deacon felt the tears start again after not feeling anything for some time, and then, to his profound relief, the massive chest heaved, and a ragged cough exited Golith's bloody lips.

"Golith," Deacon said, and moved closer to see his face.

The big alien's eyes were still closed, but as he watched, Deacon could see his breathing slowly improve. As he sat by his friend's side, he realized that noise drifted through the hatch from the equipment room. He wanted to stay with Golith, but he also needed to know what was happening, so he stood and made his way to the hatch. He was still muddled from the lack of oxygen and the beating he'd taken during the burn, but with each step, his confidence grew.

At the threshold, he saw the equipment room was abuzz with activity. The Tendari maintenance crews rushed to dress in their suits and ready tools.

Deacon entered but stayed out of the way. The Tendari were clearly agitated, and he was afraid his very presence might be enough to get him killed, especially after Golith got himself hurt rescuing him. The thought that Golith might still die wormed its way into Deacon's mind, past the walls of optimism that had protected him through the years.

The sound of what could only be the Gorski's guns firing could be heard above the general turmoil in the equipment room. Deacon clutched at the wall. He hated this forced ignorance he was in. Give him a foe he could see, no matter how scary, over the unknown any day.

Through the wall he was clinging to, Deacon felt vibrations that made him imagine a giant hand pounding on the outside of the ship. He wondered what it was that would be attacking the Tendari and didn't know if he wanted them to win or not. Sure, he was somewhat tied to the Tendari, which definitely influenced his judgment, but to see the Tendari beaten would be quite a sight, even if it were his last.

The equipment room quickly emptied, the crews going to work on legitimate repairs as they attempted to undo the damage that giant hand was inflicting. Deacon went back into the closet. He really should learn the real name of this room, he thought. He checked on Golith and was happy to see that he was still breathing, and the blood around his mouth didn't seem any worse than it had been.

Tendari were definitely a hardy species. The beating that Golith had suffered was incredible, and yet he still breathed. Deacon sat next to his friend for some time and tried to ignore the noise of battle that he could do nothing about. It was strange that he now considered Golith, his 'friend,' but what else did you call someone that saved your life?

Hearing the thunk-click of mag boots behind him, Deacon turned. Trask came to the open hatch and poked his head in.

"Grak! Good, you're not dead. I need you." As Trask finished, an explosion rocked the Gorski, nearly sending the big Tendari to the ground. "Now, boy!"

At the Sergeant's insistence and...was that fear...Deacon jumped to his feet and staggered to the doorway.

"What's going on?" Deacon asked, but Trask ignored the question. Instead, he rushed Deacon to his locker, thrusting his suit into his hands. Deacon hurried to comply, but his nerves were still on edge, and he fumbled at the neck gasket. Trask helped him and must have had a pang of sympathy because he spoke as he worked.

"The Tendari are at war." Trask seemed to realize how ridiculous the statement sounded and rushed to explain. "We are at war with another species, one that has proved remarkably strong."

Trask handed Deacon his helmet and turned to the door, but he continued to speak as he rushed from the room. Deacon had to run to keep pace with the Tendari's incredible stride.

"They are called the Marak, and their origins are far from here, but their abilities are beyond anything we have seen. They have started attacking up and down the belt, and we were called to respond to an attack on a neighboring mining facility."

The news was surprising, to say the least. Deacon had never heard of the Marak or this war Trask spoke of, but as he thought of it, it made sense that the Tendari would not advertise the fact that they were, apparently, losing a war. If that kind of thing got out, it could inspire all kinds of bad behavior among the slaves. Up to this point, Deacon, as well as all of the other slaves, saw the Tendari Empire as nearly invulnerable. This revelation worked all kinds of warring emotions in Deacon.

What if the Marak destroyed the Tendari? Would the Marak keep the slaves? Would they set them free? Or would they even be worse to them than the Tendari?

They entered the airlock and waited the thirty-seconds for it to be depressurized.

"What do you need me to do?" Deacon felt a tremor in his voice that put his fear on display.

"The Gorski's defensive array is down."

"Defensive...what?" Deacon asked.

Trask ignored him and instead clipped a tether to his suit. The tether stretched between the two, and Trask pulled on the tether that emanated from a box on his back, giving them some slack.

"Once those doors open, the buffers that keep us upright inside the ship will not help us, and we will be thrown around like pistangs with every move of the ship. This will keep us together. Do your best to keep your footing. I don't want to have to drag you the whole way."

The door opened, and Deacon's world became a violent tableau of light and movement that threatened to make him sick inside his helmet. Flashes of what he assumed were projectiles streaked across the backdrop of black space, pocked with the occasional asteroid.

He stumbled almost immediately as the Gorski shifted beneath him. He looked out toward the front of the ship and watched as the distant stars seemed to move right to left. The Gorski was obviously turning, and it was doing so far faster than Deacon thought the big ship was capable of.

As he watched, Deacon saw another ship come into view. It looked like an even larger Tendari ship, but the damage done to it was devastating. Explosions, white-hot at first, then quickly quenched of light producing fire by the vacuum of space, popped soundlessly along the giant ship's hull. Just based on the first few seconds of observation, it seemed that the Tendari were losing this battle.

"We need to get the defensive array up and running, or we will be torn apart by the Marak," Trask said, and climbed up and out onto the hull of the Gorski. Deacon followed as quickly as he could, his progress slowed by the ship's almost constant shifting movements beneath his feet.

They made their way along the hull toward the front of the ship. At first, Deacon had a hard time taking his eyes off of the scene being played out above him, but it slowed him down and disoriented him even more, so he focused on Trask's back and trudged on behind him. The ship spun and turned simultaneously, and Deacon cried out as his mag boots were pulled from the ship's exterior, and he was thrown out into open space.

Trask had felt the movement early and launched himself to a conduit that jutted from the ship's hull and latched on to it. Deacon swung dangerously at the end of the taught carbon fiber tether.

Once he got his feet secured, once again, Trask slowly pulled Deacon back to the ship. Deacon was trembling uncontrollably when he finally made it back to the ship.

"Come on Grak! Shake it off," Trask said. The big Sergeant turned and began walking toward the front of the ship again. Deacon was more or less pulled along behind him for a while until he was able to concentrate enough on walking to keep up.

They had apparently reached their destination when Trask stopped and turned to Deacon.

"Follow this conduit down into the space between the

shield plating. We got hit by a piercing round, and we're pretty sure that it severed the conduit. You need to put this splice on the conduit when you find the damage." Trask pulled a splicer out of his suit's back-case and handed it to Deacon.

"Don't drop it, or we're all dead," he admonished.

Deacon grabbed it tightly and turned to the hatch that would give him access to the space between shielding layers. The ship shimmied with another impact as he lowered himself headfirst into the dark, cramped space. He gripped the splicer tool in his left hand and the conduit with his right and pulled himself down the length, searching for the break.

The ship twisted violently, and Deacon was slammed against the outer shield wall. Luckily for him, there wasn't enough room between him and the wall to have built up much momentum, and he hit the metal with force enough to bruise but not kill. He swore and pulled himself down the conduit, eager to finish the job. He didn't know what this defensive array was, but it must be critical for them to attempt the repair mid fire-fight.

The illumination from his helmet lamp was enough to see by, but the dark, oppressive interior of the shields was foreboding. He wondered if he would rather die in a place like this than float helplessly through space. He still hadn't made up his mind when a brief flash of light lit up a space ahead. He pulled to the spot and found a hole in the outer shield wall that he could see out of. As he watched, an unfamiliar ship passed by, firing projectiles in three directions simultaneously. He marveled momentarily at the sight of it. Its design was far more sleek than the Tendari ships he'd seen, and it moved with a grace that belied its size.

Deacon watched as several projectiles flashed toward him, and he flinched as they struck the hull nearby and passed through at least the first layer of shielding, punching more peepholes further down the crevice in front of him. He swore as he saw one round strike the conduit.

"Poor design," he muttered to himself.

"Repeat your last," Trask's voice came over his comm. It shouldn't have surprised him that Trask had opened their channel

"I was just commenting on the stupidity of the design of this bagh ship," Deacon said, allowing his anger to get the better of him. He probably wouldn't have spoken so openly if he had been standing within arms reach of the Sergeant, but he figured he probably wouldn't make it out of this alive anyway. Where was the harm in letting Trask have a taste of his real feelings?

Deacon was surprised as he heard Trask laugh over the comm.

"If only you knew," Came Trask's response. "Now, are you done yet? We're getting hammered."

"I'm working on it, but they just rammed another hole through the conduit further up."

Trask unloaded with a string of Tendari curses that his translator didn't even bother relaying.

"Go as fast as you can, Grak."

Deacon felt along the conduit and found what he assumed was the original break. He positioned himself opposite the break, careful not to touch the exposed wiring inside and placed the splicer on the conduit. He ran the device down the conduit several times, and when he pulled it away, the break in the metal was gone.

"One down," Deacon said.

"Copy," Trask responded.

Deacon pulled himself down the conduit once more, hoping that a stray round wouldn't crash into him as he moved. He made it to the second break and quickly fitted the device over it, and shoved the tool back and forth. He pulled the splicer away and was satisfied that the conduit looked whole. He scanned the length of the conduit for any more breaks but couldn't see any.

Guns fired in rapid succession, so fast that Deacon couldn't really distinguish separate shots. He peeked through a hole in the outer shield wall and saw a trail of light streak out from the Gorski toward the projectiles that came from the other ship, intercepting them with bright explosions.

"You did it, Grak! The Defensive array is running! Now, get back up here," Trask yelled over the comm channel.

Deacon smiled to himself and grabbed the conduit, and backed his way out of the space. It was too tight to turn around, so he had to look past his feet to guide his way back up to the hatch. He made it to the hatch, and as soon as his foot was out, Trask pulled him roughly the rest of the way out and slammed the door shut.

"They're counting a recall! They're going to burn. We have to get back now!" Trask yelled, and he clipped the tether to Deacon's suit and began to run along the hull. The sound of his mag boots were thunk-clicking way too fast to be safe, and Deacon could do little but hold on to the tether as he was dragged behind.

He watched as the Marak ship passed close by overhead, strafing the Gorski with bursts of fire from too many guns to count. It may have been his imagination, but it seemed that one set of guns took a particular interest in their headlong flight across the outside of the hull. Rounds began to fall around them, and Deacon screamed in terror as time seemed to slow, and he watched as the tether was struck by a round. The tether parted so quickly that he didn't even feel the line jerk in his hands with the impact.

"Trask!" He yelled over the comm, but Trask kept running. He wondered if the Sergeant couldn't hear him with the sound of shrieking metal, dull explosions, and the echo of his own breathing in his helmet.

"Trask! The tether!" he tried again, but Trask kept running, and Deacon kept floating. Deacon tried to reach out to the ship as it passed by underneath him, but it was just out of reach.

"Trask!" He looked forward, wishing the alien would turn

and see him, but he didn't.

Deacon saw the end of the tether flash by his visor, and he had a thought. He pulled the tether in so that he held the very end, creating a loop and pushed the loop toward the hull, hoping that it would snag on a jutting piece of equipment or conduit that was common on the exterior of the Gorski.

"Trask!" he tried again, and this time the alien stopped and turned, seeing him. Just then, the loop caught and pulled Deacon to the ship and bounced him hard against it. He was about to drift back up and out but was just able to grip a jagged piece of metal that had been lifted up from one of the enemy's rounds. He engaged his mag boots and put his feet down, then turned back toward Trask, but he was gone.

CHAPTER 21

Deacon carefully walked along the hull of the Gorski, cautiously skirting many holes that now riddled the metal plating at his feet. He made it to where Trask had stopped and found the airlock. The door closed, and the Tendari Sergeant had already passed the interior door, running away down the corridor.

"Trask! You can't leave me out here," Deacon called to him.

There was static as a response for a time, and then the Sergeant's voice broke through.

"There's no time." Deacon heard Trask close the comm channel with a click of finality that he felt in his bones. He felt tears wet his cheeks, and he pressed a series of buttons on the control pad, hoping to guess the correct sequence. The buttons turned red with each attempt, and the door remained closed. Of all the access panels that he had memorized codes for, why had he not paid better attention to this one? He knew the answer, of course. He had not felt a need to know this one. How would this code help in his and Elijah's escape from the Tendari?

He swore, knowing that his time was running out fast. He braced himself as the ship beneath him heaved. He turned and looked out at the stars, wondering what he should do. For valuable seconds he was at a complete loss, and he spun helplessly, searching for a solution in his immediate vicinity.

The tears were running in earnest now, and he felt completely helpless.

Then he saw it.

He moved back out of the alcove that served as an entry for the airlock and back out onto the ship's hull. He moved as fast as he could and traced his earlier steps back to a large hole in the outer shielding of the Gorski. He took three giant breaths and lowered himself into the hole, careful not to snag his suit on the sharp edges of the ship's gaping wound.

Once inside, he switched on his helmet lamp and scanned the interior. It appeared that the projectile that had made this hole had continued on, though at a vastly diminished velocity, and punctured the interior shielding.

The red of interior emergency lighting spilled out of the rupture. The hole was too small for him to press through, but he pressed his face against the hole and peered through. He saw the disheveled interior of a crewman's cabin. It had been explained to him that unimportant rooms like crew cabins were situated around the exterior wall of the ship so that in the event of a puncture, the room's hatches could be closed and the ship could maintain air pressure.

Apparently, that is precisely what had happened here. For a moment, he was tempted to try and force the hole bigger, but something told him that he didn't have that kind of time.

Instead, he turned and looked down at the gap between the shield layers. The function of the shielding had also been explained to him, and despite the impressive damage done to the exterior plating, few of the projectiles had actually made it through the inside layer.

The outer shields worked to slow and break up projectiles, robbing them of momentum and, hopefully, depriving them of the ability to puncture the inner layer. In addition to these two layers, baffles were situated between the layers along key areas for added protection. The theory was that the projectile, upon being broken up and diverted into less perpendicular trajectories, would wobble and spin its way into the lengthwise sides of the baffles and stop.

Deacon came to the closest baffle and gauged its size. He hoped this would work. The burn was probably going to start up at any second. He gritted his teeth and pushed feet first into the end of the baffle. The fit was extremely tight, and for a second, he worried that he would never be able to get out again, but he told himself the tighter, the better and forced himself deeper into the octagonal tube. He prayed, to whom he still didn't know, but he begged whatever deity there might be to make it so that he didn't puncture his suit on any sharp piece of metal as he squirmed his way down into the baffle.

Finally, he had gone as far down as he could manage. The fit was so tight that his breathing was restricted, and his anxiety made him start to panic as he was unable to get a full breath. He was terrified, and he had to remind himself of the likely outcome if he left the baffle.

He waited for the burn, both wishing that it would never come and wishing it would. He felt completely restless and frustrated that he couldn't move. He twisted his head for no other reason than because it was the only thing he could move and caught sight of something.

His eyes adjusted as the too-bright reflection of the lamp nearly washed out the image before him. It was familiar. His heart nearly stopped as he recognized the symbol he had traced with his fingers nearly every day for years.

Stripes, red and white, with a blue square in the upper left of the rectangle. Fifty white spots dotted the blue square. It was the patch on his mining suit. His human mining suit.

What was this symbol doing inside the baffle of a Tendari corsair?

Without warning, Deacon was pressed against one side of

the baffle with such force that he felt like a giant was stepping on him. Grinding him maliciously into the hard-packed ground. He felt something wet stream from his nose, and in his addled brain, he thought...these suits make it impossible to wipe your nose... then blackness.

For the second time that day, Deacon awoke into blurry consciousness. His first thought was nebulous and hard to grasp, but it had something to do with the Gorski. He floated. He could feel his weightless limbs sway freely, and sudden panic enveloped him. At first, he wasn't sure why, but then it came back to him. He had been inside a baffle to stay safe from the burn. Now where was he?

In a panic, he turned his head from side to side but saw only darkness. Had he been thrown from the ship? He realized with a start that his headlamp wasn't on, and he reached up to it, feeling for the switch, but the thing wouldn't turn on. Something brushed against his arm, and he jumped in fear and then relief as he realized he must still be inside the ship, well, not inside, but in between the shield layers. He had been thrown from the baffle, but he must have weathered the worst of the burn inside it, or he wouldn't be alive.

He turned his head again and focused, trying to see any light. He used the thing he'd brushed against to turn himself more, and he slowly was able to make out vagaries of light. Most emanated from the holes in the outer shield, but above him, he could see the faint red of what he assumed was the ambient light coming from the hole in the inner shield he'd seen.

He pushed off toward it and floated several feet, and bumped into...something. As he felt the object, he decided it was a brace that helped suspend the outer shield layer. He blindly navigated around it and retargeted the red light, which was brighter now.

He made it to the opening where he'd entered the space between the shield walls and poked his head out of the hole, and looked around. No flashing explosions or bright projectiles tracing a path through space. He turned his head around and tried to see something he recognized and was pleased to see the Rock coming closer as the Gorski decelerated so as not to crash into the facility. Deacon never thought he would be happy to see his life-long home and prison.

With the added light reflected off the nearby asteroid, Deacon could see that his helmet's visor had been cracked and realized that he must have hit something pretty hard to have cracked the visor and broken his headlamp. Deacon had to give it to them. The Tendari sure knew how to make helmets.

Now that the Gorski seemed to be out of harm's way, Deacon decided that he would have to focus on getting inside before his air ran out. He resolved that Trask would not get away with his cowardice?... Treachery? He wasn't sure which it was. The Sergeant definitely didn't like him, but were his feelings strong enough to intentionally leave him outside the ship right before a burn? Deacon didn't know, but he would make Trask answer for the act.

He turned to the inside once again and moved to the hole torn into the interior of the Gorski. Red light poured out of the hole, and as he got closer, Deacon thought he could hear the emergency klaxons blaring inside, but he knew that it was probably his imagination as sound didn't travel in a vacuum. Then he realized he wasn't hearing it but feeling it. His hands, pressed against the jagged edges of the rupture, pulsed in time with what he assumed was the alarm.

He tested the metal's strength around the edge of the hole, wondering if he could make it bigger and quickly decided that he couldn't, at least not with his hands. His suit had built-in pouches that closed tight. He remembered that he had put several of his favorite tools in them as well as a roll of seal tape. As he examined the contents of his pockets, he remembered that he had put the splicer in his chest pouch to free up his hands after he had fixed the conduit.

He removed the tool and considered its functions. It should be possible, if he engaged the tool without applying it to any object, to form a bar of the material that the tool used to repair conduit. He thought the metal was titanium, the same material as the conduit and the shield plating.

He hit the button, and the tool heated up in his hand. It took him several tries. His first attempt created an unusable mass of metal that, when cooled, floated away. He concentrated and tried again. This time, by bracing himself against two baffles, he was able to hold steady enough to make a titanium bar. It was wavy and twisted up at one end, but he was proud of it and smiled at his simple victory.

He returned to the hole and began prying at the metal surrounding the hole. Portions of the shield plating had been scored and punctured with small fragments that weakened the metal, and after, what seemed like an excruciatingly long time, Deacon was able to bend a piece out, making the hole bigger.

He felt a vibration pass through the ship and decided it must have docked with the umbilical from the mining facility. He pushed back from the hole a ways and eyed it, trying to measure it in comparison with him and his suit. He didn't feel comfortable trying to wiggle through it as is and pushed forward, ready to go to work on the other dangerously sharp edges, when his HUD came up with a flashing warning. With his additional schooling from Elijah, he could now read the bright red characters.

Ten-percent. His air was down to ten percent.

He cursed and hit the most jagged pieces with the bar a few times, then cursed again as he put his arms above his head and pushed them through the rupture. His head came next, and he began to hope as his shoulders squeezed through without tearing a hole in his suit. Then his waist caught. He wiggled a little, trying to be gentle, but he seemed stuck fast.

He put his hands on either side of the hole and pushed. He

slid a little further into the ship with each push until he came free and floated the rest of the way in. He smiled at his success until he heard the alarm in his helmet again, but this time it warned him of an oxygen leak. He looked to his waist and legs, searching for the hole, but didn't see any. Then he realized that his gloves were bleeding air. Jets of pressurized air streamed from the holes in his suit's gloves where he had pushed against the jagged hole.

He cursed and reached for the seal tape in the pouch at his leg, only to notice that the pouch was gone, torn free in his efforts. He hurriedly pushed off the cot on the floor back to the hole and looked through. There it was, his roll of seal tape floating away. He tried to reach it, but it had drifted too far. He knew he could not push back through the hole and patch himself up and come back. By then, he would be out of air entirely.

He had a thought and grabbed the bar that he had let drift just inside the crewman's cabin, then went back to the hole. He used it to carefully coax the roll back to him using the curved end. When it was within reach, he snagged it and hurriedly began taping up his gloves.

The read-out on his HUD warned that his oxygen had reached a terrifying two percent. Deacon cursed again and searched the small room for something that would work for his plans. He knew enough about space to understand that there was no way that he would be strong enough to force the hatch open from his side with the air that he assumed was on the other side pushing against him. He had to seal the hole first so that he could repressurize the cabin before opening the hatch.

He looked at the floor and noticed a metal grate that looked like it might be big enough. He used the bar to pry it up and pushed it against the hole. Zero-G held the grate against the hole as Deacon tore off long strips of seal tape and layered them over the grating and the hole. The hole finally covered, he moved back to the hatch. He was afraid to even look at the oxygen read-out and chose to ignore it.

He pulled the lever while pushing on the hatch with all his might. As he expected, the thing didn't open, save for a mere crack that let in a gush of air. His own breathing was becoming increasingly difficult, but the longer he was able to hold the hatch cracked, the easier it became to open, and soon he was able to push it wide with a wave of air. With the air came the sound. The klaxons were indeed blaring.

He immediately unclipped his helmet and took a greedy lung full of air. The air inside the Gorski smelled of smoke and acrid fumes that he couldn't identify, but he drank it in gratefully. He had made it. He was alive...again. Despite the odds, Deacon had survived. He began to have faith in whatever deity was looking out for him. He decided that he would ask Elijah if the humans of Earth had a God that they prayed to, that is, if he survived, what he must do next.

CHAPTER 22

Deacon walked down the corridor carrying his folded-up suit in his right arm and his helmet in his left. He passed several sets of Tendari marines as they ran through the ship, helping where they could. Deacon also passed dead bodies, and for an instant, he was buoyed by the thought that they weren't invincible, but then he thought of Golith and felt remorse for his thoughts.

It was possible that, even now, his friend was as dead as these Tendari.

He had an idea come to him in the corridor outside the equipment room that he hoped would give him the edge he desperately needed.

When he made it to the room, he stopped in the doorway. Several crews were missing from the Tendari inside. Deacon assumed that they had been killed in the fight somehow or maybe they were already off working on repairs. It appeared that those inside were readying themselves to go back out and try to fix the ship. Deacon knew there was plenty to do.

The Tendari looked tired and moved sluggishly. Deacon was tired too, but he had anger driving him past it. He scanned the room for Trask and spotted him on the far side in front of his locker. The sight of the Sergeant made Deacon's blood heat, and he pushed down the temptation to charge at the giant. No.

Despite his feelings, he couldn't lose his head. That was one of Elijah's most important lessons. Another lesson was never to put himself in the situation that he now entered willingly.

Deacon dropped his suit to the floor. The sound of it clattering against the metal deck plating made several Tendari look up. Upon noticing him, murmuring began to rumble and spread among the Tendari until all looked at him.

He watched Trask's face as he looked up and met Deacon's eyes. The Sergeant's stunned countenance was a source of pride for Deacon. He had survived beyond any of their expectations, especially those of the piece of scum who left him there to die.

"Didn't expect to see me again, did you, Trask?" Deacon said.

Trask glanced around him with nervous energy. He obviously didn't want his colleagues to know of his cowardice.

"Grak. You are still alive," he said, with feigned happiness. Several Tendari seemed to sense the lie in their Sergeant's demeanor and scowled at him.

"No thanks to you. You left me to die," Deacon said, his rage building at Trask's attempt to brush his treachery aside.

Trask's mouth opened as if he was going to say something, then it closed. He looked around.

"I thought you were already dead." It was a weak excuse, as all could see. Trask's disquiet was plain and low growls emerged from several throats. The fact that the growls were not directed at him was a completely new and welcome experience to Deacon.

"You locked me out of the ship and scurried back to the safety of your hole." Deacon motioned to the closet, for which he still didn't have a proper name. "But I am Grak! I cannot be killed so easily."

Clicking sounded from every throat but Trask's in the way the Tendari expressed respect. He didn't look at the other aliens but kept his eyes fixed on the Sergeant. The clicking seemed too much for Trask, and anger soon replaced chagrin.

"So what if I left him? He is a human. Nothing but a weak human that is too lucky to die." With that, Trask roared and charged toward Deacon.

If this was the end, Deacon thought, then he would make it as memorable as possible.

He looked to the ends of the live wires that he had carefully fed through the visor of his helmet. The heavy wire trailed behind him, as yet unnoticed by the Tendari, out into the corridor from where he had found it earlier, severed and sparking. He held the wire in place, his hand inside the helmet, out of sight.

Trask ran the few steps to the workbench that filled the center of the room, and the big Tendari threw the heavy table on its side as Deacon had anticipated. The table was tall, and the ceiling was relatively low, so low that Trask's head barely cleared it. He would not have climbed over the table, and he would not have gone around. That was not the Tendari's style.

Tools and parts clattered to the floor and made the Tendari on that side jump back.

Deacon pulled the titanium bar out from behind his back and held it at his side. Trask saw it and smiled.

"You don't know how stupid that was," Trask said. But Deacon did know. There was so much that could go wrong with this plan. He just prayed that the Sergeant would be as predictable as he looked.

Trask grabbed one of the metal legs on the upturned table and ripped it from its mount. He smiled again and swung it experimentally, then charged again.

Deacon made as if he was unsure if he should turn and run or stay and fight, a feeling that wasn't hard to portray, and mentally readied himself for the onslaught. He schooled his breathing as Elijah had taught him, and with only feet, before Trask reached him, he shifted his stance to the balls of his feet and brought up his hands, the helmet as a shield and the bar as a sword. He had a split second to remember Leonidas and hoped he would acquit himself as those ancient Spartans had.

Deacon prepared himself for the overhand, bone-crushing swing that he knew the Tendari would lead with, and he was not disappointed. With a thunderous cry of rage, Trask took the table leg in both hands and brought it down toward Deacon, but the Grak was too fast.

Deacon dodged out of the way at the last instant. Compared to Deacon's blinding speed, Trask seemed to be moving in slow-motion, and he smiled as the giant's weapon clanged loudly into the floor.

Just as Trask lifted the weapon for another strike, Deacon shot his hand over with the wire and pressed it against the metal table leg. Sparks flew, and Trask's body stiffened, but the table leg was still moving, and the wire disconnected from the metal. Trask was stunned, but he would recover soon, so Deacon stepped forward and pressed the wire to his thigh.

Trask stiffened again, and Deacon could smell burning clothing and what he assumed was the Tendari's scaly skin beneath. He lifted the helmet and wire away from Trask, and the giant crumpled to the ground.

The Tendari looking on were surprisingly quiet as Deacon approached Trask's head and smashed the bar into the Sergeant's face several times. He didn't know if he had killed Trask or not, but he didn't care. As far as he was concerned, Trask had made his position clear. Either Deacon removed the Sergeant from his life, or Trask would do the same to him.

Brown-green Tendari blood seeped from several cuts on Trask's face, but the Sergeant was unconscious, so Deacon reluctantly stopped his barrage of blows. He turned and looked to the rest of the Tendari. They stared at him, dumbstruck. He didn't know what his future would now consist of. He didn't know if he was now marked for death, and to be honest, he couldn't blame them if he was. He had just, possibly, killed a

Tendari Sergeant, and he was a slave.

Oddly, Deacon didn't feel too upset with the prospect of being executed for his actions. He slowly turned from the room of stunned Tendari; he dropped the helmet and wire to the ground, then the bar, and walked away.

He walked all the way to the shuttle dock, and no one stopped him. He was pleased that he only had to wait a few minutes for the shuttle to arrive, and he was let onboard without a word. As he stood in his customary spot by the door, he saw his reflection in the polished metal. Dried blood covered half his face, but that wasn't the part that scared him.

His eyes were different.

CHAPTER 23

Water ran over his skin, and he could see skeins of blood swirl and disappear down the dark drain. Steam rose around him as the hot water came in contact with the cool metal interior of the shower. It was ironic that he would be enjoying the water that Trask had given him. He tried to push thoughts of all that had happened that day to the back of his mind, but he couldn't, and so he marinated in the feelings as the water washed the sweat and blood from his body.

He, oddly, felt at ease with the thought that he might be put to death for his actions. He didn't want to die, but it was almost like he had already accepted the probability as a cost which he was happy to pay. In his mind, it was unacceptable for someone to act so dishonorably, and he felt obligated to put an end to it.

After his shower, he got dressed and ran into Elijah as the old man entered the large, low-ceilinged shower room.

"I have been looking for you," Elijah said, and smiled brightly. "I have been worried all day. I saw the Gorski leave and feared the worst."

Deacon didn't know what "the worst" would be, but he smiled weakly at the old man.

Elijah held him at arm's length and looked at his face.

"What happened? You look like you just found out your dog was dead."

"What's a dog?" Deacon asked.

"It's not important right now. What happened?" Elijah asked.

Deacon sighed. He didn't want to expend the effort of recounting the dizzying events since that morning, but he knew it was unfair to Elijah to keep it from him, and so he sat on an old, broken, ore-crate and began his story. He had only made it to the first alarm that signaled the Gorski's emergency departure when Denzink ambled over, curious by what he had apparently overheard.

Deacon paused his recount and stared a question at Denzink. The fat Kupelti merely motioned for him to continue and pulled up another ore-crate that creaked dangerously as the alien eased his weight onto it. Deacon wondered if he should continue with other ears present but decided that it didn't really matter. He continued.

Denzink sat spellbound, listening with rapt attention as Deacon described the way Golith had saved him at the cost of his own well-being and possible life. When he got to the first appearance of a Marak ship, Denzink swore softly and called for his friend, Anzark, to come over and listen as well.

Deacon was annoyed as questions arose that forced him to summarize earlier parts of the story, but Elijah seemed content to just sit and listen, and despite the other's apparent surprise and disbelief, the old man sat patiently. When he described Trask's betrayal, though, all three were visibly angry, and Anzark swore a foul curse that seemed especially tailored for the Tendari species.

He plowed on and told how he had sought shelter inside the baffle during the second burn but neglected to mention the brief and somewhat surreal memory of a human image he'd seen on the interior of the octagonal metal tube. Thinking back on it, he wasn't really sure he had seen it. The memory was somewhat clouded with pain and fear, and he decided that he may have just imagined the red, blue, and white symbol.

Denzink gasped as he told of the holes in his suit and shifted uncomfortably until Deacon was able to repair the punctures with his seal tape. Based on their reactions, Deacon thought that it was like it wasn't a foregone conclusion that he had survived and sat in front of them now. He was half tempted to reassure the rotund Kupelti that he had, indeed, made it.

When Deacon told them of his fight with Trask, all three were amazed, and Denzink leapt to his feet and did a surprisingly agile dance while chanting something in his native language. Despite his melancholy, Deacon couldn't help but smile at the sight. The two Kupelti congratulated him on his incredible survival and hurried off to their cliche of friends. Deacon assumed that everyone would know what had happened soon enough, and he had a hard time feeling anything about that. It was impossible for him to see how he would survive past tomorrow, and so his judgment was darkened and more cynical than it normally was.

"Well, that was odd," Deacon said, nodding toward the Kupelti. "My conversations with non-human slaves up to this point have been limited to one to two sentences. Now, all of a sudden, they want a lecture."

"Tales such as the one you just told are rare enough to be called legends, and to a slave, the hope you cultivate in your wake is tantalizing." Deacon wasn't sure what the old man meant, but he didn't bother asking. Unlike his Kupelti audience, Elijah seemed to understand the probable retribution that the Tendari would visit upon him.

"You shouldn't go tomorrow," the old man finally said.

"Why not? It's not like they'll forget I exist, and I'd rather not force them to come to look for me. I think they'd be in a much worse mood when they found me."

Elijah thought about it for a minute.

"You're probably right," he said, trying to smile

optimistically as if both of them didn't already know the danger he was in.

"I have a question," Deacon said, as he lay down on the ground where he normally slept. He didn't feel the point in training tonight, and based on Elijah's non-reaction, the old man didn't either.

"Go ahead," Elijah said, sitting on the floor next to him.

"Why would there be a human symbol inside the baffle of a Tendari ship?" Elijah's face blanched, and he turned to him sharply.

"Don't ever repeat that. You hear me?" The old man's vehemence was surprising, and Deacon flinched, then quickly nodded his understanding.

"But..." Deacon began, but was cut off by the old man's stare.

Elijah looked around worriedly, then nodded to himself. "Listen, I will only talk more if we have some safe place to do it," he whispered.

Deacon thought for a moment and then rose to his feet. Even though he didn't logically see the point, his curiosity was piqued, and he motioned for Elijah to follow. He moved quietly to the corner where the door to Nah-leesi's warren of service tunnels sat in shadow, the only light coming from the keypad on the wall. This was the earliest code he had memorized. He was a little embarrassed now to think back on his motivation for doing so.

He entered the code and pushed the door open, and the two of them passed through. Instantly, the humm of equipment filled the air. A steady clunking noise sounded every few seconds.

"I don't think they have any listening devices here. If they did, I think the machinery would drown out anything we say," Deacon said.

Elijah looked around and, not seeing any obvious spying equipment, nodded his agreement. He turned and looked down at Deacon. The old man's brilliant eyes could even be seen in this dark corridor, and they looked serious.

"Now, listen to me," he said, gripping both of Deacon's shoulders in strong hands. "What I'm going to tell you is extremely dangerous knowledge to have in your head. If the Tendari catches any hint that you know it, they will exterminate you and everyone you know."

Deacon couldn't imagine what would be so damaging to the Tendari that they would go through such efforts to keep it hidden.

"From your reaction out there, you already know a part of it, might as well know the rest."

Elijah swallowed before continuing. "Humans were far stronger than anyone of this generation will ever know. That's the big secret, really. There was a war between the Tendari and humans two hundred and fifty years ago, and we beat them. The fact that a species so physically weak by comparison could wreak such havoc among their fleets, armies, and planets was a sore point for them, and they refused to capitulate. Humans, however, saw the writing on the wall, and just as the Tendari refused to give up, we refused to exterminate them. Genocide is a horrible thing, and we had seen enough of it in our own history to know how ugly it was, so we left them alone, sure that that was the end of it. Fifty years later, they returned. They had spent their time developing a weapon that was devastating and effective. A virus."

Elijah saw Deacon's confused look and went on.

"That's right, it did not originate on Earth. We were not the source of the weapon that had since served the Tendari so well."

"But surely that isn't the big secret they kill to protect," Deacon said.

"It is only a part. When they infected Earth, we, of course, tried to find a cure or vaccine, but the Tendari made up for their lack of technical sophistication with their biological knowledge, and a cure was not found. Once it was apparent that all of Earth was doomed, the world's leaders quarantined the planet and sent all those unaffected away. Once the Tendari started to show up to claim their new planet, we decided it was better to destroy the Earth than give the Tendari any satisfaction in their victory."

"We destroyed it?" Deacon asked, bewildered.

Elijah ignored the rhetorical question and went on. "Those left in the colonies and mining facilities in the belt were hit with the virus as well, but not all died. Those that survived were immune, as are their descendants, of which we count ourselves."

"Though we destroyed the Earth to keep it out of their hands, we could not do the same with all our ships and facilities throughout the belt. They gladly made them their own, and so it is that you find an Earth symbol inside the bowels of the Gorski, or should I call it the U.S.S. Tucson."

"You must realize that without knowing how the Tendari think, this story still wouldn't explain their need for secrecy, but you, of all people, know how they think. Can you tell me why they need this to be a secret?"

Deacon thought about it and almost gave up prematurely when he thought of the Tendari in the equipment room tilting their heads and clicking in some strange sign of respect. There was something there. He thought about it for a few more seconds then it came to him.

"We let them live," he said simply. Elijah smiled, pleased that his pupil had made the connection. He waited for Deacon to expound on the thought.

"We let them live," he repeated. "They should have respected us after we beat them instead of coming up with an underhanded way to kill us." Deacon was confident of his assessment of the Tendari, but he wasn't sure that the alien hierarchy would be forced to the same strange honor system that the individuals were bound to. Elijah nodded, confirming his assessment.

"What else?" the old man prodded.

"Tendari don't hold as much value in advantages like technology. They seem to judge an enemy on their physical characteristics, so to them, humans are inferior. With that in mind, they must be extremely embarrassed that we defeated them."

Elijah nodded. "Embarrassed, yes, but more than that. They are scared." Deacon looked at him questioningly. "They are scared of us because no other species has come so close to annihilating them. Your whole life, you have been treated like you are nothing, like you are weak and worthless, but that is a lie perpetuated in large part by the Tendari. You are strong. You are human," Elijah said, patting Deacon's chest with the palm of his right hand.

"If they're so scared of us, why don't they just kill every single one of us that they find?" Deacon asked.

"They did for a while, but they realized that an even more acceptable outcome was to subjugate us. Make us slaves that they could kick around. It helps their self-confidence, I suppose." Elijah said.

Deacon grimaced. "I think they need their confidence shaken," he said.

CHAPTER 24

Another headache greeted Deacon upon waking, and a wave of stress hit him as he remembered all that had happened. He sensed the odd feeling of Deja Vu floating around the periphery of his consciousness, but unlike the last time, he suspected his death awaited him upon his arrival at the Gorski. This time he wasn't afraid. Well, not so afraid as he had been before.

Now he felt somewhat content as if a measure of his business had been completed. Maybe it was because he had been the one to make the decision. He had chosen to confront and fight Trask. He did so, knowing the consequences. Therefore, as he went about the motions of his morning routine, basic as it was, he smiled at the thought that he had done his part to assert human strength in the minds of those that had watched him put down Trask. That, he realized, was why he must die.

To the Tendari, his victory over Trask could only remind them of their own failures of the past. Grato would have no choice but to have him put to death. He was surprised that the commander had even brought him aboard the Gorski in the first place, knowing the Tendari's real history with humanity. He guessed his original assessment that Grato had done it to needle Trask for some reason still held water in his mind, but he couldn't be sure.

Denzink called to Deacon in the ration line and motioned for him to go in front of him. The Kupelti's open kindness surprised him, and Deacon was scared to accept. He was sure those in line behind Denzink would protest and cause a scene, and he was not in the mood to deal with that. He declined the offer with a shake of his head, but Denzink insisted. After an intolerable minute of Denzink persistently motioning for him to come forward, Deacon mentally shrugged and walked forward, sure that those around him would mutiny.

Surprisingly, no one said a word, and when he made eye contact with one of them, Grimshoth, a Carexi, the slave merely nodded to him as he passed. Deacon was sure that, had he tried this before, he would have been yelled down at the very least and probably beaten. He was still contemplating the change in the slave's behavior when Denzink grabbed his shoulder and pushed him into his place in front of him.

"What's up with them?" Deacon asked.

"Oh, they just respect anyone who fights the Tendari," Denzink said, proudly.

"You told them?" Deacon said, a little exasperated. He had expected that the tale would have been spread throughout the night, but he didn't expect *everyone* to have heard it by now. "Anzark and you must have been busy last night," he said.

"It is not often that such a story can be told. It is remarkable what you have accomplished."

"Accomplished?" Deacon scoffed. "I'm all but dead," he had said it under his breath, not really meaning anyone to hear, but Denzink did.

"This is also why they respect you." The Kupelti said, looking down at Deacon with sadness in his eyes.

Deacon didn't know what to say. He found it ironic that he no longer needed to fear his fellow slaves on the day that the Tendari would likely kill him.

He was only two away from the window when the door

that he and Elijah had gone through the night before opened, and out stepped a harried looking Nah-leesi, followed a few seconds later by a gasping Anzark. He clutched his chest like he was dying and slumped against the wall, totally exhausted.

Nah-leesi spotted Deacon and made her way over to him.

"Hey, mud thumper, what do you think you are doing?" She said to him angrily. Denzink, perhaps fearing the small Kalix would soon back up her attitude with violence, stepped back a pace. Despite his mood, Deacon smiled. It was amazing what just the sight of her did to him.

"Good to see you too, Nah-leesi," he said. "I'm just getting my food, if that's what you can call this," he said as he reached the window and received his ration. He knew what she meant, and he knew that playing dumb would annoy her wonderfully and make her scrunch up her nose in that way that kept him up at night. She didn't disappoint, and as he stepped away from the window, she jabbed him in the chest with a dagger-like finger.

"You know what I mean. Are you just going to roll over and let them execute you?" Her voice rose with every word until the end of the sentence was almost inaudibly high. He looked at her for a while, knowing it was probably the last time he would see her beautiful eyes. She shifted under his gaze and was about to repeat her question, but he spoke before she could.

"I don't see how I can stop them if they want to," he said simply.

"I can hide you. There are places that I know about."

"And then what?" he asked.

"And then...well, we can figure out the rest as we go," she said.

"They will kill you and everyone here just to find one rogue human. You know they will."

She stammered and obviously agreed with his words logically but couldn't bring herself to agree emotionally. Tears started to form in her large green eyes.

"You're beautiful, Nah-leesi, and if they decide to kill me, I think I will miss your eyes the most." He walked away toward the door to the Tendari section of the facility.

He heard her sob behind him, a sobbing that transformed into a growl followed by a scream of rage as she shoved the still-wheezing Anzark out of the way and slammed the door behind her as she left the barracks.

"Remember who you are!" Elijah's voice called behind him. Deacon turned in the doorway and saw the old man standing in the middle of the barracks, fist held high. Amazingly, the surrounding aliens were silent. Deacon nodded to his friend and turned around before they could see his tears.

He moved down the corridor somber and despondent and only nodded to Gorat and Slik as he approached the door they guarded. He wondered, absently, what horrible thing they had done to warrant this prolonged guard duty. For all the anticipation that welled up inside him, nothing seemed to separate this commute to the Gorski from any other day until he was aboard the human-built ship. Damage to the ship was still very much in evidence as he slowly made his way to the equipment room, and tired Tendari faces barely registered his presence as he passed among them. He wondered if that was why he hadn't been apprehended yet. Maybe they simply had more important things to deal with. He began to hope that, maybe, his assault and possible murder would be forgotten in the turmoil when he came to the doorway and stopped in his tracks.

Golith stood in the center of the room, propping himself up, wearily, with the table.

He felt guilty as he realized that, since yesterday, he had done relatively little worrying for his friend who had risked his life for him. Despite his selfishness, he felt a wave of relief like the first breath after being deprived of air.

He ran to the Tendari and embraced him. His arms wrapped around the alien's legs and held on. He felt Golith turn in his grasp, and when Deacon looked up, the Tendari was looking down at him. Deacon knew that the action was strange. Other aliens didn't embrace or "hug," as Elijah had called it, but the act felt so comfortably human that it was hard for Deacon to let go.

Finally, Deacon pulled away and smiled up at his friend.

"I am so glad that you survived," he said. It should have surprised Deacon that Golith could even stand, but it didn't. Tendari were extremely resilient and healed remarkably fast. Still, Golith had large splotches of discoloration on his head and around his mouth.

"It would take more than an unharnessed burn to finish me off," he growled. His voice was even scratchier than normal, and he sounded exhausted. "I hear that the same is true of you," Golith said.

Deacon blanched and looked away. He scanned the room and saw that it was filled with his Tendari maintenance colleagues, and they were all looking at him. He swallowed hard and looked back to Golith. "Survival is kinda the point of life, I think," he said. Deacon felt that it was a lame thing to be one of the last things for him to say, but as he looked around again, Tendari nodded in solemn agreement to his statement.

"It's too bad that Trask died yesterday. He might have agreed with you," Golith said.

Deacon almost felt ashamed at Golith's words, but he shook it off. "Trask deserved what he got," he said. He was proud that his voice only broke slightly.

"He did indeed," Golith agreed. "He should have known better than to try to tie into a live wire like that. I guess, in the thick of things, we all run the risk of losing our heads and forgetting our training."

Deacon stared at Golith, dumbfounded.

"Well done, Grak," Golith said, and placed a hand on his shoulder.

CHAPTER 25

"I still can't believe that they covered for you," Elijah said for perhaps the hundredth time.

"Well, I'm here, aren't I?" Deacon said, letting too much of the annoyance he felt sneak through in the words.

"Yeah, I suppose there's no denying that," Elijah said, seemingly unaware of Deacon's attitude.

"Can we not do training tonight?" Deacon asked.

Elijah looked up at him. "Why? What else do you plan on doing?"

"Well. I don't know." Deacon said, lamely. A slow smile spread across the old man's face.

"Ah. You want to go see little Nah-leesi, don't you?"

Deacon felt his face flush with warmth. "Well, she deserves to know...you know, that I am still alive," he said. It surprised him how difficult it was for him to find words all of a sudden.

"She did seem very upset this morning." Elijah's smile disappeared. Well, it physically disappeared, but Deacon could still see it in the old man's eyes. "Be careful you don't do anything stupid. It seems that tomorrow's training will have to be about the birds and the bees."

Deacon had no idea what the old man was talking about, and he wondered if Elijah was losing his mind. That happened to old people, didn't it? He tried to ignore the man's amused look and turned away.

When he finally found her, Nah-leesi was again pounding on some stubborn piece of machinery with a large wrench and cursing.

"Hey, Nah-leesi," he felt stupid. What do you say in a situation like this?

When she turned, Deacon was shocked to see that she had obviously been crying. The wrench clattered to the floor, and the ringing echoed off the dark concrete walls and various undefinable pieces of machinery. She strode purposefully to him and gripped the neck of his coveralls in a tight fist, causing Deacon to shrink back. He was sure she was about to strike him, but he forestalled the reaction that his martial arts training had conditioned him to have and instead closed his eyes and readied himself for the blow. Warm lips pressed against his own. His eyes flew open, but he didn't pull away. Instead, he let his body relax, and he luxuriated in the feel of the kiss. Deacon wondered vaguely if this counted as "something stupid" in Elijah's point of view and forced himself to pull away.

"How did you...why," Nah-leesi stammered.

Deacon smiled and told her what had happened. When he was finished, Nah-leesi seemed just as incredulous as Elijah had been.

"I don't know how I feel about everyone being so keen on my death. You should have seen all the slaves stare at me as I came through the hatch." He laughed at the memory.

"I'm definitely not 'keen on your death.' I am just amazed that the Tendari like you enough not to kill you," she said.

"Ouch," he said.

"You know what I mean. They are hardly the forgiving type, especially to humans."

"That's true, but apparently, I had done them a favor in getting rid of him. Trask hadn't made many friends among the maintenance crews. Apparently, he had been court-martialed for something he'd done in the past and had been installed in the position above the crews as a slap in the face. Maintenance and repair are hardly considered honorable among a species that holds warriors in such high esteem. I guess he took out his frustration on the crews. They were only too happy to see him gone," she nodded, thinking about it. She knew all too well the disregard the Tendari gave to her specific brand of genius.

"A good mechanic is just a knuckle-dragger until you need one, then we're treated like royalty until the job is done," she paused and then smiled. "I, for one, am glad they didn't kill you."

The recent emotion that emanated from Nah-leesi, like the waves for which her planet was famous, confused Deacon. She had never seemed like the type to let something as trivial as feelings get in the way. Right now, he was happy with these emotions, but this morning he had been almost scared of her. He wondered if this was what Elijah had talked about when he said women were confusing.

"I have to say...I was pretty happy with the outcome as well." He smiled back at her.

They stood there uncomfortably for a time. At least he felt uncomfortable.

"So...you wanna show me those hiding places you talked about?"

She giggled, a sound he'd never heard come from her. "If I didn't know better, I'd think you were trying to come on to me," she said.

Yep, girls were definitely confusing. He'd only said it to try and alleviate the tension, but now it felt so much worse, and he didn't even know why. She laughed at his discomfort.

"You are cute," she said and grabbed his cheek between thumb and forefinger and gave it a squeeze. He didn't know why, but it embarrassed him. The embarrassment was followed closely by anger. He swatted her hand away and turned away.

"If you don't want to show me, then fine. I'll just go back to the barracks," he started walking away.

"Hey," Nah-leesi called.

He turned. She jerked her head in a 'follow me' gesture and started off in the opposite direction. After a very brief fight with his pride, he followed.

They wound deeper into the Rock than Deacon thought possible. The mining facility was truly massive, and as they walked, Deacon saw evidence that the humans who were here before were using the Rock as more than just a means to collect the valuable ore. They passed a long hallway which was lined with doors that Nah-leesi said were to living quarters of some kind.

Deacon's curiosity was piqued. He could have spent months down here investigating all the artifacts left strewn about. He was tempted to stop half a dozen times to take a closer look at something, but Nah-leesi moved with purpose, and he didn't want to upset her generosity with a request to stop.

"How many people know about this?" He was talking about the miles of unused subterranean real estate, and she must have guessed as much.

"Anzark knows a little, but I'm the only one I know of. I'm assuming the Tendari know since it's theirs," she said.

Deacon wanted to tell her the truth. He wanted to tell her that this entire place was first built by humans. From the look of the place, he doubted a Tendari had made his way down here since they first took the Rock. If that was the case, there probably wasn't anyone still alive that would remember it. He almost opened his mouth to tell Nah-leesi everything but remembered Elijah's admonition to keep the secret no matter what. He trusted Nah-leesi, but if knowing the details of his specie's past put her in danger, he would gladly keep quiet.

She brought him, finally, to a large, thick metal door. Metal carts sat outside the door with sealed boxes scattered over them. He kicked one that laid open. Dust clouded around his foot, and a pile of tiny packets spilled out. Deacon bent down and examined them. Each packet of clear plastic contained twenty or thirty tiny brown objects. He picked one up and held it so the dim light in the corridor could help him identify them, but he was stumped.

"Seeds," Nah-leesi said behind him. "At least that's what I assume they are."

"Why would you assume that?" To Deacon, it seemed like the most outlandish guess, given where they were. Why would there be seeds here? He looked up at her. She pointed at the door.

"You'll see," she moved to the control panel.

"You know the code?" He asked.

"Code?" She guffawed. "I don't need a code," she took a screwdriver from her small tool belt that hung at a jaunty angle on her hip. She popped the cover of the panel off in one smooth motion with it and reached in and grabbed a black wire that he could see had already been stripped. She touched it to the stripped end of a white wire, and the door slid open in a cloud of dust. That seemed way too easy to Deacon, and he kicked himself for spending so much time memorizing the various codes around the facility and on the Gorski.

Deacon waved his hand in front of his face, trying to clear away the dust that swirled before him. Nah-leesi led the way into the darkened space ahead. As they passed through the door, lights high above clicked on, revealing dark rock and dirt all around them. A wave of panic ran through him as he identified the space as a cave. In his mind, there shouldn't be any air in here. He subconsciously held his breath until logic reasserted itself.

The air felt moist, and he noticed a dripping noise echo through the cave. It was also surprisingly warm. It smelled strange, different from anything he had ever smelled. Slowly, as his eyes scanned the dimly lit cave, he noticed a row of raised rectangles filled with what he could only assume was soil. Above the rectangles hung long banks of lights that remained dark. He walked over to the soil beds, drawn to them by something indescribable.

As he came closer, he realized that the smell he couldn't identify came from them. He hesitantly put his hand into the soil of the closest bed and let the cool dirt enclose his fingers. He lifted a handful and inhaled the scent. It was strange, but it felt...right. He looked around and came to the conclusion that this dirt may have originally been brought from Earth. Its color didn't match any of the surrounding stone and ore that made up the cave walls. He looked back at the dirt in amazement.

"I sometimes forget that you have never been outside the Rock," Nah-leesi said.

He looked up and saw her staring at him, a small smile on her lips. Deacon realized that his eyes had betrayed him and released tears that ran down his cheeks. He ran a sleeved arm over his face, trying to hide the evidence of his weakness as casually as he could.

"I guess in that, at least, I am lucky," she said. "I've felt dirt between my toes. I've seen seeds. Before those mud-thumpers came, I swam in the ocean every day," she looked at him with sad eyes. "That is something you have never done."

There was silence between them for a time.

"At least I've smelled dirt," he looked at her and smiled. "You've given me that...Do you know anyone that knows a lot about growing plants?" he asked.

Her eyebrow raised.

CHAPTER 26

Deacon set up a meeting with Nah-leesi and Elijah. He had an idea that he wanted to go over with them, so they met just through the doors into the warren of corridors that Nah-leesi had come to know so well.

"Why are we meeting here?" Nah-leesi asked, annoyance edging her voice.

"I think you would agree that we don't want to draw attention to the fact that we are all meeting together," Elijah said.

"Well, we could do it in the barracks just fine. If you're worried about the cameras in your area, I turned those off months ago," she said matter-of-factly. Deacon and Elijah both looked at her, surprised. "What? I thought it was a good idea since you started working for them on the Gorski. I didn't want your day work to come back with you. If you know what I mean. It's a good thing I did too. Since you two have started your little nightly dances. It doesn't make you look all that dangerous to me, but the Tendari might see things differently," she folded her arms smugly. Elijah cleared his throat.

"I wondered why the Tendari hadn't even mentioned the training to Deacon, but how have they not noticed that their camera is off?" he asked.

"Oh, they've noticed, but they have so many out that this

is pretty far down the list. You'd be amazed at what you could actually get away with down here. Besides, they submit the repair schedule to me, and I don't know about you, but I don't like the Tendari peeking in on me. I put the repairs off, and when they complain, I tell them that if they want it done faster, they can get me some help. That always shuts them up. They don't want to have a Tendari debase themselves by coming down here to work maintenance."

Elijah smiled.

"I see why you like her," Elijah said to Deacon. Deacon nearly choked.

"I don't like her," Deacon said. Then he almost died. Elijah's eyebrows lifted, and Nah-leesi's folded arms clenched, as did her jaw. "I mean, I do, but.... " he sighed in defeat. "Never mind," he would have given anything to take back the last few seconds. Why did he feel so chaotic inside all of a sudden?

"Anyway...Let's go in then and find a place to sit. I am old and have learned to enjoy every second of leisure I can get," Elijah offered. He put an arm out, ushering Nah-leesi ahead of them. They passed back through the door and walked over to the alcove that he and Elijah had claimed for the humans. 'Claimed' may have been the wrong word, more like he had been forced into the dark corner of the barracks, but he had grown to like the little spot. In fact, he had thought many times that he wouldn't have a different spot in the whole barracks if it were offered to him, and now that he knew that Nah-leesi had disabled the cameras, he felt even more comfortable there.

They sat on the discarded ore crates that had long ago transitioned to furniture for Deacon and the other slaves of the Rock. Deacon made sure that Nah-leesi got the good crate, and he took the wobbly one that had, at some point before Deacon's recollection, been badly bent out of square. The crate tipped back and forth as his weight shifted, making a 'thunk' sound with every move. He made a conscious effort to sit still, but when he noticed that both Elijah and Nah-leesi stared at him, the tippy crate lost its importance.

They waited for him to start. He had, technically, been the one to call this meeting, but he didn't think that that meant he had to really do anything. He supposed that both had a vague notion as to why they were meeting. Deacon had filled Elijah in on what Nah-leesi had shown him. So he had assumed that the dialogue of the meeting would flow naturally and he wouldn't need to actually be the first to speak. He didn't know why their gazes would make him so nervous, but he swallowed and then spoke.

"I think we can all say that we are tired of being slaves," he paused, sure that their faces would betray the disappointment they felt in his bland yet cliche statement, but to his surprise, they both nodded their agreement and attentively waited for more. "Right now may be the best time for us to free ourselves from them. The war with the Marak has given the Tendari a priority that we could never compete with. While I don't think they will just let us go without a fight, I do think that their attention will be pulled away from us, no matter the damage we may do to their pride. Not only do I think it is our best chance, I think right now is our only chance," he looked at them in turn, and both seemed, more or less, in agreement.

"So...how do we take the Gorski?" Elijah asked.

First of all, Deacon was dumbfounded that his mentor was asking him, but second, he couldn't believe that the wise old man hadn't seen it already. "We don't," Deacon said.

Elijah looked confused.

"We have to, son," he said in a patient tone that verged on condescending.

"I don't think we do, besides, it's impossible. I've gone over it again and again for months, and I can't see a way that we can successfully take the Gorski. No...we let them come to us."

Elijah's brow furrowed in a question.

"Without the Gorski, we won't be able to leave here," he said simply.

"As much as I'd love to get off the Rock, I think we need to stay...at least for a while."

"If we don't get the Gorski, it may be a long while," Elijah said.

"Yes." Deacon agreed. "Which is why we need to try and establish some food production beforehand and make sure that all of our necessities are housed internally," he looked at Nah-leesi, who was already nodding.

"Most already are. Water extraction and storage are past the growing room deep within the facility, as are the O2 generators. The problem will be the electrical. It's routed from the panels on the surface."

"If it's solar, then there must be a battery terminal somewhere, right?" Deacon asked.

Nah-leesi nodded again. "Yes, and it would be safe within our control if I am reading your intentions correctly. It's housed down by the O2 generators."

"How much power can they store?" he asked.

"At current usage...about a week, but if we cut all nonessential use and didn't run any mining equipment...a month and a half, maybe two," she said.

"Hang on, hang on," Elijah interrupted. "I think we're getting ahead of ourselves." He did not seem nearly as excited by the conversation as Deacon had anticipated him being. "We can't really do anything by ourselves. We need them," he pointed over Deacon's shoulder at the packed barracks behind him.

Deacon looked down. "I've been thinking about that too."

Elijah's eyebrows raised. "Seems like you have been doing a lot of thinking," the old man said, not unkindly. "Go ahead then."

Deacon hesitated.

"There was a guy...from one of your lessons on Earth

history. Nepo-something."

"Napoleon," Elijah offered.

"Napoleon. Yes. He said something like… 'an army walks on its stomach'... or something like that."

"An army marches on its stomach. Close," Elijah encouraged.

"Right. I think if we fed them real food, their attitudes might change." Deacon waited for a reaction from his mentor. He could see the wheels turning in the old man's head. At least he was listening to him. He had half expected Elijah to just laugh off his ideas as childish. He wouldn't have blamed him, he didn't know what he was doing, but he felt someone had to do something. Finally, a smile spread across Elijah's face.

"I think if you keep this up, we'll have to make you general."

CHAPTER 27
Caliban

What woke him was the same thing that woke him every morning since he was conscripted. His wrist vibrated with the MACO's attempt to rouse him. If he didn't get up soon, the device would make an annoying trilling sound that was sure to anger the other conscripts that were in various degrees of wakefulness around him.

When he had first been conscripted into the Marakan auxiliary army, the barracks had been a bustle with noise. Upon waking, it seemed inevitable that the untrained soldiers would speak to one another, but the Marakan Sergeants put a stop to that. Now, only a month after becoming a soldier, Cal marveled at the silence with which the unit readied itself.

Cal was a Torg. He hated the name 'Torg.' To him, it seemed that with a name like that, they would all be brutish, unthinking, warmongers, but although they were a very large and strong species, Torg were just as intelligent as most others and decidedly less violent by nature. Most of his unit were also Torgs, but there were a few Carexi and a Bulrathi. All of them were large, as was required by the unit's special purpose. They were a breaching unit or would be once they had been fully trained.

He didn't know what more they could be taught. Each had proven that they could rip a sealed hatch from an airlock. What else was a 'breaching unit' expected to be able to do? He was a Torg, though, and he supposed he would leave his training to the much more experienced Marak.

The Marak were at war with the Tendari, and the Torg home planet of Proxima was a Marakan protectorate. Therefore, the Torg were subject to the Marakan conscription laws. It didn't really bother Cal. He figured that the Torg would have been sucked up by the Tendari years ago if it hadn't been for the Marak protection, so he was fine with the circumstances he found himself in. He might feel differently if he died, but as of right now, he felt surprisingly ambivalent.

Not all Torg felt like he did. In fact, most bristled at their relatively new 'protectorate' status and down-right rebelled at being conscripted. Most of those malcontents had been dealt with early on by the Marakan Sergeants, however, and the rest chose to keep their feelings to themselves. Despite the danger, Cal still heard the occasional insubordinate whisper. He walked a fine line. He didn't want to advertise his ambivalence toward the Marakans to his fellow Torg, but he also didn't want to seem too ready to comply with the Marakans' every wish.

Cal looked up and down the long line of Torg on either side of him. Everyone stood stock-still wearing the Marak issue jump-suit. He smiled at the many Torg whose full body fur was matted and mussed from sleep. He fully understood that his own appearance was probably just as comical, only in a different color.

Cal, or Caliban, was named for his black fur. It was extremely rare among the Torg to have pure black fur like Cal's. Legends, as old as his people, told of magical properties available to only those with such fur. There were hundreds of tales that described the impressive feats of past black-furred Torg, a fact that haunted Cal his whole life.

People expected things from Cal that were no more

possible for him to accomplish than it was for them, and when he was unable to perform to their expectations, he was looked upon with a kind of disgust, as if he were defective somehow. 'Friends' came and went in Cal's life. They came for the mystic but soon left when they discovered that there was truly nothing special about him except for his fur.

To his right, at the far end of the unit's barracks, the door slid open and in walked the Marakan Sergeant in charge of their training. The Marak people were extremely...shy? Cal wasn't sure that was the right word for the extremely powerful species. They remained hidden as much as possible, and as a result, this was the only Marakan Cal had ever seen, though he had never really *seen* this one either.

Sergeant Muzetti was, as always, fully encased in armor that covered him from head to toe, face hidden behind a heavily tinted visor. Marak were large, well, not as large as Torg or Carexi, but larger than most species.

Muzetti sauntered down the row of trainees, his hands pulled behind him in a way that lent his form formality, prestige even. Marak were nothing if not intimidating, and Muzetti was no exception.

"Spurius. You are far too strong to be cowering so."

The chastened Torg stiffened, visibly putting all he had into his posture. Cal marveled how Muzetti always seemed to remember everyone's name, and despite the familiar way he addressed them, the ability only elevated the Sergeant's frightfulness.

Most Species had difficulty differentiating Torg since most looked similar, except Cal, of course, but not Muzetti. He supposed that the Marak's seeming infallibility was yet another factor contributing to his imposing presence.

Muzetti stopped in front of a blue-green Carexi whose name Cal hadn't yet learned and pointed at his writhing, worm-like mustache.

"When I ask for stillness, I expect even this to be tamed." Muzetti flicked the end of the mustache generating a full-body flinch in the larger alien. Everyone knew that Carexi antenna moustaches were extremely sensitive, and only someone with a death wish would dare touch one, but the Carexi quickly recovered from the shock and stood still once again, back straight. Cal was impressed. Carexi weren't known to be longsuffering, and the tears in the poor creature's eyes testified to the pain he'd felt, but Muzetti was not to be opposed.

Caliban had never actually seen the Marak use violence unless you counted flicking Carexi mustaches, but everyone had readily accepted the Sergeant's complete authority over them. Muzetti continued his inspection of his newly-waken soldiers. Eventually, he reached the end and turned around. There was a long, uncomfortable silence, but they all knew better than to look toward their commander. All eyes stared straight ahead at the far wall. Cal had even picked out a smudge on the otherwise pristine graphene wall opposite him to stare at. He felt that over the past two weeks, he had become uncomfortably familiar with the smudge. It wouldn't have surprised him if he had started to dream about the thing. Muzetti finally spoke.

"Today, we will be sparring. I want you all to be sure to do your best. I know that most of you don't consider yourselves 'fighters.' Well, we are going to change that. If I feel that any one of you isn't doing your best, you will have to face me."

Cal groaned softly to himself. This is what he was afraid of. He didn't want to fight anyone. He had been fine with the idea of destroying hatches and blast doors, but striking another person seemed too...difficult. He didn't think he would dare use his full strength against anyone, let alone one of his comrades, but it sounded like that was exactly what Muzetti wanted.

"Normally, I would start conscription combat training later in the day, but I think that an empty stomach may motivate you all, and I think you big softies are gonna need all the encouragement we can give you."

Muzetti moved to the center of the long line of conscripts, hands still behind his back.

"Manius, Sargento, step forward." Two worried-looking Torg stepped forward from different places along the line and came slowly toward Muzetti.

Sergeant Muzetti positioned the two opposite each other and adjusted them into a loose fighting stance. Cal didn't know the first thing about fighting, but he could tell that these two didn't know either. Maybe they didn't even know as much as him.

Muzetti shook his head in frustration after working with the two for several minutes and stepped back. He sighed heavily.

"I suppose we shall see if you two know anything," he brought his hand down. Cal knew that something was supposed to happen, presumably that the two would begin to fight, but they just looked at Muzetti, confusion splayed across their hairy faces. Muzetti swore. It was a rare show of emotion, and the Torg's confusion turned to fear. It was obvious that they wanted to obey, but didn't know exactly what to do, so they put their arms out and approached each other.

If Cal didn't know better, he would have assumed the two were loved ones long separated. They hugged, swaying side to side slowly.

Muzetti's hand went to his shaking head. The Carexi, whose name Cal still didn't know, chuckled softly.

CHAPTER 28

"Frankly, I'm surprised that your kind are still around. How have you not been annihilated long ago?" Muzetti said. He grumbled something unintelligible and waved his hand to stop the bout, if you could call it that. It was the third sparring match that morning, and all were equally pitiful. Even Cal judged them to be pathetic, but he wasn't sure he could do any better.

"Maybe a Carexi can show you how it's done. Dorgoroth and…." Muzetti scanned the line of conscripts. "Caliban."

Cal's throat clenched, and his stomach fell. The big Carexi that Muzetti had called out earlier stepped forward with a big grin on his face. He struck his fist into his palm in apparent gleeful anticipation of the coming fight.

He had never been hit, but Cal couldn't imagine it felt good. He stepped forward slowly and tried, in vain, to hide his nervousness. They came together in front of Muzetti. Dorgoroth's grin never wavered, and when Muzetti's hand came down, the Carexi's fist came forward, right into Cal's cheek.

Light exploded behind his eyes, and static, like what's heard over an open comms channel, filled his head. Pain followed close on the heels of the strange sensation, and he felt himself stumble backward. Cal dimly was aware of another strike, this time to his abdomen, and he lost his balance and fell backward.

His large body hit hard on the metal floor, and he heard mutters coming from the Torg onlookers.

This scene was completely foreign to them, and the violence shocked them.

Cal grunted in pain. He was bewildered when the mean Carexi jumped on top of him and started using closed fists to pummel his face. Between punches and through blurry eyes, Cal could see flashes of Muzetti. The Marak stood with arms folded, obviously unwilling to intervene any time soon.

A growl rumbled in his throat as his head slammed back against the hard floor with each successive strike. He wanted to block the blows, but his hands were pinned beneath the heavy Carexi. Cal summoned his strength and wrenched his arms free, then put them between his head and Dorgoroth's fists. The defensive move seemed to do little to discourage Dorgoroth, however. Punch after punch struck his forearms. In a flash, a giant fist swung around his arms and caught him on the ear.

Pain, like he'd never felt before, lanced into his head from his throbbing ear. He pushed his arms out and swung wildly, driven to action by the thought of more pain. His extended fist made contact with the Carexi, but it was too much turmoil for his brain to realize that he had struck Dorgoroth on the temple. The Carexi's full weight landed on Cal.

It seemed that with one hit, Cal had rendered his foe unconscious or...dead. Caliban shifted under the body and extricated himself from under the limp form. Silence filled the large room. Cal panted heavily, trying to recover his breath.

"It is well that your kind can act when eventually impelled to do so. This means that there is potential there, but the amount of energy expended to urge you to fight means that we will have to work hard, harder than you have, likely, ever worked." Muzetti said behind Cal. He was dizzy, but he turned in place and saluted the Sergeant, fist to still-heaving chest.

Muzetti slammed his own fist into his chest and nodded

his approval.

"I would say, 'well done,' but I was taught to always be honest. Get back in formation."

Cal hurried to comply and was surprised to see several Torg in the line on either side of his empty spot, smiling and nodding at his success. The Torg to his right, Spurius, clapped him on the shoulder as he came into formation. They were lucky that Muzetti didn't see the friendly gestures, or if he did, he chose to ignore it. Normally that kind of break in discipline would result in some kind of near-torturous punishment, but perhaps his lucky victory had earned them a small degree of latitude.

"That was unattractive," Muzetti said. "But it gives me something to work with. You are dismissed to consume whatever it is you call food, but then you will report to Sergeant Crassus for hand-to-hand training on E deck," he focused on two Torg in front of him. "Backus and Duranus, Take Dorgoroth here down to medical before you indulge," he slammed a heavy booted foot into the metal deck plating, and the entire unit slammed their fists into their chest in salute. This move, at least, had been successfully drilled into them already.

Muzetti turned for the door, and the unit waited for it to close entirely behind the Sergeant before they surged out of the formation, completely at ease once more. It was as if some shaman had released a spell that had kept them all motionless til that point. Dozens of Torg made their way to him in the tumult of getting ready to leave the barracks for chow and congratulated him on surviving what surely could have killed him.

None of them had seen such a beating, and the blood that ran from several gashes on his face captivated them. It wasn't until Cal looked in the mirror that he understood their curiosity. He looked like he had been through a thresher. Blood matted the fur around his swollen eyes, and it glistened wetly on his furry cheeks. The smaller wounds were hidden by his fur, but the larger ones were hideously visible, and he wondered if the scars would be big enough to hinder the proper growth of his fur.

He swore an ancient oath and touched a swollen cheek tenderly. He was surprised that Muzetti hadn't told him to go to medical as well. Surely he couldn't be expected to continue on to 'hand-to-hand' whatever that was.

"You are still as ugly as ever," Spurius said next to him. Spurius was his only true friend, Cal thought. They had grown up together in the same village, and when the Marak came looking for conscripts, the two were obviously marked for service. They were by far the largest youth in the village, and although the conscription procedure was supposed to be random, everyone knew it wasn't. The Marak took who they thought would serve them the best, and to be honest, Cal couldn't blame them. Still, the incident had been a little on the nose, and the village elders caused a scene that would have shamed any Torg into capitulation, but the Marak barely acknowledged the angry elders. That was when Cal first realized how different the Marak were.

"Come on, we'd better get moving, or Marius will eat all of the tupeti again," Spurius said.

Cal put down the mirror.

"Do you think this will keep bleeding?" He asked his friend worriedly.

"I don't think you'll die from it." Spurius didn't sound too sure, however. "I mean, would Muzetti ignore it like that if he thought you'd die from your injuries?"

It was a good point, but then again, who knew what the Marak were capable of?

CHAPTER 29

Caliban was aboard the Baychimo, a humongous training ship designed to train new conscripts as they hurtled through space on their way to war. Despite the vast speeds that the Marak were able to obtain with their technology, the immensity of space made the travel time to and from the front lines a logistical nightmare. For this reason, they had come up with an ingenious solution.

The Baychimo and its sister training ships used the time to their advantage. The ship would tour Marak space, picking up conscripts at all the main ports, then begin its journey toward the Tendari. A one-way trip to the front took a little over a year, and by the time they arrived, they would be some of the best-trained soldiers in the universe. So far, however, they hadn't had enough time on the ship to really learn much.

That didn't stop the combat conscripts from thinking they were somehow better than Cal's breacher unit. Maybe it was the fact that they were mostly made up of Torg, and their incompetence at fighting was well known. Proof of that theory was that any one of the breachers were head and shoulders taller than any of the combat troops, but it didn't even seem to deter the other units from their derogatory treatment of the Torg. Maybe the new hand-to-hand...whatever would help them be more accepted by the combat units, but until then, they would just have to put up with the negativity from the others.

The later breakfast schedule put them in the chow hall at the same time as a different batch of conscripts, and Cal couldn't help but glance over and see if they were being watched. He hated that he felt so much like prey among all of these violent species. Torg were strong yet had been taught the honor of refraining from violence. Great store and prestige were placed upon the Torg, who were the most patient and wise, but here, it seemed the opposite was valued, and Cal was saddened by the increased desire within himself to go that way. He wasn't the only Torg that was beginning to feel it, he knew. Spurius and he had had this discussion already and had decided that most of the Torg in their unit were displaying a shift towards violence.

So much the better, he supposed. They were a fighting unit. Breachers, yes, but by all that Muzetti had said, they would see plenty of violence, and so they had better gain the mindset now or risk annihilation at the hands of the hated Tendari.

Though undoubtedly, inclined toward peace, Torg understood the point of fighting when great need demanded it. After all, it was all well and good to instill such altruistic thoughts in one's own populace, but they could not control the actions of those outside their reach.

Years ago, Proxima, the Torg home world, had even had a defense force. It was something Cal had even been proud of until he saw how quickly they fell to the Tendari. The Torg were swept away so easily that if it hadn't been so sad and terrifying, he would have been embarrassed. Thank Tarsus that the Marak chose Proxima to stop the forward advance of the Tendari campaign. For a while, Proxima had been savaged by the back and forth ground war that decimated cities and leveled forests, but the Marak won out and pushed the Tendari from Proxima, forever earning the Torg allegiance, little as it seemed to mean to them.

"Looks like someone had their way with your face." The

original language was in Chalcidian but was translated for Cal almost instantly. He looked up at the ugly insectile face above him. He didn't have a name for this one. The Chalcid was obviously trying to get a rise out of him, but Caliban merely laughed good-naturedly and nodded.

"Yes, you could say that," he touched his lip to see if it was still bleeding. It was. He smiled at the Chalcid in what he hoped would be a disarming way.

The Chalcid swore in an untranslatable series of clicks.

"You Torg are some of the most ugly aliens in the universe. Really the only species that are uglier must be humans. Have you ever seen one of those?" Cal shook his head. He tried to not show his anger at being called ugly. After all, it was only a matter of perspective, wasn't it?

"Really, you should thank whoever beat in your face. I think they made an improvement." Cal laughed again, but instead of being disarming, his nonchalance seemed to anger the Chalcid. His wings buzzed excitedly, betraying his frustration with this Torg.

"Did you even fight back? I doubt it. You Torg are about as useless in battle as a human, if not quite so ugly." Cal just kind of shrugged his shoulders noncommittally. As if to say, 'that's your opinion, and you're welcome to it.'

"Where is this hero who fixed your face? I'd like to congratulate him." Cal didn't respond.

"You'd have to go down to medical." Cal looked along the table at who had responded to the Chalcid for him. Blotha, the single Bulrathi in the unit, still looked down at his food tray. Between bites, he continued.

"His name is Dorgoroth, a Carexi. You'd have to wait for him to wake up first, though." Blotha said.

The Chalcid's wings buzzed again, and he clicked angrily before turning away from their table. Cal nodded appreciatively to Blotha, who ignored him and continued munching away at his food.

"Chalcids always give me the creeps," Spurius said in an undertone. "Maybe he doesn't like you because his little friends back on Proxima told him how we used to catch them and pull their wings off, then make them fight other scary-looking insects we'd found."

Cal smiled at the memory. It was, by far, the most violent thing they'd done as pups. Cal thought back to how guilty he had felt each time they'd done it, but there really wasn't much else to do for a pup in the wide rural swath of Proxima's northern forest where he lived. He wondered, absently, if there would be much new growth in those forests by the time he returned. Many of the trees in the giant forest had been destroyed by the ravages of war, but the elders had been working feverishly to restore the land to its pre-war beauty. Cal found himself almost wishing that his conscription would be longer than the three years they were all bound to, just so that his home would look more like home when he returned. Almost. As depressing as his war-torn home was, it was still home, and this place...this place was hard.

Everything about it was hard.

The Marak ships were utilitarian, to say the least, and while some might find beauty in the sleek lines and shiny metals, Cal only saw cold, hard discipline. As of yet, they had not received a single day off in their training, and the stressful routine was beginning to show on the faces of the Torg around him.

Torg were normally a happy lot. They enjoyed being alive and, by comparison with the species he'd come in contact with of late, Torg were nice even when they didn't want to be. Having the black fur of legend, Cal had been the target of many unkind words from fellow Torg, but they paled compared to the recent barrage of harassment.

Now, as he looked around the long table at his compatriots, he saw nothing but drawn and weary-looking Torg faces. Faces that just weeks ago smiled persistently now looked sullen and depressed. He'd never seen the like among his kind. Something would have to change soon.

The MACO on his wrist chimed, and he realized, with a start, that breakfast was over, and he had barely eaten anything. He knew better than to waste what little time they had to eat, and he berated himself for letting his thoughts carry him away. It wasn't entirely his fault, he reasoned. If that Chalcid hadn't come over and been so mean to him, then he might have at least taken the edge off his hunger.

He quickly shoveled heaping spoonfuls of tupeti into his mouth before reluctantly following the rest of the breachers out of the chow hall. He wiped the fur around his mouth free of the sticky tupeti as he walked away from the table. It was going to be a long day, Cal thought.

CHAPTER 30

He touched his face with a gentle hand for perhaps the hundredth time since the fight. His face had finally stopped bleeding, it seemed, but his fur all the way down to his chest was still wet with it. He must have looked horrible, and he couldn't wait until he could clean himself up.

Sergeant Crassus had taken a slightly different tack in training them how to fight. He ran them through drills where they would perform a series of strikes to the air, and he would go up and down the line correcting posture and giving other useful advice. Cal had to admit that this was a far superior way to teach, and he struck the air over and over, concentrating on the form. It seemed that the other Torg of the unit felt the same relief he had upon learning that, today, at least, they would not have to fight someone else.

"You are big." Sergeant Crassus yelled as he strode down the line. "You have impressive muscles. You look intimidating...." He stopped in front of a somewhat overweight Torg named Livius, who seemed to have a perpetual grin. "Well, most of you. So why is this so hard for you to understand? Snap the arm out." The Marak shot his arm out with such speed that Cal hadn't even seen it move. It had just appeared fully extended. "Like this," he shot the other out, equally fast.

The rhythm of the breacher unit's air strikes faltered as their attention was drawn to the Sergeant.

"How can we move on to more interesting techniques...?" He launched himself into the air, twisting and striking the air with an outstretched foot before rolling and coming up with a graceful uppercut. "If you can't even master a punch?" He had done the move so quickly and casually that it stunned all who watched, and a scattered applause broke out among the watching Torg.

"Bagh! Be quiet!" Crassus grumbled something in his frustration.

Cal was shocked. For the second time that day, he witnessed a Marak lose that characteristic formality. Crassus inhaled deeply and seemed to gather himself.

"Before we meet on the morrow, I want you all to think long and hard about how much you desire to be alive because if you do not master what I teach, you will die. The Tendari will rip this unit to shreds." Crassus turned without another word and walked stiffly from the room.

"Well, I don't think I like the sound of that," Spurius mumbled as the door closed behind the Marak.

Over the next few weeks, the breacher unit was put through hell in an attempt to harden them, and Blotha and the few Carexi in the unit began to complain at having to suffer the same rigors as the 'inept Torg,' but their protests were always under their breath and never directed at a Marak trainer.

Cal wondered how long it would be before the non-Torg in the unit broke down completely and went to Sergeant Muzetti about the strict training regimen. He only hoped that it was before open violence erupted against the Torg.

"It seems that your poor performance yesterday has earned you a three-a-day schedule for the rest of this week." Despite the unit's fear of the Marak, an audible groan rumbled through the ranks.

Cal glanced at Blotha's enraged face. He felt pity for the

alien. Blotha, counter to most of the unit, had excelled at the hand-to-hand combat training. He was obviously frustrated by the extra work that he didn't deserve. Cal felt somewhat indebted to Blotha for his help with the ill-mannered Chalcid those few weeks ago, but more than that, he was afraid that he might resort to a physical representation of his anger. Therefore, Cal stepped forward and cleared his throat.

Muzetti had been walking away from Cal, but he turned at the sound. Cal couldn't, of course, see the Marak's face as they always had their helmets on and visors down, but there was energy coiled in his limbs, an energy that could easily be converted to action. Cal gulped audibly as Muzetti turned on a heel and came back to stare daggers at his recruit, who was, quite literally, out of line.

"What, exactly, do you think you are doing, Cal?" Muzetti whispered. Cal had the sudden light-headedness of low oxygen, and he realized that he was holding his breath. He puffed out the contained breath and inhaled sharply. His massive, thick-fingered hands at his sides were shaking, and he hid them behind his back.

"I...I," he stammered. Cal's own face reflected back at him off of the Sergeant's visor, but Muzetti made no move to either encourage or discourage him, so he continued. "Blotha and the Carexi have no need of the extra training, sir. They are already far past the rest of us," he finished in a rush.

"Do you mean to say that you wish a part of this unit to not be subject to the orders given to the rest?" Cal wasn't sure what to say. It was exactly what he was saying, but the tone in which Muzetti asked the question triggered a warning in Cal's brain. He didn't respond right away, hoping that the question was rhetorical. After a wait that felt like an eternity, Cal opened his mouth to speak, but Muzetti interrupted him.

"What is this unit!" He shouted to the entire room of keyed-up conscripts, and Cal found himself chanting the litany, along with the rest, that had been pounded into them since their first day on the Baychimo.

"One body, one purpose, one objective," the entire room erupted.

Muzetti leaned forward and whispered so that only Cal could hear his words.

"Do you wish me to take your hand so that you might know what it means to separate a piece of the body from the rest?" Cal saw his own reflected mouth drop open in shock at the quiet threat. He couldn't find words, so he just shook his head vigorously. Muzetti straightened and looked down the line.

"You are all part of one body. Whatever you face, you face together!" he yelled, and without lowering his voice in the slightest, he turned back to Cal. "If you ever speak so again, I *will* take your hand!"

Cal's whole body trembled visibly, and he just managed to respond with a "yes, sir" before returning to his place in line, head down in shame.

"If Blotha and the Carexi are that much better than you, Torg, maybe they should work to help train the rest rather than complain like mewling children," he looked toward the non-Torg, who shifted their eyes so as not to look directly at the Sergeant, their body-language displayed their chastened spirits. At least they were humble in Muzetti's presence. Cal doubted that their behavior would change much once the Sergeant was gone, but he hoped that at least they wouldn't retaliate against the Torg now.

Muzetti laid out their orders for the day and then marched out of the barracks without another word. Once the door closed behind the Sergeant, Cal bent double and inhaled deeply, hands on knees.

"Well, that was stupid," Spurius said beside him. "I thought for sure you were a goner."

"My mom always said, 'can't expect an answer if you never ask,'" Cal said, between gasps.

"Yeah, but your mom is soooo nice. She's, like, the nicest person I know, and I'm a Torg. Muzetti, on the other hand...." Spurius shook his head. "Maybe he was just acting mean. You don't think he'd really take your hand, do you?"

Cal knew he would but didn't feel like answering his friend. Spurius seemed to take his silence as an answer and grunted in contemplation.

A gravelly voice spoke Bulrathi above him, and Cal stood up.

"That was very stupid," Blotha said.

"That's what I hear," Cal said, smiling at the short but extremely strong and intimidating alien. Blotha had rows of spikes that ran up and down his body. It was a body that evolution had obviously tailored for combat.

"I don't appreciate you calling us out like that," Blotha said, and as he spoke, Cal saw the three Carexi in the unit shoulder up behind Blotha, Dorgoroth chief among them. All were staring daggers at him. It seemed that Cal had succeeded at diverting the non-Torg aggression from the rest, but he hadn't anticipated it being focused on himself instead. Spurius seemed to melt backward out of Cal's periphery.

"I was trying to help," Cal protested. "I thought..."

Blotha's spike-crusted knuckles slammed into his belly so quickly that Blotha had already retracted his arm and stood ready for Cal's reaction before he even registered what had happened. Cal, for his part, was bent double once again, and retaliation wasn't even possible for him.

"Don't ever *help* us again, or you might accidentally fall out of the airlock,." Blotha grumbled before leading his small cadre away.

Cal wasn't sure what he was supposed to learn from today, and that was the most frustrating part of the whole thing.

"Boy, those guys are scary. Maybe we should work harder at fighting," Spurius put in from somewhere behind him.

"Maybe," Cal grunted.

CHAPTER 31
Deacon

It had taken months before the soil was conditioned with something called microorganisms and another couple of weeks to figure out which seeds were still likely to grow. Once they had finally planted them, Deacon was disappointed to learn that the plants took weeks before they would even break the surface and much longer before anything edible was produced. He had begun to wonder if it was all worth it, but then one of the plant's yellow flowers turned into a small, green sphere. The sight of the little ball, which Elijah said was a tomato, caused a thrill of excitement to course through him.

This little thing was, in essence, a physical representation of rebellion against the Tendari. A way in which Deacon hoped to inspire the slaves to action. A way that they could survive without their hated masters.

Slopik was the Kupelti that Anzark had entrusted to help Deacon, Elijah, Nah-leesi, and Denzink get the little subterranean farm running. Slopik had been a farmer on his home world before the Tendari took him, and he understood the basics of making the whole process work. To Deacon, despite the eternity it took to grow anything, the fact that they actually could seemed like a miracle. He would spend hours of his free time just looking at the green leaves and smelling the moist soil.

Elijah and he had taken to going to the 'farm' every evening for his lessons. There was something incredibly soothing about the place, and regardless of the danger, they were drawn to it. They rationalized that none of the slaves would go to the Tendari with any suspicions. How could they? The Tendari were so universally hated by the slaves that such a move would be the ultimate betrayal, not only to those who disappeared every night through the maintenance hatch but to their own sense of self.

Sweat ran down his head and soaked into the collar of his coveralls. The farm seemed to give him strength. He had made great strides in his training since they had begun to exercise in the warm cave, and Deacon couldn't help but feel proud of the changes his body had begun to reflect. He had always felt weak compared to other aliens, but now he only felt smaller. His muscles felt firmer and taught with repressed energy.

He knew he could now move and strike faster than any in the slave barracks, but he recognized the danger in fighting someone who could not only end the fight with one lucky blow but end his life. Elijah had felt the need to warn Deacon repeatedly against pride. He was, apparently, worried that he would start a fight, confident that his new abilities would win the day. Deacon was convinced each time Elijah would begin such a lecture that the old man still didn't know him. It would take a lot more than learning how to punch for him to have that kind of confidence.

He patted himself dry with a cloth and smiled at Elijah when the old man grunted and rolled his shoulder in discomfort. Deacon had landed several blows to that shoulder, and he knew all too well that Elijah would be sore for days from it.

"I'm getting too old for this kind of behavior. We may need to restrict our sparring sessions to once or twice a week." Deacon shot the old man a glance. It shocked him that Elijah would make such an admission, and what's more, he just proposed cutting back on sparring. What was even more shocking, however, was the fact that Deacon felt sad at the thought. He had grown fond of the exercise, admittedly only after he had gained the proficiency needed to hold his own, but still, he would miss the daily bouts.

According to Elijah's calculations, Deacon must have had a birthday and was now either fourteen or fifteen. One night, Nah-leesi and Elijah surprised him with a gift. It had been the first gift he'd ever been given, and he prized it beyond any other object. It was a circular pendant that hung from a thin but strong chain of Nah-leesi's design. On the pendant was the simple Greek letter, lambda. He knew from previous lessons that the letter was the symbol used by the ancient Spartan army. Those same ancient humans who Deacon idolized so.

He reached up and felt for the pendant through his coveralls, making sure of its safety, as he always did after a sparring session.

"Have you had to explain that yet?" Elijah asked. They had been concerned that the Tendari, specifically Golith, Deacon's supervisor aboard the Gorski, would question him about the uncommon piece of jewelry.

"No. I think that saving the ship earns, even a human, a bit of leeway."

Elijah grunted. Deacon didn't know if it was a sound of approval or just understanding.

"Well, they do owe you for all of their miserable lives." The vitriol in Elijah's voice made Deacon go cold inside.

"Yeah," Deacon agreed uncomfortably. He had mixed feelings about the whole thing. He understood hatred for the Tendari, especially from those who were still alive when the Tendari took their home worlds, but having worked with them every day gave him a slightly different perspective. Sure, the Tendari were extremely harsh and hated non-Tendari, but Deacon's small group of colleagues had grown to accept him, even befriend him.

He had to remind himself of the general despair and

death that their species had propagated among the stars, and specifically, the genocide that they had practiced against his own people, a people that he had, more and more of late, become connected with. He had begun to see himself as human now more than ever, and the affront that the Tendari caused among his ancestors had become more and more egregious to him.

Then there was Golith, possibly his best friend. Golith, who had saved his life on that terrifying day when he had killed Trask. He couldn't bring himself to feel the anger that he knew he was supposed to for Golith, so when Elijah spoke with such hate for the species, Deacon could only mitigate it with his knowledge that the Tendari were made up of individuals. Individuals with choices to make, same as the rest of them.

The next day, Deacon had to stay aboard the Gorski longer than normal and just caught the last shuttle back to the Rock. When he entered the barracks, Elijah wasn't there, and he assumed that his mentor had gone to the farm without him, so he decided to follow. There was still enough time for him to sit for a short lecture, so he put in the code to the door and passed through.

Deacon walked down the darkened corridors lined with piping and conduit. The ever-present sound of dripping water echoed down the passageways in a way that was comforting to him now.

Something, a vagary of the air to his right, made him look in that direction just as a fist came hurtling from a darkened recess in the corridor. Deacon reacted with the speed that had been pressed into him like grease into a fitting. He could not have helped but react, and he was glad he did. His head shot down, and his feet moved without thought. His stance widened, and his already closed fist came up and struck the long arm at the elbow, further deflecting the fist from its target.

He didn't stay within range of his yet unseen assailant but shuffled back up the corridor.

"You are quick. I'll give you that." The language was Tarpin, and the voice belonged to Silax. Deacon had long feared this day. He knew that the Tarpin had still harbored feelings of hatred for him, but he'd hoped that the alien's loathing had ebbed over the months since that day when Elijah had rescued him. He thought that, maybe, with the increased respect he'd gained after Anzark and Denzink had advertised his revenge on Trask that Silax may have moved on.

Now, however, he saw the alien's eyes as he stepped forward into the light. No. Silax definitely still hated him. He would hold nothing back, and so, neither could Deacon. He held his hands up in front of him in a way that might appear to be a stance of capitulation to the untrained but was actually a common krav maga defensive posture.

"Silax, I don't want any trouble," he said the words in Tarpin, a language that he had made a concerted effort to learn, and he was proud of his own pronunciation. He knew that Silax had probably never encountered a non-Tarpin with a better grasp of the complex language, and he was pleased when Silax stalled momentarily, his brain trying to figure out how the sounds that were so emblematic of his culture came out of this scrawny human. Silax's face darkened after his momentary contemplation.

"Don't try to charm me with your Tendari-loving tongue. You may have fooled them," he pointed a finger back toward the barracks. "But I know that you are just a Tendari spy. Why else would you go off each day to bow and scrape to them?"

Silax threw a left jab at Deacon's head, but he was ready for it. Deacon had seen the shift and pull of certain muscles before the alien even moved and knew how to counter without conscious thought. He dodged left, then as Silax tried to follow up with a right, Deacon stepped up onto the smooth surface of a large pipe that ran along the wall. He launched himself up into the air. Then turned as he came down and landed his right foot straight into the side of the Tarpin's knee. Deacon had planned it well, and the knee that crunched under the force of his Tendari mag-boots was the same leg that Elijah had previously injured.

It had been a long time since Elijah had inflicted that dreadful injury on the alien, but he knew all too well that wounds as serious as the one Silax had suffered took years to heal, if they did at all. From the way Silax reacted, Deacon had chosen his target well.

The cry of pain was surprisingly loud in the tight corridor, the sound reverberating off the pipes like a drum. Deacon felt bad before he had even gotten clear of the thrashing Tarpin. Silax leaned against the wall and breathed heavily while glaring at Deacon. For his part, Deacon stood silently, unsure of what to say. He had long pondered the best way to immobilize the powerful Tarpin, but he hadn't really given much thought to how inflicting such pain would make him feel. He was surprised now to recognize regret at the forefront of his thoughts.

"I wish you hadn't made me do that," Deacon whispered in Silax's own language.

CHAPTER 32

Despite Silax's fierce anger, he eventually calmed enough for Anzark and Denzink to drag him back to the barracks. Anzark informed Silax, with a smile on his face, that the Tarpin would once again be receiving half rations until he healed if he healed. They all knew the fate of those who were too feeble or crippled to work the mine, or rather they didn't. One day, the ill-fated alien would just disappear, the Tendari taking them while everyone else was on the surface, working.

The conservative theory was that the Tendari killed them. The more pragmatic among the slaves decided they were probably used for their meat. It was well known that Tendari were insatiable carnivores and had little scruples about the source of their meat.

Deacon knew how hard it was to subsist on half rations, and he, yet again, felt a pang of guilt. It was a strange feeling for him to not have the same anger and hatred toward someone who wished him dead. He felt like if Silax could just get to know him, surely he'd see that Deacon wasn't worth the effort. He tried to put it out of his mind and threw himself into his work, both at the Gorski and at the farm.

The plants were coming along nicely, and he was learning a lot. Once in a while, Slopik would trim the fast-growing herbs, and they would all chew on the pungent sprigs and leaves and grimace at the strong flavors that assailed them. Deacon had never tasted such flavor. The rations he'd been raised on were bland by comparison, and the taste of the fresh herbs seemed too strong to him, but there were a few that he really enjoyed chewing. Elijah called them mint and spearmint. Then there were lemongrass and chives, which were also good but strange.

Deacon chewed on a length of lemongrass while he used a gardening tool called a hoe to scratch and claw at the hard stoney floor of the cave. They had decided they would try to expand their growing area, and he was tasked with trying to 'till' up the practically solid rock.

"You know, this would be easier if we could use some of the equipment from the mining shed." Or even some of the smaller tools they brought below at the end of each workday and stored in the equipment room. Deacon had said this at least half a dozen times since starting the project, and each time Elijah had cautioned against it, saying: 'I don't think the others need any more reason to question what we're doing back here.' This time, however, he just grunted in annoyance at being interrupted and continued his lecture.

There had been more and more mutterings about the small group leaving for parts unknown each night among the slaves. Mainly, Deacon believed, they just wanted to be included, and he just needed a little more time before he would feel comfortable enough to share their secret. He wanted to ensure that the farm was well established and could provide at least some supplemental nutrition to all the slaves before he made their project public knowledge.

He knew that the appearance of Silax the night before being dragged through the door by two Kupelti would stir the masses, and the Tarpin's angry words would probably help sow dissent among the slaves. Deacon was afraid he wouldn't be given enough time to feel comfortable and decided that maybe he was just being overly cautious, but Elijah encouraged the tactic. They hoped that the proven success of the farm would be harder to argue with than what was, to all appearances, a pipe dream. Denzink and Nah-leesi argued that the fact that plants had grown was evidence enough that it could work, but to Deacon, the whole idea seemed so foreign that faith in the process was hard to come by. It was still incredible to him that anything even sprouted, but he had never even seen a plant before other than stink-weed, so maybe his lack of experience brought with it a skepticism that needed hard evidence to overcome. Something more than a sprig of mint or a length of lemongrass.

He hoped he was the only one among the slaves with such a lack of faith, but he knew he wouldn't be. Years of being dragged down and exposed to every manner of cruelty had a way of hardening a soul. Slaves that had become almost dead inside would find it very difficult to let any hope inside. Deacon knew from sad experience that it was a way to protect oneself. If you didn't let yourself hope, you couldn't be hurt when that hope was dashed, as it often was. He didn't want to be the cause of such pain, so he was doing everything he could to make the farm ready.

A green scale-covered hand appeared in front of Deacon's nose. It held a bright red tomato. It was beautiful. He didn't think he'd ever seen a red as bright as what covered the smooth skin of the tomato. He dropped the hoe and, gingerly, picked up the tomato. Slopik chuckled at his reverence.

"Try it. We have about a dozen already. In a few days, we'll have two dozen more."

Deacon hesitated. He wasn't sure about this. He had never known real food, with the exception of the questionable meat that Grato had given him, and he wasn't sure how he would like it. He lifted it to his lips and stuck his tongue out, licking its surface.

"Not like that boy! Bagh. Bite it," Slopik laughed.

Deacon bit into the yielding flesh. Juice exploded from the

tomato and, with the juice, flavor. He had no words to describe the flavors, but he hadn't known that he was capable of sensing something so intense.

He felt juice run down his chin, and he smiled broadly. He had wondered if all of this was worth the work involved, but now he had no doubts.

"Don't eat too much of that," Elijah called. "Your stomach is not used to it."

Deacon wanted to ignore the warning, but after his second, blissful bite, Slopik pulled it from his grasp and tossed the remainder to Elijah. The old man caught the sloppy pulp and ate the rest, laughing at the dripping mess.

"This is far sweeter than I had anticipated. The chronicles describe it as acidic, and it was used in many savory dishes, but this seems too sugary." Elijah said.

Most of the words that Elijah said were foreign to Deacon. In a life devoid of flavor, what was the use of such descriptive words? What was even more confusing was that his mentor had apparently never tasted a tomato.

"You mean you have never eaten one of these?" Deacon asked. He had been under the assumption that before being captured and enslaved by the Tendari, Elijah had indulged in other foods.

"Most of Earth's plant life was thought to have been destroyed, including tomatoes. These may be the last remnants of that wonderful planet's ecosystem."

A wave of...severity washed over Deacon. The farm became much more important in his eyes, and he looked around the cave with a new respect for the plants they had grown.

After their work was done for the night, Deacon took one of the ripe tomatoes with him, and once he was through the door to the barracks, he turned left instead of right.

"Where are you going?" Elijah asked. "It's a little late for a shower, don't you think?"

He held up the tomato.

"Silax." The one word was enough, and Elijah displayed a series of emotions in a second's time. Deacon thought that his mentor was going to reprimand him. There was a part of him that would agree with Elijah. Silax was probably not going to be amenable to anything Deacon did or said, and any olive branches or tomatoes would be summarily rejected.

Elijah nodded, finally accepting the logic behind the move.

"Be careful. An animal is at its most dangerous when it is wounded," he said, and then turned toward their alcove.

There was something else, though, that pushed Deacon toward reconciliation. He knew that in the coming months, they would need every one of the slave's hearts and minds if they were to succeed. If Silax's hatred for him grew greater than that for the Tendari, then he might turn traitor and inform on them before they were ready. Not that they had much of a chance even after they were ready. They were all likely to die in the pursuit of their freedom, but Deacon, at least, had come to terms with that probability.

As he passed cots occupied by various alien species, it struck him how differently he was treated now compared to just a few months ago. Still, despite the relatively non-hostile environment, he sensed a strange tension in the air. Guzonians watched him with their creepy reflective eyes from the dark corners they preferred and whispered to one another as he passed. Carexi, previously boisterous in their argumentative tones, quieted instantly upon seeing him.

He walked uneasily to Silax's cot, where the Tarpin lounged with his wounded leg elevated. A few other Tarpin, apparently friends of Silax, hissed as he came close. Not quite 'non-hostile,' he decided.

Without a word, Deacon lifted the red tomato and tossed it onto the cot next to Silax's head.

"Thought you might be hungry," he said in Tarpin after

a long silence between them. Deacon regretted the words as he
saw Silax's face darken.

"Thanks to you!" He nearly yelled the words, followed by
a snarl that was chorused by the surrounding Tarpin. Deacon felt
anger rise at the acquisition. Anger that would not be quieted.

"I did not hurt you on purpose! Bagh, you really are
dumb, aren't you? You were the one waiting in the dark to strike
me down. You were the one that swung first. I gave you every
opportunity to back out, but your stupid pride is why you're
hungry and in bed. Not me...Not...me."

The whole thing was said in Tarpin, and even Deacon
was surprised with the emotion behind the words. He had had
enough of cowering and letting others walk over him just because
of his size and supposed ancestry. He now realized, as he looked
around at the faces of the stunned Tarpin, that this may have
been what Elijah had warned him about. He mentally kicked
himself. The old man was right far more often than it was fair to
be, and he had long ago learned to heed his advice.

The Tarpin, surprisingly, remained silent. Their faces
remained awe-struck, far longer than his words warranted.
Slowly, a Tarpin came forward and lifted his right hand to
Deacon's head. A flash of instinct fought against another. Part
of him wanted to shift into a defensive stance, but the Tarpin's
move didn't seem threatening. Logic won out, and he stayed still
and allowed the alien to place his thumb against his forehead
reverently.

Silax exploded angrily, cursing and thrashing in rage.
Deacon couldn't follow all that he said. Much of it seemed
relevant only to the Tarpin. Something about 'the rights' and
'kindred tongue.' Some of the others seemed upset as well, but
most were somber.

"He has mastered the kindred tongue. You heard it. He
must be given the rights. I will not betray the Race just because
you are angry." An older Tarpin said from the back of the group,

which parted to make room for him. "You should know better, Silax," the old voice chastened, and to Deacon's astonishment, Silax reacted as if struck.

The old Tarpin came forward then and also pressed his thumb to Deacon's forehead. He felt a little foolish as, one by one, each of the surrounding Tarpin mimicked the gesture. After the last one retreated, everyone stood silently for a while. Deacon wasn't sure what had just happened or what was now expected of him, so, after what felt like hours, he made to speak, but the old Tarpin held up a finger forestalling him.

Deacon closed his mouth and fidgeted uncomfortably. Slowly, he became aware of a tension flare among the Tarpin. No words were spoken, and yet eyes darted nervously toward Silax's cot. Finally, after another eternity, Silax sighed and gingerly lifted his leg over the side of the cot and rose on his one good leg. He hopped over to Deacon and sighed again. He pressed his thumb against Deacon's forehead in exactly the same place the others had.

Deacon could tell that the act was far more painful for the alien than it had been when he had smashed his knee in the corridor, but after his thumb came away, Silax looked down at him without any anger in his eyes.

"Brother," he said.

Deacon made his way back to the alcove after the surreal tableau with the Tarpin, totally at a loss and yet completely satisfied.

Elijah noticed the strange expression on his face and grunted a question.

"What's wrong with you?"

"Uh. I think I'm Tarpin now."

CHAPTER 33
Caliban

The Baychimo shuddered slightly, and Spurius groaned.

"I will never get used to space travel," he moaned and put a hand against the bulkhead for stability. The ship was almost entirely steady. Only sporadic subtle vibrations passed through it when they passed through some unknown space turbulence, but Spurius acted as if they were aboard one of the village's fishing scows during a storm.

Cal just smiled at his dramatics and prodded him forward.

"Come on, we need to get to training before Blotha hunts us down and pounds us to dust." The words had the desired effect of encouraging his friend on his way even though the Bulrathi had warmed considerably in the months since he had started training them personally. He now only struck them out of anger on occasion rather than daily. Cal suspected that Blotha had softened, if that's what you could call it, out of a sense of futility rather than morality. He had even said: 'You Torg can really take a hit' in a strangely complimentary tone. The problem was that they couldn't seem to muster the emotional fortitude to strike back, and that, more than anything, is what angered Blotha time and time again.

"I'm here, wasting my time trying to knock some fighting

spirit into you two, and you have the stones to show up late? On my free time, no less." Blotha steamed upon their arrival. Cal glanced at his MACO. They were not late, but Blotha often sought any reason to be angry at them, and today wasn't the first time he used this excuse.

"Sorry, Blotha. Spurius isn't feeling one hundred percent," Cal said.

"Oh, I'm sorry to hear that," Blotha said to Cal's surprise. Blotha came closer to Spurius, a concerned look on his face. "Would you like a nice warm cup of kathar? It's supposed to be good for the stomach."

Spurius glanced nervously at Cal before answering. "Uh, sure...do you have one?"

Blotha's face scrunched in utter disbelief. "No, I don't have a cup of kathar. Why would I...aaagh." The stocky alien threw his thick arms in the air. "You Torg are beyond anything... anyone. You're all Tendari meat, and there's nothing that anyone can do about it," he was babbling in his rage, and neither Cal nor Spurius had any idea what had worked him up. They shrugged at each other. Blotha put his head in his hands and looked like he was in physical pain. Cal was tempted to comfort him but hesitated. Since they had no idea why he was so angry, maybe it was better if he didn't.

"Okay, I guess we'd better get this over with," Blotha said. He sighed dramatically and moved to the center of the room. "Spurius, let's go."

Spurius stepped forward and assumed the customary stance, and waited for Blotha to start the bout.

"Hit me." With that invitation, Spurius made one of his standard half-hearted jabs that Blotha blocked contemptuously. "Come on, you furry idiot! Hit me!" he yelled. Spurius made another attempt, only marginally better but nowhere near Blotha's high standards.

Blotha growled in frustration and dodged, then followed

up with a strike to Spurius's face, obviously trying to encourage him to action as he had every day since he started their personal training. Spurius reacted as he had every other time and covered his head with his massive arms while peeking through the gap between them at his assailant.

"Hit me, you useless mountain of fur." Blotha leaned back and came forward with a heel into Spurius's exposed side. Cal winced as the air audibly left his friend's lungs. Spurius, however, wasn't spurred to any offensive action by the violence and instead stood, hunched, unsure of where he should guard against the next assault.

Blotha was exasperated, as he always was with his Torg comrades, but today was different. He seemed more...sad. Like he genuinely felt their failures inside himself.

Their bulky Bulrathi trainer turned and began walking away from Spurius. He muttered, more to himself than to anyone else. "Your ancestors must be ashamed of you." It was said quietly, but Torg have exceptional hearing, and Cal stiffened at the offense.

Spurius clearly heard the barb as well because he, too, stiffened, then roared his anger. It was a rare thing for a Torg to roar in such a way, and it was a sight to behold, even for a fellow Torg. His fur bristled down his spine, standing straight on end and giving his friend the appearance of an even bigger specimen. Spurius's sharp teeth were bared, and his face was scrunched in a snarl.

Blotha turned in surprise at the unexpected sound, momentary worry crossing his face before logic reasserted itself. He was undoubtedly reassuring himself, remembering the countless times he had sparred with Spurius, so his worried scowl changed to a smile.

"Well, well." Was all he got out before Spurius charged.

Cal's friend dug gouges in the steel decking with his claws as he propelled himself toward Blotha. Blotha, for his part, readied himself, unmovable like the stone his species resembled, but as Spurius closed the distance, the Bulrathi shifted his weight and moved to grab Spurius on the way by in what Cal recognized as a tumbler, a move taught to them by Crassus.

Spurius, however, shifted his course at the last instant and hit Blotha squarely, sending them both cartwheeling into the far wall. The Torg, his ire kindled past the point of feeling pain, recovered first and began raining heavy blows down on Blotha, who could do nothing to protect himself. What could only be described as 'chips' flew off Blotha's pummeled stoney skin with each blow.

Cal ran forward and pulled on his friend.

"Leave him! He didn't know," he yelled into the ear of his incensed friend. He yanked and pulled and had to repeat himself over and over until, finally, Spurius allowed himself to calm slightly.

After several minutes of cajoling, Blotha was able to stand.

"What was that?" he asked.

"Our ancestors are sacred," Cal responded, deciding that more specifics were unnecessary.

"I'd say so," Blotha rasped.

CHAPTER 34
Golith

It surprised Golith how much he had grown to enjoy his time with the little Grak-human. He had been raised to believe that all other species were inferior to the mighty Tendari, but everything Grak did seemed to show a value that far exceeded that of most of Golith's compatriots. Especially that useless scum Trask. Golith hadn't been surprised when the team had decided to protect Grak and finish off Trask as he lay wounded on the equipment room's floor that day. It should have, but it didn't.

Trask had made too many enemies, and Tendari held grudges, so the Sergeant's days had been marked from early on in his...leadership. That was the word that should be used for Trask's position, but it didn't fit.

There was a back story for every maintenance crew member. After all, it was not a position that Tendari sought. It was a position that Tendari were punished with. Golith had always suspected that Trask had been sent to the team because he had stepped on too many toes higher up.

Golith couldn't blame him there. He was a part of the team for much the same reason, though his reasons for stepping on those toes were diametrically opposed to the reasons that Trask had.

Golith had been sent to the maintenance team because, as first lieutenant, he had refused an order to execute a group of refugees from the battle of Cintaur. The only reason he hadn't been put to death for his insubordination was the court-martial and assignment to maintenance were considered worse than death. Golith, however, had grown to enjoy the work, demeaning though it was meant to be, and those with whom he worked, especially the little Grak.

He had always been soft-hearted. His commanding officers had called it cowardice, but Golith had learned long ago how false such a description was. He maintained that the real cowardice had been committed by those who would disgrace themselves by killing defenseless refugees. He recognized the same kind of hidden strength in Grak. He had been impressed when Grak had returned the very next day after Trask had beaten him almost to death. Grak's bravery and fortitude that day was why Golith talked the facilities quarter-master into giving Grak more water rations.

Golith shifted his feet on the scorched metal surface of the Gorski's hull. Little Grak and he had been patching holes in the hull and repairing the shield baffles for months. Golith had assigned his whole maintenance team to the daunting project, dividing the ship into sections for which each team of two was responsible. He and Grak were nearly finished with their section, and even though they had taken months to do it, they had accomplished it twice as fast as the next fastest team.

Golith would like to take the credit for the speedy repairs, but he knew, as did the rest of the team, that most of the praise belonged to the little Grak. He scurried about the hull, delving in and out of holes that the smallest Tendari wouldn't be able to fit a leg through, fixing the internal baffles before exiting and helping Golith patch the outer shield. They had developed the most efficient processes through intuitive action, hardly needing to speak, though they did plenty of that.

The little Grak liked to talk, especially after Trask was out of the picture. Most of the time, it was hypothetical questions about different ship functions that Golith did his best to answer, though some of his questions were too advanced for even him. Sometimes, however, the questions were of a more personal nature. Tendari didn't generally talk about their personal lives, and at first, the queries felt like an invasion of his privacy, and Golith tended to ignore them, but as their undeniable friendship grew, he couldn't resist the obvious interest that Grak had in his life experiences.

Grak seemed extremely interested in the fact that he was nearly twenty-eight cycles old, and Golith had to remind himself constantly that this little Grak was a mere toddler, which only made him more impressed with his abilities.

"That baffle is done," Grak said in near-perfect Tendari. Golith smiled at the use of his own language by this tiny creature. It was surprising that such noises could come out of something so small, let alone with near-perfect diction. He wondered, not for the first time, why Grak bothered learning other languages. With the embedded translators that they were all given at birth, there really was no need, but the effort was appreciated nonetheless. Grak's Tendari had ingratiated him with the whole maintenance team.

Grak wiggled out of a particularly small hole, being careful not to snag his suit on the still-sharp edges. He grunted tiredly and swung stiff arms around his head as Golith pulled the plate they had planned to use to patch this hole from the Gorski's hull. They used magnets to fix the plate and other tools to the ship while not in use to keep them from floating away on an endless sojourn across the galaxy. Working in zero gravity held many such difficulties that Golith had still not gotten completely used to, but there were benefits to the environment as well. For instance, he was able to lift the heavy plate with no effort at all, something that he would have struggled with despite the relatively small sheet of metal had there been gravity.

He held the sheet in front of Grak, and the boy removed the magnets that clung to the opposite side before Golith lowered it into its destined position. Without a word, Grak readied the impact drill and the self-tapping bolts that would hold the shield patch in place while he adjusted the angle of the patch for maximum strength. After the patch was secured, they both clicked off their boots and relaxed their bodies.

Slowly, Golith and Grak floated away from the Gorski twenty or so feet until the slack in their tethers lessened, and the carbon fiber bands arrested their ascent. They drifted, comfortably relaxed. They had developed this form of relaxation as a reward for a long day's work, and Golith wasn't sure of a more peaceful way to end a day. Golith looked at the time on his HUD and mentally set a timer. As Sergeant, he had to maintain a higher standard of work ethic, so he only allowed breaks at the end of the day and for only fifteen minutes at a time.

"Why did the Tendari kill my people?" Grak interrupted the silence. The question surprised him. Not the fact that the little Grak had asked a question since the boy seemed to do nothing else during these breaks, but it was the question itself. They had never really broached the subject before, which, now that he thought about it, was strange. In the two-hundred-plus years since the purge, Golith hadn't heard of a friendship between a Tendari and a human, though he supposed that if one existed, it would only be natural that they would discuss the brutal past between their two cultures.

Now, however, two explanations warred with one another inside him. Golith didn't have many friends. Tendari culture, as a rule, didn't allow for friendships in their competitively brutal society. That's not to say that friendships didn't exist, but when they did, they were deemed more than merely friendships. Brotherhood was a more apt description of a Tendari friendship, and Golith felt such a bond with this little Grak-human of all creatures. So, as Golith pondered the version of events that he would share, he was forced to recognize the bond between them as a qualifying exception.

"What I tell you is not to ever be repeated," Golith said. "If you do, we will both be killed," he added to emphasize the severity of the statement. Grak nodded, somberly.

Golith began with the Tendari-human war that ended with the disgraced Tendari shaming themselves by not recognizing the human victory.

"They were blinded by the rage they felt at being beaten by such an inferior species." Golith shrugged at Grak to take the sting out of the words and continued. "The humans showed mercy in not annihilating us when they could have, but the Tendari of that generation, my grandfather among them, chose to seek revenge at any cost. We are the ones that developed the virus…a most non-Tendari tactic. To our greatest shame, we used it and continue to use it. Most Tendari believe that the virus was human, to begin with, and we just weaponized it for our own means. It seems, to me, a small difference, but to them who seek absolution, it is enough to assuage their souls." Grak was silent, and Golith searched his face for an emotional response. It was there for certain, but not to the degree that he had anticipated. This little human was strong.

"We sought the total destruction of your people and the conquest of your world, but the humans, in a most Tendari fashion, chose self-destruction to capitulation. And so you see… to our great shame, the Tendari were weak when you humans were strong. That is the great secret. That is what you must never repeat. We Tendari hold long grudges and have longer memories. Our culture could not survive if such a secret were generally known among us."

Golith was surprised by how much he had shared. He had not anticipated telling all, but as he had started, it felt as if the weight of his grandfather's disgrace was lifted slightly as he confessed to this human. Oddly, Golith felt embarrassed, an emotion that Tendari rarely experienced. He glanced up at Grak, afraid of how he would react.

Tears were wet on the human boy's face glistening in the light from the distant star Sol. Grak nodded at him as if Golith's truth had somehow confirmed their brotherhood to him.

"Thank you," Grak whispered.

"Not all Tendari hate humans." Golith hesitated a long moment before continuing. "Some of us hate ourselves far more."

"And those… they put in maintenance," Grak said, and the chill in his voice made Golith tremble.

CHAPTER 35
Deacon

It was amazing what a little real food did for people's spirits and what it did for Deacon and Elijah's reputation around the barracks. Deacon had gone from being worse than a pariah to being openly respected. He had even begun to develop tenuous friendships with various slaves.

Part of the change, Deacon suspected, had been his adoption into the Tarpin clan. He still wasn't entirely sure what all his new status with them entailed, but he was beyond happy to be rid of the constant stress that being marked for hatred brought with it.

Preparations for the coming 'revolt' had been moving at a faster pace than he could have hoped for. It seemed that once the slaves were given a choice and a purpose, they bent to their goal with a determination that startled Deacon.

For some reason, everyone had begun coming to him with questions and at first, Deacon tried to shunt them off to Anzark or Elijah, but one night, his mentor came to him and explained the situation to him.

"You are a born leader. Whether you like it or not, God or fate or the cosmos has deemed that you should be the leader of these men," he had said. Deacon had been unconvinced and scoffed at the notion, but Elijah wasn't done. "Despite the curse of hatred that you were born to bear, you have gained this entire barracks' trust, no, not just their trust...their respect. When I first came here, I was determined to give up. I did not want to continue this charade of strength. I had been beaten down and thought I hated everyone until you forced me to like you. What's more, you reminded me of the strength that we humans have. In spite of the opposition, we keep on."

"You won over Nah-leesi with your persistence, though I suspect you wish it had been your charming good looks that had done it." The jibe hadn't been far from the truth, and it had torn a laugh out of him.

"After Nah-leesi, you won over Denzink and Anzark with your bravery and value of life, all life. With them, the rest of the Kupelti followed. Then...." Deacon had been embarrassed and raised his hand.

"I get it. Please, no more." The old man held up his hands in mock surrender.

Now, even though he sincerely wished for the contrary, Deacon found himself making decisions, and for some reason, no one questioned them. He and Anzark queried the entire barracks about what professions the slaves had before being captured by the Tendari and set out to give them all jobs in the areas where they would be most useful regardless of species.

There had been some hesitancy at first as the orders broke up the little cliques that the various species inevitably formed, but the wisdom in it was clear, and the mumblings dissipated quickly. Slopik had been the obvious choice to be in charge of the farm, but there were a dozen or so farmers that were eager to help. Several had experience with hydroponics, which Deacon knew nothing about, but it was apparently something that would help their efficiency immensely.

All of their work had to be done after their work at the mine, and they were all warned against slacking on that front.

They did not want the Tendari to catch wind of anything suspicious because they were all missing their quotas. Still, they were able to accomplish a surprising amount with the little time they had each night.

Nah-leesi came to him one day, excited. Her beautiful face glowed, and Deacon gulped hard. It felt like there was something caught in his throat as she smiled warmly at him and placed a slender hand on his arm as she spoke. He shook himself mentally and asked her to repeat herself. She blushed, evidently aware of the reason he was distracted, and did so.

"Koolig and I have figured it out!" Koolig was a Guzonian electrician, and the two of them had been working on making batteries that they could charge in the event the Tendari cut their power from the panels on the surface. They had hit a stumbling block involving chemistry and a lot of words that he didn't understand, but now, apparently, they had made a breakthrough.

The news was worthy of her uncharacteristic blitheness, and Deacon got caught up in it, grabbed her in a bear hug and lifted her off her feet. She laughed, and Deacon thought he'd melt. She had a sweet lilting laugh that sent a thrill through him. He caught Koolig's expression out of the corner of his eye and quickly put her down.

Koolig, obviously confused by Deacon's exuberant display, nevertheless wanted to participate and held out his hairy arms, waiting for Deacon to lift him up as well, an innocent smile on his face. Deacon shrugged and lifted Koolig, laughing. Instead of laughing in return, a rumble vibrated from Koolig's chest, and Deacon nearly dropped the Guzonian. He set him down instead and realized that the rumbling sound was some sort of non-verbal que. Happiness maybe?

"How many can we make?" He directed the question back at Nah-leesi, hoping Koolig would stop his strange, disquieting rumble if he ignored him.

"As many as we need. Almost all the materials are natural

resources here. We just had to put them in the right order."

"Good. How many people do you need to make it happen? I want as many batteries as we can produce and charge as soon as possible."

"If I could get five or six Guzonians, we can get a lot done. They're the only species besides us that have small enough fingers to be of any use to me."

"He nodded. I'll see what I can do," he said.

Koolig had stopped his rumbling. Unbidden, Deacon's hand went out to the Guzonian's head. He didn't know why, but he felt the desire to pet Koolig. What was more strange was that Koolig pressed his head into Deacon's hand before he could pull it back in embarrassment. The Rumbling started up again. Deacon smiled as the Guzonian luxuriated in the touch. It was strangely soothing for Deacon as well.

"What are you doing?" Nah-leesi asked. Her tone implied concern. As if she suddenly questioned his sanity.

"Uh, nothing." Deacon jerked his hand back and tried to look nonchalant. "How many batteries could we get charged in, say... a week?" He asked. Nah-leesi passed the question to Koolig.

"About five," The Guzonian spoke with a soft purr behind the words, then, when it became clear that Deacon was done petting him, he began licking the back of his furry hand, evidently trying to portray his own nonchalance. His body language said he couldn't care less if this human didn't pet him.

Elijah walked into the room they had made into the effort's headquarters with a large bundle in his arms. He came to the large table in the center of the room and dumped the bundle on it. It made a loud clatter, and a few sharp glinting pieces of metal poked out of the cloth wrapping. Without a word, Elijah threw back the cloth, exposing a large pile of crude but effective-looking weapons.

Nah-leesi whistled.

"Someone has been busy," she said.

Deacon agreed. "When did you find the time to make these?" he asked.

"I've been making these since the day I came here. Same way I did the one I used so long ago to save that little crying human who got himself in too deep."

"I wasn't crying," Deacon said defensively. He looked at Nah-leesi, who had a hint of a smile tugging at the corner of her mouth. "I wasn't," he said, more adamantly. Deacon remembered crying quite clearly, but he wasn't about to admit it with Nah-leesi present. He looked back at Elijah, who made a face. Deacon chose to ignore it.

"How did you get them all back to the barracks without being seen?" he asked, more to take the pressure off of himself than due to a need to know.

"A piece at a time. In the case of the larger ones, literally a piece at a time. I had to assemble them once I had all of the pieces here," he pointed at one especially long sword that would be perfect for a Carexi. It had been segmented, and small rivets held the pieces together. Deacon knew from experience that the titanium rivets would be strong enough. He was impressed.

"These will help," Deacon said, fingering a sword that looked like the ancient Roman gladius that Elijah had drawn for him on the dirty floor of the barracks.

Nah-leesi had apparently been eyeing her own favorite and reached down, picking up a slender, razor-sharp sword that looked like a stylized cutlass.

"Can I have this one?" she asked the old man.

"As long as you stick a Tendari with it," he said. She smiled with evil eyes.

"I'm glad you're here," Deacon said to Elijah. "I want to run something past you." Deacon wondered where such confidence came from. He had never spoken like this to anyone, let alone his mentor. 'Run past you.' like he was doing the old man a favor.

He mentally chided himself, but Elijah didn't seem to have even noticed the pompousness.

"What has been turning in that devious mind of yours," Elijah said the words like it was a compliment.

"I may have an idea of how to take the Gorski."

CHAPTER 36
Caliban

Under Blotha's tutelage, Spurius and Cal made progress after that violent day when Spurius tried to kill the Bulrathi. Blotha, to his credit, held no grudges and only wanted to know the exact source of the motivation. Cal informed him in detail the reasons why Spurius felt obliged to try and pound his stoney face to powder.

Torg had no religion per se. They did have a connection with their ancestors that rivaled the most fervent of religious zealots, however. Torg lived and died in the hope that their ancestors might be proud of the way they had acted while alive. Their culture was steeped in that drive. It is what encouraged patience and kindness, gentleness and friendship above all.

Blotha listened with surprising interest and then asked a pointed question, one that Cal fought to not be offended by.

"What do you think your ancestors think of this war?"

His question was sincere, so Cal overlooked the mention of his ancestors by a Bulrathi. Cal gave the query the contemplation it deserved and didn't answer until he was sure he had done his due diligence.

It was accepted and even lauded that Torg had fought in the distant past. There had been previous wars, always with other species, that ensured Torg freedom and dominance on Proxima, but after that security was ensured, peace had reigned for centuries among the Torg. The actual act of fighting was not disgraceful when the need was clear. Was the need clear? Was their enemy worthy of violence? The Tendari were, perhaps, the most worthy of Torg violence in his species' long history. His mind finally made up, he nodded.

"They would want the Torg to fight as hard as they had in the war of Punderi or the battle of Trathar." Blotha, not knowing anything about Torg history, nodded his understanding even though his face displayed confusion.

"Did they fight hard…then?" He clearly hoped that they did but seemed doubtful.

"They fought like titans. The Torcians feared us by the end. I mean really feared us. Tell your pups scary stories kind of fear." Blotha smiled, the first such expression Cal had seen on the Bulrathi's face.

A few weeks later, the breachers were doing their normal, pitiful best under the watchful gaze of Sergeant Crassus. The only problem was it wasn't their best. Spurius and Cal were sparring when Crassus came up to them. They both came to attention when he spoke.

"At least two of you are making some progress. The rest of this lot are nearing the end of my patience. If they don't progress soon, I think we'll have to send them out of the airlock rather than take them into battle. Better that than letting them embarrass us." Crassus grumbled, more to himself than to them, but they felt inclined to answer in any case.

"Yes, sir," they said, in unison. Cal thought for a second as Crassus started to walk away again. He glanced across the room at Blotha, who was watching them. He nodded at Cal as if he knew what he was thinking.

"Sir," Cal called to Crassus. The Sergeant turned, surprised at the forwardness of this Torg. He tilted his head. Cal took it as permission to continue.

"May I have a moment of the unit's attention?" Crassus thought about the request for a moment, then gave in and nodded his consent. Cal nervously stepped to the center of the large room around which pairs of trainees were spread. He cleared his throat, attempting to get the unit's attention, but his voice was far too quiet to overcome the chorus of grunts and heavy breathing that accompanied the exercise.

Cal thought of Borthos the fierce, a black Torg like himself from whom he had inherited his rare black pelt. His parents were particularly proud that Borthos was their distant ancestor and had told stories of his courage and strength all of Cal's life. Cal squared his shoulders and inhaled deeply.

"Soldiers!" he yelled. He was so keyed up that the echo of his own yell made him jump. The pathetic sparring came to a staggered halt, and the combatants looked in his direction. Many of them looked back and forth between Cal and Crassus, sure that the Marak would put a stop to his grand-standing. Cal gulped and pushed on.

"Fellow Torg! What is it that we fight for? Is it for the Marak?" From the corner of his eye, Cal saw the Sergeant's body language shift. Crassus would be asking himself if he had made a mistake in allowing this. Cal had very little time, so he hurried on.

"Do we fight for our home? Thanks to the Marak, Proxima is safe. So what, then? For what do we fight?" He had everyone's attention now. "What would our ancestors have done when faced with the Tendari threat? Would they have left it alone and allowed others to fight in our stead?"

"No!" Several Torg yelled in response.

"Then I say we fight for them. We fight to bring pride to our forefathers. As they see our strength and courage, they will smile and say, 'That's Caliban, son of Lucius, son of Mamarcus, son of Titus, son of Quintus, son of Borthos the fierce!" he ended in a near yell because the Torg in the room were cheering and chanting ancient ceremonial battle songs that, until this moment, hadn't been fully understood by his people for centuries.

Cal turned to Crassus, who was looking at him. At least, he assumed the Marak was looking at him. His face, as ever, was covered by the visor, but his body language told Cal that Crassus was assessing him. Weighing him like a merchant did his coin.

"If this little speech improves their efforts, I will put you in for advancement," he said under his breath, careful that none of the surrounding Torg would over-hear.

After that day, the Torg in the unit progressed smoothly and excelled even, and Cal got his advancement. He was now a Lance-Corporal which, Cal learned, made him the ranking conscript in the unit. When a Marak was not present, Cal was in charge of the breachers. The advancement both scared and pleased him.

He didn't know, all of a sudden, how to act with his fellow conscripts, especially Blotha. He was the one that deserved the promotion, not Cal. Still, the Bulrathi handled the situation with entirely more grace than Cal would have given him credit for having.

They continued their private lessons with Blotha, though both Spurius and Cal's skill had all but caught up to the Bulrathi's. They had just finished an especially taxing session when Cal asked Blotha how he felt about his advancement.

"I mean, you're the one that deserves it, not me," Cal said, trying to soften any anger Blotha might have hidden under his literally stoney surface.

Blotha smiled for the second time in Cal's presence.

"You're assuming that I want it," Blotha said. "I can't imagine something that I would want less than to be in charge of this lot." There was a long pause while Cal contemplated Blotha's reasoning. He didn't have to think long. Blotha enlightened him.

"You know that the Marak kill you if you lead the unit to

destruction, don't you?" Cal suddenly felt nauseated and bent over, breathing heavily, sure that he would wretch.

CHAPTER 37
Deacon

The plan Deacon outlined for Elijah was daring, and he wondered if anyone would even volunteer to make it happen. Elijah seemed impressed by the plan and spent the rest of that night questioning it, testing it from every angle. They had returned to the barracks hours ago and sat in the dark of their secluded alcove. The old man finally sat back against the wall and sighed.

"Well, it seems that it is a very sound plan, and I admit that from where we are at the moment, it is the best plan we can come up with. Let's sleep on it, and tomorrow we will see what the others think." The 'others' he had referred to were the small cadre Deacon had trusted from the beginning and consisted of Nah-leesi, Anzark, and Denzink.

Surprisingly the others were supportive, even excited by the plan. They asked many of the same questions that Elijah had the night before, and Deacon answered them patiently, but everyone seemed to skirt around the obvious hindrance to his own plan. Maybe they were afraid of the answer like he was. Finally, he broached the subject.

"So…who is going to lead the Alpha team?" Silence filled the space between them.

"I suppose that besides you, I have the most experience

with that sort of thing," Denzink said. Everyone else chuckled nervously. Deacon offered his fat, scale-covered friend his hand. Denzink took it.

"The whole plan hinges on your team. We'll hash out all the specifics before asking for volunteers." Denzink nodded his agreement. Deacon could see that he was nervous. He couldn't blame him. Alpha team would bear the brunt of the risk, but Deacon knew that many species might jump at the chance for the greater degree of glory associated with it. Since he was…adopted by the Tarpin, he had learned that the species sought glory much like the Tendari. They valued bravery and self-sacrifice. It was possible that they would be excited to join Denzink's team.

At first, the slaves of the barracks were every bit as reluctant to join the Alpha team as he had feared they would be, but as soon as they heard Deacon's role in the plan, his Tarpin friends clamored to join the team. It wasn't glory for glory's sake that drove them to it as Deacon had imagined, but their loyalty to him. It surprised him just how different the Tarpin were with him now. He had never had a family. He had never had a sense of belonging. Under Elijah's tutelage, he had gotten a sense of… purpose, a connection for sure, but he wouldn't go so far as to call it belonging, especially now that he had a taste of true belonging.

The Tarpin protected him, told him jokes that could only truly be understood in their native tongue, and served him. He did his best to fit in with them, but they seemed unphased by his ignorance, accepting him for who he was. It was strange but not unwelcome.

In the weeks that followed, Denzink and the Tarpin practiced during the day, careful to not be observed by any functioning surface cameras, and Deacon found himself beginning to worry for his new family. As the time drew near, he wondered how many of them would die. He worried for more than just the Tarpin. He worried for Nah-leesi and Elijah, Anzark and Denzink, and he even worried for Janisar the Bulrathi, who, despite everything, still seemed to treat him with little better than contempt.

The entire operation was his responsibility. He felt obligated to worry, and there was good reason to. There was a good chance they would all be killed, exterminated by a vengeful Tendari. For the thousandth time, he wondered if it was worth it. He felt he wasn't qualified to judge since he had never experienced freedom. The best he could do was go off what everyone else said. Elijah never wavered, convinced that he would rather die than live out the rest of his life as a slave, and so, Deacon was reassured.

When the day that had been decided upon finally came, the tension in the barracks could have been cut with a knife. Deacon felt it the moment he woke up, and when he was getting his rations, a sea of nervous eyes stared at him. They had decided to leave all talk of their plans out of the barracks, but as Deacon saw the distraught expressions on those normally stoic faces, he felt that he needed to address it.

"Today, we prove ourselves." It was simple, and he felt foolish saying it, but the nervousness, although still there, was less somehow. He walked over to where Denzink stood with a handful of his Tarpin team members. Deacon needed to be assured that his friends were ready for the day.

"Big day," he said. "Are you ready?" He was sure there was a political way of asking, but Tarpin, at least, reveled in brevity and bluntness.

"We are ready," Denzink said. The words sounded confident, but his eyes betrayed the fear there. Deacon clapped him on his wide back.

"I'm sure you are."

"We going to crush those red demons," Torax, the oldest of all the Tarpin in the barracks, said. Deacon grinned and nodded.

Deacon next visited Elijah and Anzark, where a similar scene unfolded. The difference was that Elijah seemed as calm and cool as black space. Deacon was tempted to remind the old man what day it was and why it was significant. Maybe his age was finally catching up to him, but no, Elijah knew what day it was. He knew today was death or freedom, and he seemed to accept either outcome as being decreed by fate. Deacon wished he could be as calm as his mentor. He knew that many of those around him looked to him, but if they recognized the slight tremor in his voice or the cold sweat on his forehead for the fear that it was, they didn't say.

Deacon shook hands with the old man, praying it wouldn't be the last time he saw his friend. He left the barracks. Each step closer to the Tendari made him feel worse and worse. He stopped just around the corner from where Gorat and Slik stood guard and vomited violently. A chill ran through his body, and he righted himself, shivering. He was still wiping his mouth when he came around the corner and saw the two Tendari glaring at him.

On a normal day, he probably wouldn't have seen anything suspicious about the two as they glared at him. In fact, for Tendari, they seemed glad to see him, but in his current nerve-wracked state, he could only see two enemies who could see right through him. He was convinced that at any moment, Slik would pull the shooter from his hip and send a pulse of energy burning through his body. He didn't, though, and Deacon passed through like normal and was soon waiting for the shuttle.

He stood as the tell-tale sound of the arriving shuttle groaned and clicked into place on the other side of the airlock doors. He made sure to stand to the side to allow the Tendari priority as they exited and entered the shuttle, but instead of the usual crowd, dozens of fully armored troopers ran out, weapons drawn. Deacon's heart sank as they searched out and surrounded him.

He raised his hands in the universal sign of surrender but refused to show the fear that threatened to overwhelm him. To do so would almost certainly invite the nearest Tendari to tear his throat out. He could tell that the soldiers were keyed up, and the only thing that kept them from making good on their violent desires was the military discipline that had been pounded into them.

"Did you really think we did not know about your little revolution?" The voice was Commander Grato's, and as Deacon searched for the source, the officer stepped off the shuttle into view. He was smiling, his sanguine tongue snaked out between razor teeth to lick scaly lips.

"It's a pity. I had such high hopes for you."

CHAPTER 38

"Lieutenant, take your platoon and help Captain Toth cleanse the facility. I want them all dead, you understand?" The Lieutenant nodded. "We'll have to bring in more slaves, but they are cheap." Commander Grato coughed out a disturbing laugh that made Deacon shiver.

The majority of Tendari marched off with the Lieutenant to do what they did best, and Deacon worried for his friends left at the barracks.

One Corporal stayed behind with Grato and kept his gun pointed at Deacon.

"Come on then. I haven't got all day," Grato growled and motioned for Deacon to lead the way onto the shuttle. The ride to the Gorski was silent but for the indeterminate docking sounds as the shuttle connected to the larger ship. When the doors opened, Deacon was surprised to see another platoon of soldiers, garbed and ready for battle. After Deacon was pushed roughly from the shuttle, the platoon marched in. It seemed that Commander Grato was taking no chances. He clearly wanted the threat resolved quickly.

Deacon was surprised that they hadn't bound his hands in any way as they pushed him down the corridor. They obviously didn't see him as a threat. The Corporal pushed at his back with the barrel of the energy pistol, coaxing him through an open door into a small room. There was a small table and a single chair, surprisingly human-sized, in the middle of the room. The walls, floor and ceiling were brushed stainless steel, easy to clean, Deacon thought.

Grato closed and locked the door behind him with his command key card that hung from his neck. Deacon sat in the chair when Grato motioned him down.

"The sooner you answer my questions, the sooner we can all get on with our day," he began, but Deacon knew that Grato didn't intend for him to have a day to 'get on with.'

Elijah hadn't anticipated the Tendari so soon, but he had long been a student of the adage 'those who fail to prepare, prepare to fail.' They were ready, and the only thing that the Tendari's early arrival accomplished was allowing them less time for their minds to work against them. It was better this way. His men were largely untrained, and they didn't need the extra time to stew.

He had assigned the Guzonians as scouts, given their natural abilities at silent movement, and Koolig purred a warning over Elijah's earpiece. They had gutted the comms out of their mining helmets so that they could communicate, and Koolig's words sounded calm, almost lazy, to Elijah.

He relayed the warning over to Nah-leesi, and a few seconds later, the lights went out. According to Deacon, Tendari liked it bright and warm, so their plans included making the facility as dark and cold as they could.

Almost as soon as the lights went out, Elijah heard the snarling hiss of the Guzonians as they ambushed the first Tendari to the fight. The flash of energy guns discharging reflected through the open door, and Elijah could tell from the haphazard sound the shots were fired too quickly, the result of undisciplined fear. Elijah smiled.

The Guzonian ambush had been more about psychology than tactics. Aliens used to bright light would naturally avoid the dark, perhaps even fear it. The Guzonians thrived in the dark. Their black fur and large eyes were tailored specifically for the environment, and they could move like ghosts through the inky blackness. Such creatures were anathema to Tendari, perhaps because they recognized strength where they were weak.

The Guzonians weren't meant to do significant physical damage to the platoon, but Elijah hoped that the psychological damage that they inflicted would last through the rest of the battle. After only a few seconds, the lights came on, and as the Tendari realized there were no targets, the gunfire died away. Confused muttering could be heard as the Tendari unit attempted to gather its wits.

Another brief report from Koolig informed Elijah just how many Tendari were on the way. Three full platoons. Grato must be nervous, Elijah thought. He gave the signal for the Guzonians to fall back, and almost instantly, shadowy figures passed through the open door to the corridor where the Tendari had been stalled.

Elijah sat in the corner of the barracks, holding a thick cable with two exposed wire ends sparking. He stood and ducked into the doorway leading to the vast subterranean facility that would prove a death mire for the enemy, a maze of danger within which Elijah hoped they could hold out for days. He muttered into his comm mic, and the lights went out again. The cable stopped its flashing, and he dropped it into the pool of water covering the entire barracks floor. It was ironic that the Tendari had given Deacon the very water that they were now going to die in.

The first of the Tendari cautiously made their way through the doorway and into the barracks. Brief flashes of light shone as nervous soldiers shot at imagined glimpses of fur or gleaming eyes. Elijah smiled. They were so focused on hunting the elusive Guzonians that they barely registered that they stood in ankle-deep water.

In the dark, it was difficult for Elijah to see how many Tendari had come in, but the closest of the soldiers would notice him soon.

"Let there be light," he whispered into his mic. The lights came up, the cable jumped, and sparks flew. Twenty or so Tendari spasmed like a grotesque marionette show, their muscles involuntarily squeezed triggers, and energy blasts shot wildly through the room, making an already deadly situation worse. Elijah watched them dance for a few seconds, then signaled for the power to be cut once more.

The dark returned, and Elijah whistled into the silence. Guzonians ran forward in the dark and splashed through the water, retrieving fallen weapons. Elijah had stressed speed when going over this part with the scouts. Within seconds, most of the Guzonians had retreated past Elijah with armloads of energy rifles and pistols. Two of the Guzonians were not fast enough, however, and a furious Tendari blasted them with his energy rifle from the doorway where twenty of his comrades had just run through. Elijah swore as the two aliens were pierced by concentrated light. The heat left in the gaping wounds caused the corpses to hiss when they hit the water, and steam rose from them, obscuring Elijah's view of the far doorway.

Elijah ordered the lights back on and retreated down the corridor. The electricity should hold them for a while, long enough for him to prepare for the next stage of their defense.

Denzink peered up at the Gorski high above. It looked small, like the size of his thumb on an outstretched arm. He had looked up at it every day for weeks and thought the same thing every time. It's impossible. Every day before had had the benefit of not being the day they attempted the impossible, and so he'd managed to continue on, holding his doubts and fears in check with the 'yet to come.' It was no longer 'yet to come,' however, it was the 'here and now.' There was no future to hide behind. He now had to face his fears and do the impossible.

For the hundredth time, he checked the straps on his thruster assembly, then turned and eyed the rest of the Alpha team. They seemed excited, but it was hard to judge their faces inside the dark interior of their helmets.

During practice, they had gone back and forth on the risks and benefits of having everyone tethered together during the jump, and those that wanted the comfort of being tied together won out, but Denzink had his doubts. The danger was that if one person went off course, he could drag the rest with him.

"It's time." Denzink almost didn't recognize his own voice.

"It's time to secure our spots in history," Torax amended. The rest of the Tarpin grunted their approval. Denzink rolled his eyes. Tarpin could be so melodramatic.

"Okay, let's go. Torax, start the count." So much about their practice had been hypothetical since they couldn't practically simulate the jump they were doing now, it was just too high, but they had practiced their lift-off so much that each person knew his place without question. Torax was last in line and could see each person as he left the surface of the Rock, so he would give the count that they would all go off of. He would also try to correct the team's overall course if needed. When Denzink had been placed in command of the team, he had quickly realized the old Tarpin's value and had made him his second. All of the Tarpin respected Torax and followed his wise counsel, which made Denzink's job easier, all he had to do was convince Torax, and he would do the rest.

"One-one-one, jump." Denzink jumped and hit his thruster switch. He lifted into the void they all feared.

"Two-two-two, jump. Three-three-three, jump," Torax's low voice continued, setting the ideal spacing between team members.

Once off the surface, each member was to cut their thrusters, with the exception of Denzink, who would slowly take up the slack in the tether, towing the team toward the Gorski. This is where the hypotheticals came in.

He didn't know exactly how to go about it. He nudged the controls of his thrusters and slowly built up speed. He felt the tether tighten behind him, and he had a brief vision of the carbon fiber strip tearing, leaving his team floating in space while he careened off at an uncontrollable speed. He banished the thought and applied more pressure to the switch, using his right hand to pilot the joystick that controlled his direction.

Successive jerks signaled the tether becoming taught down the line of Tarpin, and he took a second to adjust his mirror. He had rigged a rudimentary arm that jutted off his left shoulder and held a mirror where he could see behind him. He glanced at it and saw the surface of the Rock with a trail of small figures dangling behind him. He gulped and fought a wave of fear. He had already come far. He would have to watch his speed. It wouldn't do to pull the team into the side of the Gorski at such a speed that they became smears of Tarpin and Kupelti blood across its hull. The worst part of that scenario was that Deacon would be abandoned. Left waiting, exposed at the airlock for the team that had failed him among those Tendari scum.

Torax's low voice came over the comm.

"Torlig, come right half a count." Denzink looked in his mirror. Sure enough, Torlig, the Tarpin directly in front of Torax, had drifted out of line and needed to correct, but as the suit's side thruster engaged, it seemed to sputter and then explode in a wild fury as a cloud of vapor billowed out of his left side sending him in a wild spin.

"Cut your thruster!" Denzink yelled. He doubted that Torlig could hear over his own screaming. Denzink had been there, he had experienced the terror that Torlig fought, but if he didn't get a handle on this, he could kill them all. Denzink felt the jerks of the Tarpin's thrashing, twisting body through the tether, and as he turned his attention back to the Gorski, he could see that the malfunctioning thruster was pulling them off course at an alarming rate.

Denzink tried to compensate for the erratic movements and managed to at least get them pointed, more-or-less, in the right direction, but the increased use of his thrusters had the side-effect of adding more speed to their already dangerous velocity.

Denzink patched into Torax's private comms.

"Torax, we need to get him under control now."

Torax was silent for half a second. It felt like an eternity.

"I will take care of it," was his simple reply. He was about to encourage him to hurry but held back. The old Tarpin would know the danger they were in. His own anxiety would do nothing to help the situation. He watched in his mirror and saw Torax engage his own thrusters. His second in command had his thrusters wide open, and he blasted past Torlig's spinning form.

At first, Denzink wasn't sure what the old Tarpin's goal was, but the realization wasn't long in coming. They had all chosen weapons from the stash that the cunning old human had made, and Torax drew his sword from where it had been tied on his back.

"Don't do it, Torax!"

"No other way." Torax flashed straight for the tether. He had chosen his target well and sliced the carbon fiber that connected him and Torlig to the rest of the team.

Denzink immediately felt his own control increase and set about correcting their course for what he hoped was the last time. Once he was confident that they were safe, well, as safe as any of them could be, he searched his mirror's reflection for signs of the two Tarpin, but they were gone.

"Bagh! Torax, where are you?"

"Don't worry about us. I'm going to try and get Torlig, and we'll meet you on the Gorski." Denzink knew that the likelihood that he would ever see the two again was extremely low.

"I'll see you on the Gorski," he said.

He focused on the problem at hand, which was that the Gorski grew bigger too quickly. At this rate, they'd smash into the hull far too hard. He switched back to open comms.

"Who's in the rear now?" He should have known without thinking who it was, but he was agitated and didn't want to divert his strained concentration on remembering the team order.

"Bolax," came a nervous voice over his comm.

"Bolax, we're going to need to slow down, so you're going to have to reverse thrust. Can you do that for me?" Denzink forced himself to speak slowly and with as much calm as he could muster.

"But, Torax…"

"I know we were all counting on Torax being here," Denzink interrupted. "But he's not, so you have to do it. Just angle your body exactly in the opposite direction of our course and give me short thrusts."

There was no response.

"Bolax!" Denzink's restraint snapped. "Do it, now!"

"Yeah, uh. Okay."

Denzink glanced in the mirror and saw Bolax reorienting himself, using the tether to position his thrusters back toward the Gorski.

Denzink looked ahead, and what calm he had forced upon himself vanished. The Gorski was looming ahead. Details appeared along the ship's hull, and he soon could no longer see the black of space in his periphery.

"Now, Bolax!"

Denzink felt his tether snap tight behind him, and his stomach lurched as his body slowed quickly, but not quick enough. The hull zoomed closer, and it was all Denzink could do to pull his legs around before he hit.

He hit the ship's metal hull with surprising force, and his

legs crumpled beneath him. He tried to roll with it, but after he
hit, he was floating once again, flipping head over heels. The face
shield on his helmet struck something and cracked. He heard
nothing but his own panicked breath coming way too loud in
his ears. He knew that if someone on the team didn't clip to
something fast, they were all lost.

He tried to focus on the hull as it passed his field of vision,
but it was going by too fast. He heard the grunts and curses
as the other team members suffered the same fate as him. One
by one, they crashed into the hull and were sent skipping off
again, spinning in uncontrollable tumbles that made securing
themselves to the Gorski an impossibility. Denzink's arms flailed
wildly, searching forlornly for anything to grab, when his body
was jerked to a sudden stop. He spun in a half circle as the
momentum of his heavy body strained against the carbon fiber
tether.

He turned his head from side to side, searching for what
had arrested his flight. He found it. His tether had caught on
some type of communications equipment that jutted from the
hull below. As he watched, the tether grated dangerously against
the sharp metal of the broken equipment, fraying and cutting the
tether with every movement.

A low moan escaped his mouth, and he pulled himself,
hand over hand, toward the structure. He reached the equipment
and gripped the metal tubing, and took a breath. He then took
the tether and pulled it away from the sharp metal, and wrapped
it around his left arm. That way, if that weakened spot did break,
he would still be tied to the team.

He searched for his men and couldn't see any along the
hull of the ship. His gaze tracked up the tether on the other side
of the communications equipment to where his men dangled
like kooloksi on a string. Some of the Tarpin floated limply, and
he silently prayed that they were knocked unconscious and not
dead.

"Status check," he managed between gulps for breath.

Two were unresponsive, which left five beside himself able to continue the mission. After hearing his team's report, he assessed his own injuries and wondered how much good he would be after all. It felt like he had broken his left leg, but he mentally shrugged it off and began climbing down the comm tower toward the metal hull of the Gorski, careful to keep the tether wrapped around his arm.

When he finally reached the hull, he clipped his chest strap to the tower's base and began pulling his men in. As he pulled, the Tarpin floated and bobbed, again reminding him of the delicious Kupelti delicacy. His massive stomach rumbled inside his suit at the thought of the kooloksi, and he grunted a laugh.

"What are you laughing at?" One of his team members called over the comms.

"You all look so delicious, I could eat you." Those that were conscious joined in. It was the kind of laughter that didn't need anything truly funny to be let loose. It was like a relief valve letting off the intense pressure they had just experienced and beyond all odds, survived.

CHAPTER 39

"I will ask you again, what is the plan to take the Gorski?" Deacon grimaced at Grato, but refused to answer. He breathed heavily through clenched teeth. In retaliation for the silence, the Tendari commander reached forward and snapped another finger on his left hand.

Deacon took pride in the fact that this time, he didn't scream. Grunts and foul curses exited, but not anything he would qualify as a scream.

"You have strength. I am told that the Tendari you work with have a name for you. Grak… it is fitting, I admit. I originally put you on the maintenance team because I hated Trask. After he died, however, I'll be honest, I forgot about you."

Deacon began to laugh. He couldn't help it. Grato looked confused, then angry. He finally slammed his massive fist down on the table in frustration at not understanding the source of the humor.

"Why do you laugh? Has your puny mind broken?"

"No," Deacon managed between chuckles. "I killed Trask." A few more chuckles escaped as the commander scowled in deeper confusion. Deacon had said it so matter-of-factly that he felt it lent it enough credibility to be believable even by Grato.

"I killed Trask, then the team covered it up and said it

was an accident so I wouldn't be executed. To be honest, it was an accident. I didn't mean for Trask to die, not really, but I guess what can I expect from such a weak species."

Grato reacted as if Deacon had just broken *his* fingers. He jerked back as if in pain, and then the rage hit, and Deacon wondered if he had gone too far. Grato gripped the edge of the metal table in one powerful hand and flung it across the room like it weighed nothing. The Corporal just managed to jump out of the way before it smashed into the wall. Grato leaned down, and roared into Deacon's face, obviously hoping that he would flinch, but he knew this game and sat as unperturbed as possible. If he showed weakness now, it might be the last thing he did.

Grato restrained his anger with great effort and began pacing the width of the small room just in front of Deacon. As he did, Deacon massaged the three broken fingers on his left hand. The seal tape on his hands had just begun to wear off, and he wondered if he would have to re-wrap them. He mentally shrugged. Survival seemed like more of a concern at present than his broken fingers.

"Do you wish to know just what the maintenance team thinks of you?" Grato growled. Deacon looked back up at the scowling Tendari. He had obviously used the time to think up a come-back that was worthy of the situation. Deacon refrained from mentioning just how long it had taken. With no visible reaction from Deacon, Grato continued.

"Who do you think informed on you?"

Deacon swallowed. Grato, apparently pleased by his reaction, smiled.

"It was your very close friend Golith, of course. I'm told that he even risked his life to save you once, so imagine his anger when you betrayed him, stirring up the slaves to rebel against his people." At Deacon's blank stare, he clapped his hands together excitedly. "Don't believe me?" He asked, then swiped his card at the door. It clicked loudly, and the Commander opened it and spoke to someone out of view. "Sergeant, come in, please."

Golith entered the room, and Grato closed and locked the door behind him.

"As you can see, your friends are not as close as you think they are." Grato had won. He knew it. It was written across his face, as vibrant as the red scales.

Deacon turned his head and spoke to Golith. "Took you long enough."

"What do you mean it 'took you long enough'? I don't have a key card."

"I guess that is the whole point," Deacon conceded.

Grato looked from Deacon to Golith, then back to Deacon, dawning realization emerging ever so slowly across his ugly face.

Golith pulled the energy pistol from behind his back and tossed it to Deacon. He gripped it in his uninjured hand and sent two bolts into each of Grato's kneecaps. At the same moment, Golith advanced on the Corporal who shot at him. It was a hurried shot, born of fear and surprise, and it passed harmlessly over Golith's left shoulder, bounced off one gleaming stainless-steel wall, then another before it arrived back where it started and burned a hole in the center of the Corporal's forehead. His gun fell from lifeless fingers.

Golith took a quick step back, then let out a bark of surprised laughter. He turned to face Deacon, a grin plastered across his face that was so wide that it lent his features an air of innocence that he didn't deserve, like what Deacon imagined a child might have.

"You have one sick sense of humor, Golith," Deacon said.

His Tendari friend roared with laughter that sounded more human than Tendari. It was infectious, and Deacon laughed as well.

"Why." Was the only word that Grato managed between clenched teeth. He pressed his hands against his legs as if stemming the blood flow, but there was none. Energy rounds cauterized as they went, and Grato's hands did nothing but hide the ghastly wounds from himself.

"Why did Golith 'inform' on me?" Deacon asked. Grato nodded. "Simple." Deacon leaned forward and pulled the master key card from around Grato's neck.

"We knew that you would lock down the ship as soon as any threat from the slaves was reported, so we needed your master key," Golith said, obviously pleased with himself.

Golith retrieved the Corporal's weapon and stuck it in his belt. The pistol that Deacon held was so large for him that he held it more as you would a small rifle. The fingers on his left hand throbbed, but he could still support the end of the gun with it and stood eye level with Grato keeping the gun on him as the Commander sat on the floor, holding his legs.

"Time to go," Deacon said and began to turn toward the door, but Grato, perhaps seeing his last chance or perhaps too angry to care, lurched forward and gripped the palm of Deacon's left hand in his razor-sharp teeth. He gave one violent jerk with his head and ripped Deacon's hand from his arm.

There was so much blood. Deacon froze in complete shock. He stared at his arm in disbelief. Vaguely, he registered that Golith finished the Commander with a shot to the head, but it all seemed far away. He slumped to the floor, and Golith knelt beside him and began working on his arm. Trying to stop the blood, so much blood.

"I guess I won't need to wrap my fingers," Deacon stammered. His teeth were chattering for some reason.

Golith left for a time, and to Deacon's bleary mind, he wondered why his friend was trying to help the Corporal, but then he was back, doing more to his arm, hand…no…where his hand had been. Deacon felt a stab in his shoulder and looked over. Golith had just stabbed him with something, but Golith was his friend, wasn't he?

Then a rush of…something ran through his veins. It felt

hot at first, and then his pain vanished.

"What was that?" Deacon asked.

"It will take the pain away," Golith said, and as he spoke, Deacon's head began to clear.

"Wow, that stuff is...good." Golith chuckled and poured a rubberized beaker of something over his stump. It bubbled and smoked and smelled terrible, but after a few seconds, the precious blood was no longer leaking out of him, and Golith removed the tourniquet that Deacon didn't even know he'd put on.

"Lucky the Corporal had a med-pack with him," Golith muttered.

Deacon suddenly felt great, and despite Golith's protests, he lifted himself to his feet and hopped around, swinging his arm around.

"I feel wonderful. What was in that stuff you gave me?" He felt more energized than he ever had.

"Well...." Golith seemed to not want to answer. Finally, he shrugged. "It's a stim-jab. It takes away the pain and gives you energy, but it was meant for a full-sized Tendari, not a young human. The dosage is pre-mixed, and I couldn't control the amount I gave you, so I gave it all to you, but...it could explode your heart." At Deacon's blank stare, Golith hurried on defensively.

"You were in shock, which I figured could have also killed you and at least this way, you can keep going in the meantime."

"Okay." Was all Deacon could manage. "We've got to get going. Alpha team will be waiting."

Golith nodded and followed him to the door but paused at Grato's corpse. He bent down.

"Do you want to keep this?" Golith asked. Deacon turned to see his friend holding his bloody hand.

"No! Bagh! That's disgusting."

"Sorry, I don't know what kind of customs humans have in situations like this," he dropped the hand unceremoniously to the floor.

"Neither do I, but I'm pretty sure they don't keep lost appendages."

CHAPTER 40

It had taken the Tendari less time than Elijah had hoped it would to get past the electrified barracks floor. He had been surprised and, grudgingly, impressed by their solution. All the Tendari had to do to survive the journey across the electrified floor was turn on their mag boots.

"Smart" was all he could say about it. The negatively charged magnets repelled the negatively charged electrons and protected the Tendari from the worst of the electric shock. The first across the room pulled the cable from the water, and the rest crossed without incident.

Elijah quickly gave an order, and steam began pouring out of the pipes that lined the corridor. Elijah ran and made it to the end of the corridor before his visibility was reduced to zero. The Tendari, However, slowed down when the steam hindered their vision, uncertain of what awaited them and was soon stalled once more as bolts of energy, fired from the newly recovered energy weapons, blasted into their closely packed ranks.

The slaves waiting at the end of the corridor had grinned as they unleashed volley after volley down the corridor. They could not know, but for the cries of stricken Tendari, that their bolts found targets because of the steam, but each time a cry of pain echoed down the hall, their enthusiasm spilled out in whoops of joy.

Energy blasts soon started flashing out of the steam, however, and their whoops were silenced as two of their number were cut down. The Tendari must have retreated back into the barracks, though, because their shots soon failed to produce even a whimper from the soldiers. Elijah motioned for the mad barrage of shots coming from his team to stop.

"Janisar, fire one shot every ten seconds. No use overheating our guns if we won't hit anything." The Bulrathi nodded and sent a blast down the center of the corridor.

Elijah had been surprised at how fast the rest of the slaves had accepted him as leader of their defenses. It seemed that once they had accepted Deacon, Elijah had been kind of grandfathered in. Maybe it was the fact that Elijah was Deacon's mentor and therefore given a degree of the boy's earned respect. Whatever it was, he was glad for it.

He set two fire teams at forty-five-degree angles to the corridor's opening and asked Nah-leesi if she had eyes on the enemy. She had gone through, the night before, and 'repaired' the disabled cameras and patched their feeds into a console deep in the heart of the facility. Thanks to some creative wiring and ingenuity, Nah-leesi could control much of the facilities functions from that console, a fact that Deacon had been immensely happy about. He had been afraid for Nah-leesi's safety and pushed for her to be far from the fighting.

"They've moved back into the barracks and look madder than a nonapod with a sore tentacle. They look like they're arguing," her excitement was electric and pulsed through his comms with every word. He couldn't help but smile at the report. Good, Elijah thought. Hopefully, Deacon's team could finish their job before the Tendari decided it wasn't worth it, and the Gorski called down hell-fire on them.

The airlock control chirped as Deacon swiped the master key. The lock's operational status went from red to green, and Deacon scanned the corridor in both directions, sure that any second, a platoon of angry Tendari would descend upon them. The hall was clear in both directions, and he turned back toward the airlock.

He couldn't see any sign of Alpha team, and the lump in his throat grew as worry flooded him. Alpha team was the crux of the plan, but they also had the most difficult task. If Alpha team, or at least most of it, didn't come through those doors, Deacon's plan was sunk, and their lives were forfeit. The Gorski would continue in the hands of the Tendari, and Elijah's team would either be beaten and executed or blown to pieces with the ship's massive cannons.

Deacon banished the negative thoughts and forced his trembling legs to still. Man, that stuff was strong. He felt like his skin was dancing, and he couldn't keep from moving. His hand, no...his arm, throbbed despite the painkiller, but it was negligible given the situation. He resisted the urge to hold his stump. Such a fragile posture would be disgraceful in front of his Tendari friend, and so he swung it casually instead.

"It's lighter now," he said, smiling.

"Grak, you say I have the sick humor. I say that it is you who has it." Golith said, clucking his tongue in rebuke. "It is okay to mourn that part of you that is lost."

Deacon was surprised by the Tendari's stance. He glanced back at the airlock.

"Not right now, it isn't. We have work to do."

Alpha team pulled themselves around the lip of the airlock's entry carefully, gripping handholds wherever they could find them. Lacking the Tendari mag-boots, the team had made slow progress across the outside hull of the ship, but they had made it. Deacon counted them as they appeared over the lip and was shocked when the number stalled at six. He had expected more. Well, that wasn't really true. He hadn't honestly given himself the luxury of expectation. Instead, he had hoped, and he had decided that if any made it, they would probably all make it. He realized, now, just how naive that logic had been. What was worse was how he felt when he realized that one of those not present was Torax, the old Tarpin who had been instrumental in his adoption into the clan. He fought the feeling that he was responsible for him and Toolig, the other missing Tarpin. If he went down that road, he would soon be reduced to a mumbling, bawling mess. He had to keep it together and forced a smile to welcome his friend, Denzink, and the Tarpin as they passed into the Gorski.

They quickly and silently removed their suits and armed themselves with the weapons Elijah had made. Deacon noticed that several of them favored limbs that he presumed were injured in the crossing. Denzink himself limped badly as he came over.

"Is six enough?" Denzink whispered, worry in his tone.

"We have eight, Kupelti, and one of them is a Grak, and another is a Tendari," he had said it as if he were insulted by Denzink's lack of faith. Deacon had been worried that Golith would be difficult for Alpha team to accept, and he didn't need him making it harder. He tried to jump in before Denzink had time to take offense, but he underestimated the Kupelti's abilities.

"I don't know what a Grak is, but a Tendari isn't much to count on," Denzink fired back.

"If Tendari are so weak as you say, why is it that all of your worlds are now ours?"

A growl of incredulous anger rose in a chorus from every member of Alpha team, and even Deacon bridled at the comment.

"Golith!" Deacon shouted, his frustration overpowering his desire to remain unnoticed by the Tendari still aboard. "You watch your tongue! You have proven yourself to me time and time again, or I would have taken true offense at that comment." To his relief, Golith bowed his head in shame at the rebuke. He turned to Denzink. "The Tendari are obviously formidable, or you wouldn't be worried if our numbers were sufficient!" Denzink's rage ebbed slightly at either Deacon's logic or his tone, and he had the sense to look penitent.

"Now..." Deacon continued. "We have a job to do, so if you two are finished, we will get about it." They both nodded their heads.

Denzink pulled Deacon's short sword from behind his back and gave it to him, hilt first. He smiled and handed his oversized pistol to Denzink in payment. The Kupelti looked confused.

"Don't you want the gun?" he asked.

"I can't really handle it one-handed," he said and lifted up his left stump in explanation. Denzink nearly fell over in shock.

"How?" was all he could manage.

"Let's just say, Grato got a snack before my friend here finished him off." Deacon pointed at Golith with his stump.

"You killed Grato?" Denzink asked, surprised. Golith nodded. "I envy you that," Denzink said.

"I believe most people who knew him would envy me that," Golith said.

"Let's go," Deacon said, and turned to lead them toward the ship's bow. Just then, a team of Tendari came running around the corner at the end of the corridor far ahead.

"Bahg," Deacon grumbled. "Back," he called and turned.

Golith had taken up the rear and had also turned, now leading the small team. They started in that direction, and Denzink fired past Deacon at the Tendari closing on the rear. He heard one call out, and then a short volley of poorly aimed shots sparked into the walls around them. A cry of alarm sounded from the Tarpin in front of him, and he looked ahead, straining to see past the huge alien bodies in front of him.

A second team had come around that corner, effectively trapping the team between the Tendari soldiers. Deacon tried to think his way past this problem, but he didn't have time. The energy bolts had started in earnest, and they had been lucky that no one had been hit yet.

"Bahg," Deacon swore. They were well and truly trapped.

CHAPTER 41

Lacking very many options, the Tendari in the barracks soon decided on the predictable course. Brute force. Elijah watched from the barricades behind Janisar and the fire teams armed with energy weapons as the largest Tendari he'd ever seen burst through the swirling steam, roaring in unintelligible pain and anger as round after round was absorbed by his massive body. He'd made it the full length of the corridor, leading the way for the rest of his platoon and protecting them from the enfilading fire. The giant finally fell to his knees in defeat and obvious agony, but he'd achieved his purpose, and the rest of the Tendari platoon flooded around him into the room, firing their energy weapons at whatever moved.

The three-person fire teams went down quickly, but Janisar, being Bulrathi, seemed mostly unaffected by the energy weapons. His rough, stone-like skin absorbed or deflected the shots causing only casual grunts of discomfort as the force of the impact struck.

"Retreat to the Warren," Elijah called. They had named the maze of corridors, rooms, and machinery the 'Warren,' and it was the last, desperate stage of their defensive plan. "Janisar! Fall back!"

The Bulrathi didn't listen. He laughed as he shot down

another Tendari, unaware or uncaring that he was being surrounded by soldiers and would soon be overwhelmed. Elijah drew his long knives and danced in. He was too fast and small to be noticed by most of the Tendari, who had their attention fixed on the resilient Bulrathi, but two soldiers targeted him with their energy pistols and shot.

The bolts went wide, and Elijah's jinking dance made him nearly impossible to hit. He dodged the point of the gun closest to him as the Tendari fired once again, and it was over. He was within the enemy's defenses and ran the length of the razor-sharp blade in his left hand across the soldier's belly. He followed up with a quick stab to the Tendari's lower back, into the spine, as he moved past.

Next, he spun and used the now kneeling Tendari he had wounded as a shield for the energy bolt that came at him. He didn't give the gun time to cycle but climbed up the back of the kneeling Tendari and launched himself off the alien's shoulders, straight at the other soldier. He flew through the air, and everything seemed as if it were in slow motion. He flipped his blades around as he fell onto his target. He slammed both knives into the alien's trapezius muscles on either side of its neck at a slight inward angle so that the blades met at the heart deep inside its chest. The beast's eyes went glassy, and he pulled his blades free and jumped clear as the huge body crumpled to the ground.

Elijah felt a stab of heat in his back and smelled pungent smoke. He looked down. There was a large black mark on the front of his jumpsuit that the smoke emanated from. His knives clanged to the floor, and he realized his hands were nerveless and unable to maintain a grip. He wanted...needed to keep moving, but his legs betrayed him and went limp. He fell to the floor.

"I hope that boy is doing better than I am," he said to no one.

———————

"Here! In Here!" Deacon called to his team and rushed to a closed door. It was locked, and he stepped out of the way while Denzink smashed the lock and used his heavy bulk to knock down the door. When he was done, the thick metal door was nearly folded in half, leaning against the far wall.

The team filed in. One of the Tarpin was struck by an energy bolt as he passed through the door, and he cursed loudly in untranslatable language as he hopped into the room. Deacon didn't have to tell Denzink and Golith to guard the door. Being as they were the only two with ranged weapons, their available strategy was severely limited.

They chose their targets and conserved the weapon's battery. It wasn't looking like they'd get replacement guns any time soon, and with every second they were stuck in this room, the already dismal odds of success dwindled. Deacon knelt and examined the wounded leg of the Tarpin that had been hit as he came into the room. Portex was his name, and he growled a warning as Deacon reached for the wound.

"It's okay, friend. I will not hurt you without your permission," Deacon said, in perfect Tarpin. Portex relaxed slightly and allowed Deacon to look at the hole in his calf muscle. The wound smelled like the meat that Grato had given him those many months ago, and when he lowered himself to be level with it, he could see straight through. He cursed, and Portex smiled.

"I have taught you something," he said. Deacon was surprised to realize he had said the same untranslatable phrase that Portex had howled upon being shot. He returned Portex's smile.

"Everyone has something to teach," he said.

"Especially you, tiny Tarpin," Deacon almost flinched at Portex's compliment.

"Like what? How to doom everyone you care about to

death?" He asked. His tone was even more miserable to his own ears than what he had intended.

"No, my friend. You have saved us all." At Deacon's disbelieving shake of the head, Portex went on. "You brought hope where there was none, unity where there was only strife and vegetables where there was only Tendari slop." Deacon laughed at the last one, but Portex was apparently serious about the vegetables.

"Thank you, Portex, but I'm not feeling very admirable at the moment."

"I understand. Once we have the ship, you will feel better," Portex said with pure conviction.

Maybe Portex was slow in the head, Deacon thought, but he didn't seem like it. Deacon didn't have the heart to tell him that that wouldn't happen now. There was no way for them to break out of the room, let alone take the ship. His somber cast must have been response enough for Portex.

"I know you think we are stuck here, but have you tried using that one attribute that humans are apparently blessed with in more abundance than we, other species?" Deacon looked at him, confused. Portex reached out with a long, muscular arm and tapped Deacon lightly on the forehead. "I have a theory that, if you are any judge of the rest of your species, humans must have bigger brains than the rest of us. It may be the only thing that is big on you, but it is enough." Portex smiled. Deacon smiled and looked around the room.

It was quarters for low-ranking officers, two by the number of beds. It was odd seeing the living space. It seemed too... nonviolent. He didn't know what he expected, maybe bloody racks of unknown meat hanging from the ceiling or excessive weapons lying around, but from where he stood, it was just a well-organized room. Comfortable even.

"Search for more weapons," he said to the four Tarpin who stood by the far wall, craning their necks trying to see out the door and the action beyond. Despite their interest in the firefight, they jumped to obey Deacon's order. He didn't think they'd find anything and wasn't surprised when the search turned up nothing. Regardless, he continued scanning the room, not sure why, then it hit him.

In the corner was a vent through which air was cycled throughout the ship after it passed through the myriad filters and rebreathers that allowed it to attain its highest level of efficiency. The network of ducts were human-sized, or rather, Deacon-sized and not Tendari sized, and so he had been inside the network several times, fixing minor problems that his taskmasters had put off for the sole reason that they were hard to reach.

He grinned.

"Lift me up there," he pointed at the vent, and one of the Tarpin bent down, scooped him up, and effortlessly lifted him to the ceiling. He felt the edge of the vent and looked at the screwheads that ringed it.

"Golith! I need a screwdriver," he called, and the Tendari paused in his shooting long enough to retrieve one from his work vest that he still wore. He tossed it underhand to Deacon, and he set to unscrewing the vent. After the last screw fell to the floor, he pulled the vent down and tossed it on one of the beds.

"Higher." Deacon requested, and he was inside the ductwork.

"Tiny Tarpin, what is your plan?" Portex asked, hopping over.

"You'll see. Be ready to move," he pulled himself along, away from the chorus of follow-up questions. To be honest, he had no idea what he was doing, but he knew it was necessary, whatever it was.

He came to a junction that he recognized and turned right, then left. When he came to the vent access that led to the equipment room, he tapped it with the butt of his sword, testing its resistance. After repeated entries into the network from this point, they had begun to be lazy and only tacked the vent in place, with four out of the dozen normally there. He turned his sword around and started prying the vent out with the tip when Srak's giant frame came into view through the grate.

Deacon paused, unsure what he should do. Would the big Tendari call for the soldiers when he realized who it was, or would he just kill him and have done with it, taking the credit for the kill. Deacon had assumed that with the ship in lockdown, the maintenance teams would all be off performing some emergency preparations standard during such a scenario, but he had been wrong, clearly, as more and more of his colleagues inched into view below.

Maybe they had been confined to the equipment room by Grato. After all, he probably didn't trust the crew, having previously judged them as cowards. Deacon flinched as Srak lifted a pry bar and ripped the vent cover down with a single yank, stripping the screws in the process.

"It looks like we named you true. A Grak for sure," he smiled and lifted his arms, waiting for Deacon to descend into them. He slowly, nervously, did so. He still wasn't sure what the Tendari meant to do with him, and his apprehension was evident to the big alien.

"Do not worry, little Grak. I will not eat you," he laughed at his own joke and sat Deacon on the floor gently. He had obviously noticed the sword gripped in Deacon's right hand but didn't mention it. Deacon turned, surveying all the faces around him. None of them seemed threatening, and a swell of emotion welled up inside him, and he hurriedly brushed a tear from his cheek with his stump. When the Tendari saw it, many of them gasped, including Srak.

"What happened, little Grak?" he asked, concern evident in his voice.

"Grato was hungry." was his simple reply. Srak spat on the ground at the words and swore dreadful curses on the dead commander's name. "I wouldn't worry about all that," Deacon reassured him. "He's dead now." Srak clapped Deacon with a little too much force on the back in pleasure.

"I have to go now," Deacon said, threading his way past the mountainous Tendari on either side of him. Any one of them could have reached out and stopped him, but they didn't. He was shocked. He knew they had a rapport, but their inaction seemed too much for him to believe. "Aren't you going to stop me?" he asked, incredulous.

"Why should we? You fight your enemies. We are not enemies…so why should we stop you? You do what you must." Srak seemed like it all made too much sense to him, and several of the others nodded at his succinct explanation.

"I see," Deacon said. He smiled at them and turned to the door, swinging his sword in anticipation of what was to come.

CHAPTER 42

Deacon cautiously looked out of the equipment room before walking out and turning left toward the sound of energy weapons. At the next corner, he stopped and poked his head out, looking down the hall to his left.

The Tendari on this side of his trapped friends had pulled random objects into the corridor and created a barricade behind which they sheltered from the occasional energy blast. It seemed like they were prepared to wait it out, knowing that the enemy were trapped. If Deacon wasn't so nervous, he would have smiled at having caught the enemy by surprise. Elijah would be proud, he thought.

Now that he had flanked the enemy like the hero in one of Elijah's lectures, he wondered what he would do with them. It seemed suicidal to attack, but what other options did he have? He tried to remain calm and breathe normally, but the jittery, amped feeling had only intensified since the injection, and he was now beyond energized. He ducked back behind the wall and removed his mag-boots so that only the cloth wrapping he used to protect him from the friction of the boots dressed his feet.

He poked his head back out. There were eight...no, nine Tendari crouched behind the barricade, but every eye was facing the other direction, and so, with a nervous sigh, he stepped out from behind the corner. Sword in hand, he crept forward. He kept the wall of the corridor against his left side. He reasoned that it was better to have a wall to your back than a Tendari.

Deacon was surprised that no one had heard his heart pounding. In his own ears, his heartbeat thundered away to the point that it was all he could hear. The trek across that expanse that separated him from them seemed to take forever, and at the same time, he was standing behind the furthest left Tendari before he wanted to be. He hadn't come to terms with this mentally. It felt like murder, but it was necessary.

That word seemed to be cropping up more and more of late. Necessary. For who? His stimulated brain flashed scenes before his mind's eye so quickly that he couldn't register all of them. They were his friends. His fellow slaves. Elijah was there, as was Nah-leesi. The last vision he had was of his earliest memory. His mother, and then of the Tendari dragging her away from him. The images were over in only a fraction of a second, and yet they served to stiffen his resolve.

He brought the sword forward with all the strength that he had. The Tendari, like all of them behind the barricade, was crouching and holding an energy pistol propped on a jumble of debris. His armpit, therefore, was exposed, and Deacon slammed the tip of his sword into the vulnerable spot with such force that the entire length of the blade disappeared into the Tendari's side. The rest seemed to pass in slow motion to Deacon's ultra-stimulated senses.

He heaved the blade free and swung it, backhanded, into the Tendari on his right. The blade bit into the giant's abdomen, and though the wound looked severe, this particular sword was meant for stabbing, not hacking, and the strike wasn't lethal, so he brought it back around point first into the Tendari's lower back. He'd angled the blade up and knew this wound would be fatal.

A corner of his brain assessed the situation continually,

and he knew that his presence was now known to at least most of the rest of the Tendari, and they had begun to react. The next Tendari in line had begun to rise to his feet, and so Deacon ran up the sagging figure he'd just dispatched and lept off of the giant's shoulder, blade held high. His sword came down as the Tendari rose, and the blade slammed into the giant's skull. Normally he wouldn't have chosen such a tough target, but his blood was up, and he felt like he could do anything, and in fact, the sword sank deep into the Tendari's head. Too deep. Deacon rode the crumpling corpse to the ground, the whole time trying to pull the blade free, but it was stuck. He felt a sudden stab of intense heat in his left shoulder and cried out. Looking up, he saw that at least three of the remaining Tendari had their weapons pointed right at him. He turned and jumped behind one of the previous corpses he'd made just as the heat of more bolts passed too close for comfort. Several more blasts struck the immense body behind which he sheltered.

Deacon felt at his wound.

"Bagh! You might as well take the whole thing off now!" he yelled in frustration. The pain had already subsided, the injection going to work there, but Deacon kept his hand over the ghastly wound. Several of the Tendari laughed at the little human's predicament, and Deacon heard their footfalls as they made to gain a vantage point from which they could finish him off. He cursed again. Then he heard it.

Around the corner where he had left his boots came Srak, big and fierce, armed with a huge wrench. On his heels were the rest of the maintenance team. They, too, were armed with their tool of choice and were upon the Tendari soldiers before they knew it. They beat and stabbed, and pummeled the soldiers into submission.

Deacon was overjoyed at the sudden events but felt too weak to stand. It seemed that either the stimulant had run its course and left him exhausted, or his heart was failing him.

Regardless, he smiled at Srak as the big Tendari lifted him to his feet and helped support his weakened body.

"We need to go help Golith. They're trapped down that way." He pointed a shaking arm toward the room where his team was holed up, but before they could move, Golith and Alpha team came into view. Denzink was in the back, firing toward the other barricade at the far end of the corridor. Golith and a few of the Tarpin could vault the barricade easily enough, but the wounded needed help over while the maintenance crew, now armed with energy weapons, covered them.

It took Golith and Srak working together to pull Denzink to safety, but when they did, he laughed and slapped Srak's massive arm in thanks.

"Good thing I've lost weight recently, eh?" All three laughed, and Deacon was glad to see the camaraderie. Golith came over to Deacon, who Srak had leaned against the barricade while he helped lift the Kupelti.

"That was not part of the plan," he said, and Deacon could hear the frustration in his voice. He obviously didn't like the fact that Deacon had left him behind.

"No plan survives first contact with the enemy," Deacon quoted from one of the lectures he'd heard Elijah give. He knew he'd gotten the gist of the quote right, but he had no clue who had said it. He'd have to ask Elijah later.

"That may be, but I still would prefer something resembling a discussion next time," Golith whined.

"Okay, next time, I'll ask them to stop shooting at us long enough for us to discuss what we're going to do next." Deacon knew it had been too harsh and wished he could have the words back. He knew that Tendari didn't react well to sarcasm, and the words had stung Golith's pride.

"I'm sorry, my friend. I think the injection has made me a little short-tempered."

Srak overheard the exchange.

"If you can do this to Tendari soldiers when you are 'short-tempered.' I'd like to see what you can do when you are full-angry." The big alien coughed out a laugh and slapped Deacon on the back again, which knocked him face-down on the ground. Srak's laughter broke off immediately, and he began apologizing while being berated by Golith for his lack of control.

They both bent and lifted Deacon to his feet once more. A bolt came too close for comfort, and the two Tendari crouched.

"What now?" Golith asked Deacon, any bad feelings were apparently forgotten.

"Now, we attack," Deacon replied. A weak smile tried to hide his fatigue, but Golith wasn't convinced.

"Not you, Grak. You are not well. Leave it to us." Deacon made as if to protest when he heard a loud thud followed by a series of clicks. He recognized that sound and looked down the corridor toward the airlock.

"Bagh," he muttered. It seemed someone was at the door, ready to come in. "Grato must have called for reinforcements when he locked down the ship," Deacon said. The thought of a platoon of Tendari unloading right in front of their eyes filled Deacon with an overpowering depression. He felt tears well up in his eyes, and he didn't care when they ran down his cheeks. It was just too much to handle, and the stress, combined with his unrelenting fatigue, forced him into a very dark place very quickly. Where just minutes ago, he was overjoyed. Now he fought to even care if he lived or died.

A thunderous pounding sounded at the airlock, and Deacon looked up. That wasn't expected. Something was trying to force its way past the inner doors, but for the life of him, he couldn't figure out why. The Tendari reinforcements wouldn't need to break down the door, would they?

The Tendari at the far barricade crossed over their jumbled mess of objects and approached the airlock doors. Two of the Tendari kept their weapons leveled at Deacon and his team while the rest focused on the airlock door that shook and shrieked as whatever behemoth on the opposite side did its best to tear through the bending metal.

There was a pause in the cacophony, and then one giant crash sounded as the door flew back into one of the Tendari soldiers, and right behind it came a giant black...thing. It was the largest creature Deacon had ever seen, and it roared so loud that he thought his ears would burst. The Tendari seemed too stunned by the sight to react, and the thing took advantage and pressed into the group. The black thing had fur that covered its entire body and stood head and shoulders above the Tendari.

To say that the thing 'tore into' the Tendari was an understatement and, at the same time, quite literal. It was hard to see exactly what was going on, but Deacon did recognize... pieces. Soon the Tendari turned and ran. Some even came in their direction, so overcome with fear of this new threat that they forgot they were even there. Golith and Srak reminded them with twin bolts that felled the fleeing Tendari.

"Cowards," Golith mumbled in disgust.

A few other creatures similar to the first, though not so large and with different colored fur, came into the corridor now, and Deacon realized that these must be the Marak.

"Put down your guns!" Deacon called to his team. The big black one was looking down the hallway at them, and Deacon said it again. A few of his team were reluctant, and he motioned with his hand to drop them. "The enemy of my enemy is my friend," Deacon said, another of those useful human quotes. Finally, everyone on his team had laid down their arms and stood nervously as the giants approached.

The furry beasts came within twenty feet and stopped. The big one roared another piercing roar, and Deacon was proud that none of his team ran, though from the looks on their faces, a few wanted to.

"We are your friends," Deacon said. Holding up his hand

and stump to prove that he was no threat. The thing seemed surprised that Deacon had been the first to speak and came closer to him. Tendari blood matted the thing's fur to its massively muscled body. It began to speak, but the translator was of no use. His growling, grumbling language must not be in the translator's database, Deacon realized.

Regardless of Deacon's inability to understand the beast, he seemed to understand Deacon, though he looked suspiciously at the Tendari in the group as if he didn't believe that they were capable of being friendly.

"It's okay. They're friends too. We all rebelled against the Tendari. We were slaves. Are you Marak?" he said. The giant's face was split by a wide grin that seemed completely at odds with what he knew of this creature so far. Deacon wondered if, by showing his teeth, this species meant something completely different than what he was used to.

The black-furred creature spoke into the display attached to its forearm, and within a minute, the corridor was flooded with more alien species than Deacon had ever seen. Another minute and an alien that looked to be about the size of a Tendari came over. It was wearing a sleek-looking suit that covered the alien's features from head to toe. A helmet and visor covered its entire head, but when it saw Deacon, it stopped, and everything in its body language indicated surprise.

It paused for a long while, staring at him, unmoving.

Deacon, feeling uncomfortable under the scrutiny, spoke. "Are you Marak?" He had a feeling that his guess was right. The suit matched the sleek-looking ship that wreaked such havoc among the Tendari ships. The alien didn't respond. Instead, it turned and started pushing prompts on the display attached to its arm.

Minutes passed as he and his team stood awkwardly waiting for what they did not know. Another alien in one of the sleek suits came into sight, but this one had a series of colored squares on its chest and little gold stars on its shoulders. All of the aliens that it passed became rigid and saluted, and when it saw Deacon, its fluid march missed a beat.

"It is true," it said, in Deacon's own language. Deacon was stunned.

"How do you know my language?" he asked, incredulous. After a long hesitation, the alien responded.

"That is not all we have in common." Before his eyes and to the astonishment of everyone, including the giant furry creatures, the alien's suit...folded away, revealing a human on the interior. At least it looked similar to him. He guessed this was one of the women that he had never seen. Her body was different, as was true with almost every species, but her skin was a tone somewhere in between Deacon's and Elijah's. She seemed quite a bit older than Deacon, but that was no surprise.

She stepped down from the opened suit and approached Deacon. Confused muttering rumbled around them, but it didn't seem to phase her. Over her shoulder, Deacon saw the other 'sleek suit' lift his visor, revealing human features as well.

The woman stopped in front of the barricade and waited. Deacon motioned his request to Golith, not trusting his voice at the moment, and the big Tendari, along with Srak, pushed a gap in the myriad of heavy objects that separated the two...humans. She did not move closer but allowed him to approach her in his own time. When he was face to face with the third human he had ever seen, she reached out and touched his face.

Deacon would have thought such an intimate gesture would be strange, but it felt right. He had longed for human contact for so long that this moment seemed almost too surreal to be true.

"I have so many questions," Deacon finally managed.

"As do we."

To be continued....

Coming Soon

A DEACON NOVEL

A NEW
BEGINNING

L. J. STUBBS

BY THE AUTHOR OF A FORLORN HOPE

L.J. Stubbs has always been drawn to futurism and the wonder inherent in 'what could be.' The possibilities are literally endless, and he loves contemplating the myriad paths that humanity can take. L.J. Graduated from Brigham Young University in 2009 and married his lovely wife shortly after. They now have three rambunctious boys and live along the Snake River in Idaho.

L.J. Stubbs enjoys writing full-time, which is a lifelong dream come true. When he is not writing, he can be found reading a book or working on an art piece that he uses to channel what he calls his 'creative juices.' L.J. is known for putting himself into his characters and takes pride in the connection that his readers make with those personalities.

www.ingramcontent.com/pod-product-compliance
Lightning Source LLC
Chambersburg PA
CBHW050724180626
46814CB00002B/588